35.95

THE PLAGUE LORD

THE PLAGUE LORD

Paul Doherty

headline

First published in Great Britain in 2002
by HEADLINE BOOK PUBLISHING

10 9 8 7 6 5 4 3 2 1

Cataloguing in Publication Data is available from the British Library

ISBN 0 7472 6268 3 (hardback)
ISBN 0 7472 6953 X (trade paperback)

Typeset in Trump Mediaeval by Palimpsest Book Production Limited,
Polmont, Stirlingshire

Printed and bound in Great Britain by
Clays Ltd, St Ives plc

HEADLINE BOOK PUBLISHING
A division of Hodder Headline
338 Euston Road
London NW1 3BH

www.headline.co.uk
www.hodderheadline.com

To Camilla Gauci and her family
of Woodford Green, Essex, great friends!

AUTHOR'S NOTE

Ever since I was a boy, I have had a passion for Marco Polo's incredible description of his travels and stay in late-thirteenth-century China. Marco Polo was a rich Venetian merchant who travelled overland to China (1271–75) and then spent seventeen years serving Kublai Khan before returning by sea to Venice, where he died in 1324. His master, grandson of Genghis Khan, was Mongol Emperor of China until his death in 1294. Marco Polo's account of the Kublai Khan's magnificent court and the glories of that ancient civilisation were a joy to which I constantly returned. I was just as fascinated by what Marco Polo deliberately omitted as by what he described. Which novelist could resist the temptation to fill in some of the gaps?

I have tried to be faithful to the contemporary spellings of different cities and provinces though, of course, this can be difficult. I am very grateful to Mr Cheong of Woodford Green (not to mention his wife, Evelina and, of course, Baby Matthew) for their assistance.

P.C. Doherty

PROLOGUE

The Hour of the Rat

Venice, Winter 1322

In his large, forbidding house overlooking the Campo San Lorenzo, where the canal water, swollen by autumn rains, lapped under lowering grey skies, Marco Polo, nicknamed *Il Milione* ('the millionaire'), stared into the flames of the pine-log fire. His white, cropped hair was sweat-soaked, his sallow face flushed. He clutched the jewel-encrusted goblet, holding a potion mixed with wine, which the physician had prescribed for the seventy-year-old man to calm his raging fever.

'I am for the grave!' Marco whispered.

He shifted in the high-backed chair, tugging his robe about him. He wasn't afraid of the dancing shadows. They were welcome ghosts, evoking memories of the past – but what memories . . . Dark-blue pagodas against white, thick clouds; the terraced fields; the canals like so many snakes cutting through the ground. The gorgeous panoply, the exotic temples of Cambaluc.

3

The brilliant pennants and banners, garments saturated with jewels and diamonds, chambers full of gold and silver.

'*Tien Hia.*' He murmured the name for Cathay. 'What does it mean? What *does* it mean?' Once he had been so conversant in the tongue: he could think, dream and speak in it, but the passage of years had wiped out the marks, covering with dust the memories of his youth. 'Ah, that's it!' he remembered suddenly. '*Tien Hia* means the Home of the Celestials, the place beneath the sky. *Sz Hia!*' He spoke another name for Cathay, the Country within the Four Seas. There was a third name, surely? Marco smiled. 'Ah yes, *Chung Kwoh*, the Middle Kingdom!' House of the Lords of the Pure Dynasty who had Heaven's mandate to rule the *La Min*, the black-haired people.

Marco closed his eyes. He saw a white, winding path; on either side, peach blossom covered the countryside surrounding the fabulous city of Cambaluc – a carpet of pink which stretched as far as the eye could see. Along the dusty track outriders galloped, clad in robes of great richness which caught the early morning sun. On their heads were gorgeous caps with tails or plumes. They were the vanguard of a glittering cavalcade: their mounts were the finest Mongolian ponies with white glossy coats and flaring manes. Jewelled saddles and cumbersome stirrups, gem-studded or lacquered in many colours, glinted in flashes despite the clouds of dust which threatened to cover them. The horsemen passed. A good distance behind marched soldiers under tiger banners. These preceded a huge gold sedan chair, its sides emblazoned with the imperial dragon. Behind its silver-brocaded curtains sat Kublai Khan, King of Kings, Lord of the World, staring impassively out at the hazy blue hills on the far horizon. Gongs clashed to the rumble of tambours, their hollow beating from nearby drum towers filling the air with a thunderous sound. Marco felt the heat of the fire and relaxed as if it was the warmth of that long-ago sun. Other, darker images intruded. The House of Serenity on the outskirts of Cambaluc, its painted doorway-screens protection against the demons, as were the upturned corners of the eaves or the bronze mirrors which hung over every entrance.

'Why did they do that with mirrors?' Marco murmured, trying to remember.

He stared at the one across the chamber. That's right! The black-haired people believed a demon could not enter a room containing a mirror lest he see his own reflection and frighten himself away. Marco smiled to himself and sipped from the cup. His mind was definitely failing! A few months ago he wouldn't have asked himself that question. He'd have revelled in the memories and wondered how such superstitions could protect anyone against the real *Kwei*: those powerful demons who flew like wild geese through the air and interfered constantly in the affairs of men.

Marco stared at the logs crackling in the hearth and thought of another consuming fire. Faces came and went. Su-Ling so perfect, those beautiful, lustrous eyes, her shorn head, saffron-coloured hood and travelling robe of slate-grey. Tears wetted Marco's cheek. Next to her was Raphael, the Franciscan, with his long, smooth face, tonsured head and the earnest eyes of a child. From the smoke, curling like some wraith, rose the faces of Lin-Po and Wei-Ning – true *Kweis*, real demons, helpmates to Azrael, the great Baron of Hell.

Marco pushed back the chair. These faces were returning to him more and more often in the last few weeks. Memories he'd buried deep now thrust through the dust of years. Why? Were they harbingers of his own end? Marco shrugged to himself. He was not frightened of death, not if Su-Ling's promises were true! He would pass through the chambers of Hell and he would

5

drink the wine of the Goddess of Mercy, which blotted out the memories of souls and prepared them for a new turn on the Wheel of Life. If Su-Ling, not the Church, was correct, they would all meet again: Marco, Raphael, Su-Ling and Mai-da. He smiled at the latter's name: his treacherous concubine had taught him so much of the pleasures of love-making. Would they also meet Lin-Po? Or had his soul been blown into nothingness, his dust buried in the very depths of Hell?

Just then, Marco heard a creak behind the arras and he froze. A nightmare sound: the scrabbling patter of rats' feet. He breathed a curse. Time and again he had ordered both his wife, Donna Donata, and his daughters to be most vigilant in that one matter. There must be no rats in his house! Venice might have its picturesque canals, its beautiful, broad lagoons, but it was also a breeding ground for vermin, offering sustenance and comfort to these harbingers of Marco's nightmares. He had spent good silver, buying all sorts of noxious potions to keep the house clear. He'd even hired a servant, armed with rod and sack, his one task being to keep the house free of any rodents. Marco sighed: it was like trying to catch the sunlight.

Easing himself up, he grasped the poker and walked over to the arras. He jabbed at it like a swordsman would do an enemy but nothing was there. Shaking and shivering, Marco went back to his chair. He pulled it closer to the fire, hands stretched out towards the flames. Why all this now? At night, why did he dream of million-coloured chambers and Lin-Po's face, ghastly in the light of a blue lamp? Why did Tanglefoot, the old beggar, come hopping towards him, sacking tied round his mangled feet, pretending to dance to the cacophonous sound of blind musicians, their eyes and noses disfigured by the pox? At other times he found himself alone in the slums of Cambaluc, his nose and mouth full of the awful stench from the rat-eating houses.

He'd roll around the bedclothes in sweat-soaked fear and the images would go. Next he'd feel the fresh air of the countryside and be gazing at some pagoda, drum tower or deserted temple built on the lee of a hill. He'd hear a sound behind him and, when he turned, there they would be – Lin-Po, Wei-Ning, Su-Ling, Raphael.

Marco sighed. He dozed for a while. This time his sleep was dreamless then he started awake at a knock on the door.

'Come in!' he shouted.

The figure slipped into the room but walked purposefully across to him, the heels of his boots rapping on the wooden floor. Marco turned in the chair and gazed up at the face of his friend, the man who had written and published his memoirs.

'Rusticello!' he murmured in pleasure.

'I'm here from Pisa.'

His visitor pushed back his cowl and crouched by the chair as if Marco was a priest about to hear his Confession. Despite the heat Marco shivered: Rusticello's face was grey with fear.

'It's started!' he exclaimed.

'What has?' Marco was confused.

'Ten days ago a ship docked in Genoa, bringing with it stories of a great plague in the East, spreading like a black cloud. The contagion spares no one. Marco, they are talking about whole cities of the dead.' He grasped his friend's wrist and squeezed. 'You said Lin-Po and Azrael were banished to the furthest Hell?'

Marco crossed himself and stared up at the crucifix nailed on the wall above the hearth.

'Su-Ling said it would come,' he replied slowly, 'but not as fierce as it should have been.' He glanced sideways at Rusticello. 'And for that we should give thanks.'

PART ONE

The Hour of the Snake

Chapter 1

Brother Joachim of the Order of St Francis was sleeping in his anchorite cell built into the hard marble walls of the Church of St John Lateran. Joachim was old – so old, he could remember men who ate and drank with their great founder Francis of Assisi. The monk groaned in his sleep, knowing that the visions were about to come! He was tense, half-awake and, rolling over on the smelly horse blanket which covered the straw-filled mattress, he blinked and his mind slipped into the visions of the night.

Dark clouds were rolling towards him. The clouds parted and different suns appeared. The first sun was many-coloured, its rays like streams of blood. It flashed, sending out jagged bolts of lightning, and belched thick clouds of bloody snow. Joachim was confused. The suns now massed into one and hung like a rose-red orb against a yellow sky. Plumes of black smoke ascended to blot it out but the image changed. The sun rose higher, and the clouds disappeared like a mist breaking up in the noonday heat. Countryside emerged into view – dark-green fields with strange temples, a winding trackway. All was quiet, no birdsong, no animals; nothing moved in this landscape from Hell.

The skies grew dark, thunder rumbled in the far distance. Joachim felt a breeze, a stench of corruption. A man appeared walking along the trackway. Was he really a man, Joachim dreamily thought, or a demon coughed up by Hell?

The monk felt himself moving forward. He was walking but he had no sensation of his feet touching the ground. Joachim stood on the trackway facing the man. The stranger was tall with a gloomy face and eyes of burning coals. His hair rose up like arrow-points. His mouth seemed to be cavernous, the teeth jagged like rocks on a seashore. He was dressed in the cloth of death, and Joachim noticed that his fingers were formed like sickles. The man lifted his strange hand and pulled aside the shroud, to reveal a body of molten copper. Joachim watched as this phantasm changed, wings sprouting like those of a vulture. The man stamped his feet. Great clouds of yellow dust rose. Again he pounded his right foot and the gate to the Underworld opened. Joachim stared in horror as the rats, a jerking, moving carpet of velvet, covered the earth.

The vision changed. Joachim was in cities where the dead were piled as high as the walls. The corpses lay strewn like those on bloody battlefields. No one had been spared to bury them. Instead the rats feasted on the rotting flesh: they bared their teeth and grinned at Joachim like demons. He left the cities. In the countryside, serpents, scorpions and every form of abomination thrived and grew. Then the earth caught fire and the flames fell like rain from Heaven.

'Where am I?' he murmured.

As if in answer, the phantasms and the nightmares disappeared. Instead the fields were being tilled by peasants. The roads were full of horsemen, palanquins, sedan chairs. Joachim smiled in recognition. He was in the Middle Kingdom, the land of Cathay, the Home of the Celestials, where he had laboured so long as a young Franciscan. But then the sky clouded over, a savage wind howled, hot and fiery like the blast from a dragon's mouth, and the flesh of all those around him burnt and shrivelled. The countryside changed into the pastures of Hell, thronged by skeletons, the ghosts of the dead. Joachim, who had seen so many of these visions, who had travelled beyond the Silk Road, now knew the portent of these dreams. He opened his eyes, rolled back on his bed, then screamed at the hideous face glaring down at him.

Nicholas IV, Servant of the Servants of God, Bishop of Rome, and Pope of the Universal Church, sat in the small sacristy which could be reached through a side chapel of the cavernous Church of St John Lateran. The Pope, the first Franciscan ever to be elected to the seat of St Peter, was dressed in the simple garb of his Order: a brown hooded robe bound by a white girdle at the waist with open sandals on his feet. Only the papal rings on his left hand were indications of his power and status.

Today, Nicholas's usually cheerful face was solemn. One elbow resting on the arm of a chair, he picked at a spot just beside his left ear and stared at old Brother Joachim. The visionary's eyes were a milky-white. His toothless mouth had a drool of saliva trickling out of the corner but this did not concern the Pope. To some, Joachim was merely a sickly old man who dreamt dreadful dreams; a Franciscan who lived more in the world of visions and prophecy than among the harsh politics of the Eternal City. Nevertheless, Pope Nicholas trusted him implicitly. Was not Joachim his confessor? And had not Joachim warned him, time and again, how the sins of men were now being answered by Hell: how the Abomination of the Desolation was about to appear? A great plague would sweep the earth and reduce to nothing the work of man and, if it succeeded, the redeeming grace of God.

The cardinals, those lawyers who administered the Curia, and the courts of Rome, would only laugh at such prophecies. Nicholas, however, believed them – and not just because Joachim had insisted that they were true, oh no. The Pope had heard similar stories from visionaries and mystics elsewhere. They all sang the same hymn. They all described the coming nightmare. True, their accounts were vague, more shadow than substance, but Joachim had now identified the place: the Middle Kingdom, the Land of Cathay which his Order had visited with varying degrees of success.

The visionary was staring sightlessly up at him. 'You must do something, Holy Father.' The grating voice cut through the silence.

'I *will* do something, Brother Joachim,' the Pope replied. 'That is why I am here.'

'No fat cardinals.' The visionary wheezed with laughter, his shoulders shaking. 'They would have old Joachim taken to the madhouse and flogged for his pains.'

Nicholas turned to the other two Franciscans who sat halfway up the table. One was old, venerable, white-haired, his bony hands already mottled with the dark spots of age. Brother Angelo was an ascetic; his sharp-boned face bore elegant testimony to that. Nevertheless, he was a fiery preacher and one of the Order's greatest scholars – a *peritus*, a man skilled in the culture, customs and tongue of Cathay, the Middle Kingdom and its new Mongol overlord the great Emperor, Kublai Khan. Had not

Brother Angelo worked for years in the provinces of Hunan and Szechuan? He had seen emperors commit suicide and the great Mongol warlord bring all of Cathay under his rule. Beside Brother Angelo sat his pupil and disciple, a young man with a long, olive-skinned face and dark, soulful eyes. Nicholas drummed his fingers on the tablecloth. Angelo was weak but wise; the younger one, Raphael, he was strong but had he learnt enough? Would he be able to cope with the task in hand? The Pope pushed back his chair.

'I have heard enough,' he declared. 'Brother Angelo, Brother Raphael, you will be my emissaries to the great Khan. You will be furnished with money and passes, but my message you must commit to memory. It is to be given only to the great lord himself. You are to take the most solemn oaths that you will warn him: the gates of Hell have been opened. A great demon is about to appear on earth who will level all kingdoms and faiths. He will walk from the distant seas of the East to the shores of the Western ocean. He is Death – and all Hell will follow close behind!'

Chapter 2

The Nunnery of the White Bird, the Buddhist convent overlooking the willow-ringed Lake of Eternal Peace on the outskirts of Cambaluc, lay quiet under a dark velvet sky. Its Garden of Perpetual Spring slept quiet under the moon. Its doors, guarded by images of the Diamond Kings of Heaven, were firmly closed and barred. The roof of glazed jade tiles, intricately carved in the upturned fashion, was surmounted by terracotta statues of dragons and phoenixes which, the Abbess hoped, would protect those within against the wandering *Kwei* or demons. Its side entrances were guarded against similar malevolent forces by screens covered in magical formulae and a huge brass mirror. Similar defences had been constructed around the trellislike windows, with their lacquered screens and oiled paper shutters.

Deep in the temple complex, however, the nun Su-Ling was not free of turbulence and disharmony. For her, the magical symbols, incantations and signs were no protection against the nightmares and phantasms of the dark. She lay on her bed in

17

the Chamber of the Eternal Moon and tossed restlessly; eyes tightly closed, small deft hands raised as if she might push away what was plaguing her mind and soul. Su-Ling was asleep, yet conscious. She wanted to wake but could not. She was about to experience a nightmare, one of those visions which came with increasing frequency to disrupt her sleep. She had confessed these to the Lady Abbess. Her superior sat, Buddha-like, legs crossed, vein-spotted hands on her knees, and listened without interruption: no flicker in her eyes, no change of expression.

'Tell me again, Su-Ling,' she'd whisper. 'If these dreams recur, tell me again.'

She had given Su-Ling a special copy of the *Girdle Classics* to place under her bed, a sure defence against wandering devils, but this had provided little value. Su-Ling returned and the Lady Abbess had increased the spiritual protection, placing amulets and charms on the black and gold lacquered furniture in the Chamber of the Eternal Moon, a room specially set aside by the nunnery for meditation and peace. Indeed, the Lady Abbess was quite concerned: screens depicting the Pearly Mountain of Eternal Peace had also been placed round Su-Ling's bed and her pillows of plaited rush were covered in floss silk, specially blessed by holy ones, but none of this had helped. Su-Ling was experiencing visions three or four times every week, be it this season or that season, be it a day of good fortune or one, according to the nunnery almanac, which had to be avoided for ill luck. Su-Ling's dreams did not concern themselves with such matters. Time and again they returned. The Lady Abbess had taken careful advice and received the appropriate answer.

'Perhaps these dreams,' came the reply of the Holy One, 'are not the work of devils or demons, but a gift from Heaven. Moreover . . .' At this point, the old Buddhist priest, his skin yellowing with age, had spread his hands. 'As you know, Lady

Abbess, Su-Ling is extraordinary. Perhaps these dreams are truly warnings from Heaven?' The Holy One had closed his eyes and gone back to thumbing his beads, lips moving wordlessly. The Lady Abbess had sat patiently.

'The foundations of Hell have been rocked.' The old priest opened his eyes. 'In temples, nunneries and monasteries throughout the Middle Kingdom, similar visions are being experienced, though none as clear and precise as Su-Ling's.'

'What is Your Holiness saying?' The Lady Abbess tried to conceal her own disquiet.

'Warnings from Heaven,' the old priest repeated. 'We must convey them to the Celestial One, the Son of Heaven, the Great Khan. The Lords of Hell are about to walk the face of the earth, so shouldn't he, who has received Heaven's mandate to rule all the peoples of the earth, be informed?' Again he paused. 'But for the while, let Su-Ling sleep and dream. Take careful note of what she says. If there is no change, when the Bright and Clear Season arrives, we will take action.'

Su-Ling was not aware of this as she tossed and turned on her bed. She'd experienced visions in the past about her nunnery and the brethren who lived there, but these were different: chilling and frightening. She wished she could move but could not. The dream was more precise this time. She was standing beneath a towering tree staring across a bleak landscape. A column of fire was racing towards her then it disappeared. A yellow mist seeped up from the earth, then dispersed to reveal fiery clouds which echoed with the sound of heavy thunder. Rainbows broke the clouds. Su-Ling realised it wasn't thunder but a boiling sea which swept across the land. She was on a seashore, staring down at the crashing waves, where loose rocks swirled amongst masses of seaweed. The atmosphere was hot, heavy and oppressive.

The column of fire reappeared, whipped up by the winds, so

it seemed like one of those terrible typhoons which often swept the shores of the Middle Kingdom. She wanted to run but her feet were trapped by the rocks as if the earth had opened and closed to hold her fast. A voice spoke from the swirling smoke. The tongue used was *Hwa Yen*, the flowery language of the Middle Kingdom. Su-Ling strained her ears. Sometimes the voice, when it had thundered before, spoke in a strange tongue which, the Lady Abbess had informed her, was the language of the barbarians who lived in the far West: the Frankish tongue. Now the voice was that of a Middle Kingdom scholar, its intonation clear, the words perfectly enunciated.

'A time of terror!' The voice swirled about her. 'For all living things on the face of the earth, an end to the doings of men! The Season of the Plague Lord is upon us!'

Then all became calm. The sea, the column of fire, the rocks on which she stood, disappeared. They were replaced by a sun with a huge raven in the centre: a moon beside it, with a rabbit standing on its hind legs, pounding rice in a mortar. Then all turned to blood, and the sun changed to a huge throne: on it sat *Hwang Shang*, the Lofty One, clothed in black, a green and red mask on his face. A voice called out: 'Look at the dragon face!'

The throne vanished. Su-Ling was moving like a ghost up the vermilion path to the golden house where the Mongol Lord of Lords, Kublai Khan, stared up at blood-filled skies. The entire vision finally dissolved, leaving Su-Ling and the Lady Abbess walking along the packed, sordid streets of the slums of Cambaluc. Su-Ling no longer knew if she was still in the dream, or whether this was reality.

'Why are we here?' she asked.

'To sing the Mass, the *Ta Tsiau*, to appease the ghosts.'

The two women moved on. The streets of the city were covered in canvas awnings, and festoons of brilliant silk hung from balconies. Strange candles of glass were suspended in the air and thousands of lanterns provided light as bright as the sun. Tables were laid out, groaning under bowls of fruit, rice, fish, meats, all to feed the hungry ghosts. A gong sounded and a blue-grey pagoda, its fretted turrets jutting above a swirling yellow mist, rose up from the ground. Drums rattled out. Su-Ling staggered and stared around looking for the Lady Abbess but she had gone. A great bat with greying fur and open rotting stomach soared through the air. Mangy, high-tailed dogs appeared in the streets as if by magic. All went silent.

At the far end of a pathway stood a man. He had lank hair, black and oil-drenched, his gown was made of night, and a young woman was beside him. What truly frightened Su-Ling was the grotesque creature hiding behind them. It had wings like a bat and the body of a rat, its face enveloped by a hideous red mask. The man started walking towards her; his face was insolent, hands swinging by his side. He was like a champion swordsman striding to meet an opponent. Just then, something brushed her feet. Su-Ling stared down at the ground covered by teeming hordes of black-furred rats, packed so close together they seemed like one. Wherever she looked, these hordes moved, destroying everything in their path. Su-Ling could take no more. She opened her mouth and screamed, crying out for comfort against such horrors of the night.

Chapter 3

In the honeycombed caves on the great outcrop of rocks which lay to the north of the city of Sachiu on the borders of the Great Desert, Lin-Po waited for death. This self-proclaimed sorcerer, Demon-Father of the Water Lily Society, exiled to this desolate place by imperial decree of the tyrant, Kublai Khan, could do nothing. Lin-Po stared at his helpmate, his wife Shunko: her oval face was pallid, her black hair now straggly, clothes torn and rent. The pair had been tricked and trapped into this underworld city of caves and passages. Once again Lin-Po cursed his own misfortune. Had he not learnt this as a sorcerer? How it was the weak, the little ones of life, who posed the most danger to people like himself – he, Lin-Po, who could read the minds of men and who had been so close to summoning up the Plague Lord. He and Shunko had wandered these caves for days. The entrance remained blocked and, despite the weak fires and torches they had lit, he had declared himself lost. He took the comb from his long, black hair and shook it free. In a sign of mourning Lin-Po picked up a handful of dust, streaking his face and garments, moustache and beard.

'We must prepare to die,' he told his wife. 'It is all my fault!'

Shunko stared impassively back. Yes, he *was* to blame! When he wished, Lin-Po could read minds but he had not exercised this gift when the *Tipao*, the headman of the village, had invited him and Shunko to the caves to celebrate a local feast. Lin-Po and Shunko should not have come. Since their exile, they had kept themselves apart, Lin-Po still making secret sacrifices to the Demon Lord. Perhaps they had not exercised enough caution. Perhaps the *Tipao* had realised that the two women who had disappeared from the village had not been abducted by bandits. Lin-Po blinked up at the rocks above him. Well, at least they would never find the corpses. The women had served their purpose: the blood sacrifice had been made but the Plague Lord, the great Baron of Hell, had not answered.

In an attempt to reassure the *Tipao*, to maintain cordial relations and harmony in the village, Lin-Po had accepted the invitation. The feast was supposed to last two days. Lin-Po could remember the fires, the food. He closed his eyes. And, above all, the drugged wine. It must have been drugged. When he and his wife had regained consciousness, they found themselves buried alive in caves beneath the earth. They had been left a little food, a sealed jug of rice wine and the tinder to make a fire.

Surprisingly Lin-Po had found dry plants, pieces of brushwood and wondered what these caves and caverns had once held. The *Tipao* had not shown mercy. The gifts were a petty cruelty to prolong their lives, make them anticipate a lingering death in all its horror.

'You must make the sacrifice,' Shunko whispered, 'and you will live. Call on the *Wen Yi Kwei*, the Demon Lord. He will help.'

Lin-Po smiled at her, his handsome face a mask for a heart as black as night. Shunko was the one person for whom he felt the slightest spark of affection. He was about to refuse when his mind was tugged as if he was falling into a sleep. It was clear of all distraction. He saw the palaces of Cambaluc, the power of the Khan. Anger seethed in his heart. Then the voice came, like a breeze, soft, importunate.

'Make the sacrifice, Lin-Po. I shall come to you and you shall come to me.'

Lin-Po opened his eyes and stared round. 'Did you hear that, Shunko?'

She was now lying on the bed of rock, staring up into the darkness above them. The small torch was already fading, its yellow flames blue-tinged.

'Make the sacrifice!' she whispered.

'If you both die,' the voice taunted, 'what profit then? Make the sacrifice, Lin-Po! I will come to you and you shall come to me!'

Lin-Po grasped the knife. He stepped forward and, in one cutting blow, drove it deep into Shunko's heart. Her body jerked, the blood spurting out of her mouth. Lin-Po rested on the hilt of the dagger. He felt a brief pang of sorrow, as he whispered the secret words of farewell. Then he drew the knife out and stared at the blood seeping along the hilt.

'One day,' he hissed, 'Shunko's death will be avenged!'

He would settle with Cambaluc for his exile, his own foolishness and this desolate emptiness. Lin-Po stood for a while watching the cold, stiffening corpse. He recalled the voice but nothing happened. His temper boiled.

'Are you here?' he screamed. 'Was this a trick?'

No answer. His words echoed hollowly through the cavern. As Lin-Po wiped the knife on his wife's gown, the torch finally guttered out. He groaned and crouched down, arms across his chest. His magic had deserted him. Was this the end of the great sorcerer? Locked like some animal in a trap? He held the knife between his hands. Perhaps he would take the same road as Shunko? Better that than starve.

The next minute he was asleep, or at least he thought he was. He was aware of dreams. He was in a cavern and a creature was coming towards him, a long black rat the size of a fox. He could make out twitching ears, the slightly slanted bright eyes, the quivering nose. The rat was moving slowly like a fox stalking its prey. Was it a were-fox – one of those strange creatures? A demon could assume any form of disguise. Lin-Po watched, fascinated. The creature didn't frighten him. In fact, he felt strong, as if he had slept well, had eaten a good meal and drunk deeply of rice wine. A power surged within him. The rat drew closer and then it changed. Lin-Po smiled. It was Wei-Ning, her fingers as delicate as young twigs, her skin as white as paint, neck slender as a worm, teeth like the seeds of a pumpkin; her forehead was broad as that of a grasshopper, her eyebrows like the antennae of silkworms. She was dressed in dawn-pink silk, her beautiful black hair held up by glowing jewelled pins.

'Where have you been?' Lin-Po asked.

Wei-Ning had been his close confederate in the Water Lily Society: an audacious witch who had plotted with Ahmed and the rest. A sinister yet beautiful young woman who kept her own secrets and whose mind, despite all his gifts, Lin-Po couldn't read. When Ahmed had been killed, the Water Lily Society hunted down, and he and Shunko arrested, Wei-Ning had simply disappeared. He breathed in her perfume.

'Where have you been?' he asked. 'What have you been doing?'

'Looking for you, Demon Father.'

Lin-Po opened his eyes. He shook his head in surprise. Wei-Ning was standing before him, but she was not dressed in silk.

She wore a peasant's dark-brown shirt and trousers, had sturdy sandals on her feet and carried a bag in one hand. She was staring at him.

'I have been searching for you, Demon Father.' She smiled, and looked over his shoulder. 'Shunko is dead?'

'Yes,' he replied heavily. 'I made the sacrifice.'

'And that is why I found you.'

'What is this?' Lin-Po reasserted himself: he rubbed his face in his hands.

'I was sent to look for you,' she explained. 'I have travelled all the way from Cambaluc. It took me some time.' She drew closer, ignoring Shunko's blood-soaked corpse, and pressed her body against Lin-Po. 'I discovered what had happened.'

'How?' Lin-Po asked suspiciously. 'Who sent you?'

'Why, Demon Father, the Plague Lord. A simple message on a piece of oiled paper left in the house where I was hiding told me where you had gone, that I was to bring you back, and other things.'

'How did you find me here?'

Wei-Ning swayed her hips provocatively.

'The *Tipao*, the headman of that village, he was as lustful as a cricket, lecherous and hot . . .'

'And did you please him?'

'Oh, yes – he soon told me about the secret entrance. When we had finished I cut his throat.' She stepped back, put the sack carefully on the ground and crouched down beside him.

'You could have come sooner,' Lin-Po accused her.

'I had other tasks to do.'

'Such as?'

Wei-Ning smiled. 'I cannot tell you now, but the Plague Lord waits for us in Cambaluc!'

PART TWO

The Hour of the Dragon

Chapter 4

The junk, *The Boat of a Hundred Fragrances*, was large and emblazoned with silken tiger banners. Imperial soldiers dressed in gold and blue manned its oars, steering the junk through the early morning mist. A light breeze stirred its coloured pennants. Marco Polo, the Venetian, friend of the Celestial Son of Heaven, principal magistrate in the Prefecture of Cambaluc and the provinces around, sat in his throne-like chair in the prow. He smelt the perfume of the dawn and revelled in its serenity as this gorgeous vessel cut through the carpet of bobbing green lotus pads which covered the Lake of Eternal Peace.

Marco's fellow magistrates, seated comfortably on silken cushions before him, murmured their appreciation at being allowed to share his pleasure. The sun had not risen but the eastern sky was tinged with red: the grey night was receding into the west in trailing streamers of mist and cloud. Birds, of various kinds and brilliant plumage, flew over their heads calling mutely as their feathery wings stirred the cool air. Ahead of the junk, the packed field of lotus pads swirled back and forth. Marco relaxed and the magistrates clapped their hands at this singular honour and unique way of beginning the business of the day.

Behind the junk came two smaller craft filled with singing girls clothed in a colourful array of silks. At Marco's signal they began their high-pitched morning hymn to the sun: this was echoed by other singers gathered on the Rainbow Bridge which spanned the Lake of Eternal Peace. In the distance above the trees rose the curved roofs of Marco's villa, known to all the magistrates of Cambaluc as the House of Serenity.

The Venetian was at peace. He felt like composing a poem but decided this was not yet the place nor the time. The rowers paused as bowls of cornflour cakes, sugar beans and candied fruit were served, along with delicate cups of porcelain containing jasmine tea. They all ate and drank. When Marco finally wiped the corners of his mouth with his fingers – a sign that he had finished – so did the other magistrates. There were belches of appreciation. The servants withdrew into the stern and Marco clapped his hands.

'Look now.' He spoke slowly to avoid giving insult, and so shattering the *ying-yang*, the harmony of this occasion. The junk moved gently forward. Marco rose and pointed.

'Watch them,' he murmured. 'Let us observe the ceremony of the lotus kissing the sun.'

His fellow magistrates studied the buds of the lotus nestling in the centre of their bed of green, small and fat, bursting with life. The grey mist had now lifted, the lake glowed like shimmering glass. The red disc of the sun made itself felt, bathing the sky in a rosy pink. A rower coughed and hung his head in shame. All eyes were now on the lotus buds which were opening, hundreds and thousands of them as far as the eye could see. As the sun rose higher, the buds of the lotus began to move. The red orb in the sky was now turning gold, rays shooting through the trees; the buds opened and their delicate odour swept across the junk.

The magistrates moaned in collective pleasure at such beauty and openly preened themselves; the Khan's favourite had deigned to share this unique moment with their humble selves. The opening buds were like the tiny hands of babies, their petals the soft pink fingers. The perfume was now stronger, wafted by the wings of the birds soaring above them. The magistrates exclaimed in surprise. They could hear, they were sure, the very opening of the buds: they were even fortunate enough to see white blossoms amongst the pink, a sure sign of good luck. The sun was now higher: its lances of light turning the lake into a disc of glittering silver.

Marco retook his seat. 'I have a poem,' he declared.

The magistrates 'oohed' and 'aahed'. This was pleasure heaped upon pleasure, one great honour following another. Marco smiled to himself but kept his face impassive. He loved this lake, the early morning and the ceremony of the lotus kissing the sun. Above all, he was pleased he could flatter these powerful magistrates. They would gossip for days about this privilege and, when they met, make his task easier.

The Venetian cleared his throat, a polite sign for silence.

'How long, o Sun, have you honoured Heaven with your
    presence?
I lift my cup and question the blue dawn sky.
On the wings of the wind I desire to visit thy paradise.
Yet I fear the warmth of your jade and crystal palaces!
Better to remain on earth and watch you entering
    our halls,
By painted doors and latticed windows,
Taking the sleepless by surprise.

Just as we mortals suffer joy and sorrow,
You, o Son of God, suffer joy in light and darkness.
You are round and full and brilliant
But sometimes dull like the eyes of my beloved.
Here is proof that perfection exists neither for God
　　nor men.
And the best you can wish is that you and I may enjoy
　　life together.

The magistrates quietly applauded and then, as one, knelt and kowtowed before the Venetian. Marco lifted his hands and turned his head away. A public sign of humility.

'This moment,' he declared, 'is made more precious because I have had the unique privilege of sharing it with you.' He sighed. 'But the Hour of the Dragon is almost over. My lords, the business of the day awaits!'

The magistrates retook their seats. Marco gestured to the Captain of the Guard and the junk turned, leaving the fields of lotus blossoms and heading back to the quayside and the waiting servants.

A short while later, just before the Hour of the Snake, the magistrates squatted on cushions flanking Marco Polo in his Chair of Judgement in the Court of Pure Justice at the far end of the House of Serenity. The Venetian had continued to show them great honour. He had led them back from the lake through his Garden of Perpetual Delight shaded by chestnuts, cedars, walnuts, firs and pines. Swallows, white-ringed crows, warblers and robins swooped and played amongst the branches whilst silver-gold pheasants strutted on the lawn. The air was made sweeter by the song of golden-yellow thrushes perched in their silver cages which hung from the branches of stunted trees above ornamental pools full of golden carp and yellow fish.

As courtesy dictated, the magistrates had paused to examine the chrysanthemums and searched for crickets to feed the songbirds, before gathering in the Phoenix Room. Here, the early morning meal was served on small, black lacquered tables: shrimp mixed with boiled rice and delicious slivers of roast goose; grilled tortoises, with shoots of bamboo and rush; minced carp; snails' flesh, browned and preserved in spices. The doors to the Moon Terrace had been thrown open and lit with dozens of coloured lanterns in every shape and size, of porcelain and precious shells. While the magistrates ate, they could contemplate the tastefully decorated screens of subdued colours which extolled the greatness of Confucius whilst their ears were soothed by musicians sitting on scarlet cushions on the terrace.

The ringers, with their buttercup bells of blue glass, of silver and rose porcelain, began the musical interlude. They played lilting tunes which were taken up by softly plucked lyres and gently beating drums. There were thirty-six musicians in all, clad in green robes, under the direction of the Venetian's Master of Music with his baton of scarlet satin. He conducted both the musicians and the singing boys, resplendent in their sky-blue cloaks and black conical hats. It was a soothing, peaceful experience. The magistrates ate in silence, their jade chopsticks delicately lifting the morsels of food, eyes dreamy, faces composed. They all worked at the feet of the Son of Heaven but was not this foreigner, by divine mandate, the Celestial One's favourite? Had he not been appointed as both their Superior Prefect and Governor General?

After the meal was finished, they all processed into the Court of Pure Justice where the Venetian would place before them the cases referred to him before he reported directly to the Celestial One. He would look on the Dragon's face and give him the sum total of their wisdom: they had been feasted and pleasured, now they had a duty to give their wisest counsel and best advice.

Marco had waited until they were all seated, making sure they were comfortable, their rolls of paper, documents, pens and inkpots carefully placed before them. The magistrates sat, heads bowed, not wishing to give offence and stare directly at the face of one who was blessed with the continual vision of Heaven's Son. Any envy on their part was overcome by awe.

The magistrates were all native-born, the black-haired ones, but the Khan was Mongol; so was his Chief Magistrate, this light-skinned foreigner with strange eyes whom the city urchins regarded as a 'Fwan Kwei', a foreign devil. The magistrates would not even dare to refer to such an insult. The Celestial mandate had chosen this Venetian and dressed him in purple silk: he was in the exalted third grade and lived directly in Heaven's shadow. His highly prized purple gown was edged with gilt, bound by a gold girdle and fastened with silver buttons which bore the Imperial Dragon. In a far corner rested Marco's official purple and silver parasol: on the table before him lay the stiffened gold tablet, the physical manifestation of the Khan's pleasure and confidence. All the other magistrates were dressed according to their rank in vermilion, green or turquoise. Despite the Venetian being their superior, they had all been greeted by him at the Gate to the World, the main door of the House of Serenity. Each had been allowed to process in, seated in their sedan chairs, their retinues of clerks, banner-bearers, gong-beaters and heralds following behind.

Marco gently belched but kept his face impassive. He really wanted to burst out laughing at these pompous, self-opinionated men who could so easily be flattered by good food, compliments and a trip on a lake. They all replied with belches to show they had eaten well. Marco bit his lip. He must not laugh or smile:

that would give great insult. Nevertheless, the magistrates did sound like a collection of bullfrogs! Whatever way Marco looked, smiled or spoke would be carefully noted and reported back. The slightest infraction of etiquette would be discussed in detail. The Kublai had insisted that Marco's task was to maintain harmony amongst these powerful men who implemented the Khan's justice and ensured that his peace was kept intact.

Marco prided himself: he had been in the Middle Kingdom for years and had absorbed its customs like a sponge does water. The ceremony of the lotus kissing the sun was original, however. Uncle Nicolo and Raffeo, on their return from Hunan, would hear of it and be pleased. Marco stared at the basket of flowers in the centre of the room. In the meantime, he reflected, he must be prudent. Something was wrong at court: messengers kept coming and going in the dead of night. Was a crisis emerging? Was it about him? He rubbed his shaven chin and stared down at the mirror-like surface of the red lacquered table. He wore no hat, an eccentricity he cultivated, though he kept his black hair cropped and, unlike his uncles, shaved daily, both his upper lip and chin.

'A Chinese face,' the Son of Heaven had teased.

This was more flattery than truth. Marco, with his rounded cheeks, broad chin and dark, well-spaced eyes, could not hide his true origin. Was this the cause of the crisis? Had his foreign ways alienated some mandarin or court noble? Marco blinked; that was impossible. The Great Khan had surrounded himself with men of different faiths and customs. Was not Sanghra, Head of the Central Secretariat, overseeing the Government of the Right and the Left, the civil and military jurisdiction of the Khan's sprawling empire, a foreigner, a convert to the Muslim faith? Marco, following his uncles' advice, always tried to keep himself free of court intrigue, the constant whispering, the silken treacheries, the fawning smiles and envious looks.

'Discuss no one,' Uncle Nicolo had warned him, 'with no one else. Do not give an opinion on a man's personality, his manners, his dress. In all things we are the Great Khan's servants. If we bask in his smile, if we enjoy his confidence, we are safe.'

Marco had treasured this advice, and eventually, his shrewdness and tact had won the eye of the Great Khan. At first Marco had been entrusted with this or that petty task but, as time went on, he was appointed one of the Khan's judges, trying cases in the city and in the countryside beyond. He had kept himself free of bribes. He showed himself resolute in the face of threats and undue influence.

'I dispense the Khan's justice,' was Marco's constant phrase. 'If you have difficulty with the Khan's justice, then you should appeal to the Son of Heaven himself.'

No one dared do that. Thus Marco's fame had grown. In the Year of the Horse, in the twelfth moon, just after the festival of the Little New Year, he had been appointed Chief Magistrate or Prefect.

When he glanced up now, his colleagues were waiting. They sat with bated breath. The great lord must not be disturbed as he prayed for Heaven's wisdom and reflected on matters of state. Marco smiled, bowed and breathed out, his breath slightly clouding the table before him. He clapped his hands softly.

'We will begin, under the watchful eye of Heaven's Son.'

Immediately the clerks entered and sat down behind their masters. These were led by Marco's own scribe, Purple-Skin, called this because of the wine-coloured birthmark which stained most of his face. Purple-Skin squatted down next to his master. Marco turned and smiled, a gesture of appreciation. Purple-Skin was the finest clerk in all of Cathay. Originally from Soochow, he had a proper name but refused to answer to it and had continued to do so in the years he had served Marco in the House of Serenity.

'My face is the punishment of Heaven,' Purple-Skin had declared. 'If I bear it well, in my next reincarnation I shall be beautiful as the lily.'

Purple-Skin was of aboriginal blood, broad-browed, flat-faced, his eyebrows mere puckers of skin. Some would describe his features as coarse, with his pug nose and thick lips, but his eyes were sharp and shrewd. He had a mordant sense of humour and had proved himself to be a shrewd judge of character. He loved rice wine and the soft-skinned courtesans of the city, almost as much as he loved learning. He could get drunk as a sot and lecherous as a dog on heat. He could swear and his language was coarser than any labourer from the slums but Marco trusted him implicitly. Purple-Skin was a man of integrity. When it came to justice he could not be bought or sold.

Purple-Skin had arrived in the House of Serenity about the same time as the concubine and courtesan, Marco's lover, the svelte-skinned, dove-eyed but passionate Mai-da. Marco suspected that there was some link between them, not amorous, more a blood tie. Yet no two people were so dissimilar, Mai-da with her butterfly loveliness and Purple-Skin, hunched, none too clean in his habits, and when drunk, colourful in his language and abuse towards the other servants. This morning, however, Purple-Skin was behaving himself. He loved such occasions, secretly delighting at how this foreign devil, whom he deeply liked, could put the fear of the Dragon into these self-important officials. Purple-Skin was Marco's adviser, skilled in the law, shrewd in his judgements. He would, when asked, give his opinion and do so in a sonorous way, imitating the sages of the court though Marco knew he was secretly ridiculing them. Now was no different. At a sign from his master, Purple-Skin picked up the golden tablet from the table, the *Bulla* or imperial warrant which gave Marco his power. Purple-Skin held the tablet of gold so all could see it, resting it against his forehead.

'By the strength of Eternal Heaven!' he intoned. 'May the name of the Khan be holy and reverenced! Who pays him no obedience is to be slain. He must die for his sin!'

The magistrates bowed. Purple-Skin deliberately kept the tablet of gold raised that little bit longer and, turning his head, grinned at his master. Marco glared back.

'These proceedings must begin!'

And so they did. Marco thoroughly enjoyed his task, fascinated by the different cases referred to him. The first, from the town of Qufu, involved the murder of a tax-collector who had been bitten to death by a mob of citizens.

'He was unpopular,' the magistrate declared. 'Bullying in his ways, and corrupt in his practices.'

'But why bitten to death?' Marco asked.

'Master,' the magistrate replied, 'if they had slain him with a knife or axe, those responsible would have faced summary execution.'

Marco nodded in agreement. Purple-Skin was about to break in. Marco lifted his hand and, as he did, admired his long painted fingernails. He repressed a smile. If those in Venice saw him now they would report him to the Council of the Eight but Venice was Venice, and this was Cathay, a different world!

'Your Excellency.' The magistrate kept his head bowed as he gave advice to this Favoured of Heaven. 'If Your Excellency will recollect: the Board of Punishments,' he was referring to the imperial ministry which ran the prisons and execution grounds, 'makes no mention of capital punishment for biting someone to death.'

Marco smiled, a sign for the rest of the magistrates also to laugh softly at the cunning of these murderers.

'Moreover,' the magistrate continued in a hurry, 'it would be hard to discover who actually bit and who did not.'

Again Marco chuckled and the atmosphere lightened.

'And you wish me to rule on this?'

At this, the magistrate responsible stared blankly back. Marco quietly cursed even as Purple-Skin fidgeted noisily beside him. He'd made a mistake; he was here to rule, not appear in doubt.

'Your collective wisdom,' Marco smiled at his companions, 'is much valued by me. However, I have decided on the punishment.'

The magistrates sat in silence, wondering what this foreigner would decree.

'The tax-collector had a wife?' Marco asked serenely though, to be quite honest, he was making it up even as he spoke.

'A wife and three children,' came the reply.

Marco looked wisely at a point above their heads.

'The corpse of the tax-collector cannot be examined,' he declared. 'To a certain extent he deserved his death, since corruption and bribery, malpractice of any sort cannot be tolerated.'

Again silence.

'Nevertheless, an imperial servant has been killed and a lesson must be learnt. The widow and her three children are to be carefully weighed. All those who were at the scene of the crime must, from the Season of *Ching Ming*' – here Marco referred to the festival of Pure Brightness – 'pay, for the next five years, the weight of the widow and her three children in rice.'

The magistrates gave a collective sigh. This was the sort of wisdom they appreciated.

'They are also to be fined the exact amount the tax-collector should have received. This, too, is to be paid to the widow and her children. They are also to pay double the tax they should have done to the Imperial Treasury, but just for one year.'

The magistrates were still staring at him.

'They are also to arrange for sacrifices to satisfy the ghost of their victim.' Marco knew he had hit his target fair and square now. 'And, above all . . .'

The magistrates were squirming with pleasure: this was the sort of decree they could analyse and discuss in the teashops and restaurants of the city.

'The widow of the tax-collector is now left defenceless.' Marco paused for the murmurs of approval. 'She has three children. The community responsible for the murder of her husband must produce a bachelor of good family and reasonable wealth, for her to marry.'

The magistrates clapped their hands.

Purple-Skin's pen was racing across the oiled paper. His master had made a mistake in asking for advice but, oh, the foreigner had compensated for this a hundred times over. The sentence showed wisdom and wit, proper balance and harmony. The Great Khan would be pleased.

Other cases were now brought forward. A man had hated his enemy so much that he'd committed suicide outside the door of that enemy's house, intending that his spirit would haunt the family for years to come. Marco decreed this to be an evil and malicious act: the local Buddhist monastery would be paid to exorcise the place and placate the spirit. An act of cannibalism was deferred for later discussion as the magistrate of Kifonge brought in an interesting case which taxed their minds. A man named Ko, and his newly married wife, took up residence in a house belonging to a graduate named Yang. Ko followed the respectable trade of a table-server in a beancurd cookshop: because of his job, he was often away from home in the evening. Before long he began to suspect that scholar Yang was paying too much attention to his wife and sought to reassure himself by creeping back and listening outside the window. As it happened, all he heard were the wise words of Confucius Yang was imparting to his wife. His suspicions, however, continued, giving rise to gossip in the neighbourhood so, on the advice of his family, Ko moved to the house of a close relative whom he bribed to watch Yang and his wife.

Shortly afterwards, Ko was seized with the symptoms of poisoning. On his way home from work he had stopped to eat some dumplings at a cake vendor's shop. By the time he reached his wife, he was so ill that she went out to a local apothecary but the medicines she brought gave no relief. Ko died, a choking sound in his throat, his lips bubbling with white froth. Ko's mother appealed to a local official: an examination was made of the corpse which led the petty magistrate to suspect that Ko had died of poisoning. A physician was called in: an opiate drug was suspected but the physician argued how certain livid blisters on Ko's corpse pointed to arsenic. This opinion was partly confirmed when the physician pierced the body with a silver probing needle and a green stain was observed.

'The physician,' the magistrate concluded, 'then made a terrible mistake. He neglected to wash the needle with a prescribed concoction which,' the magistrate lifted one slender finger, 'obliterates all stains from the needle except those produced by arsenic poisoning.'

Marco sat fascinated. 'Proceed!'

The magistrate bowed his head.

'Excellency, my official,' and now the magistrate was following the rules of the game, when the mistake of a subordinate had to be acknowledged and accepted by his superior, 'put Ko's wife to torture. She confessed that Yang had given her arsenic.'

'And what did the scholar say to that?' Marco demanded.

'He denied it, so he, too, was tortured.'

'And the corpse?' Marco insisted.

'Eventually I intervened and Ko's corpse was exhumed. Five learned physicians were called. They pointed to no reddish discoloration on the surface of the skull whilst the upper and lower bones of the mouth, the teeth, jawbone, hands, feet, fingers, toes, nails and joints were all of a yellowish-white colour.'

'In other words,' Marco interrupted, 'no sign of poisoning could be detected?'

'Your Excellency's conclusion is as wise as it is short,' the magistrate conceded.

'This is a case,' Marco pontificated, enjoying himself, 'where a minor official has first reached his conclusion and then has worked backwards to prove it. This is to be deplored. There is no evidence that Ko died of poisoning. His wife is to be freed. She is to be compensated and the same reparation paid to the scholar Yang.'

'And the official?' the magistrate asked.

'I have not finished.' Marco glared at the magistrate who hung his head. 'We are in a forgiving mood. The man cannot be truly blamed for an excess of zeal. He is to be reduced to a lower grade – a warning,' Marco wryly concluded, 'to those who work with him as well as his superiors.'

The magistrate lifted his head, a look of relief on his face. Marco decided that the proceedings had gone on long enough. He whispered to Purple-Skin: servants brought in trays bearing porcelain cups of tea and delicate sweetmeats. Marco used the occasion to consult with Purple-Skin though he caught the eye of the Principal Magistrate of Cambaluc who, throughout the proceedings, had seemed concerned and withdrawn. When the servants left the room, Marco raised his hand.

'Kunzu.' He smiled at the Cambaluc magistrate. 'You have jurisdiction in the area between the new city and the old around the Vermillion Path near the North Gate?'

'It is kind of Your Excellency to notice me,' Kunzu replied.

'And there is a matter which concerns you, is there not? I can read your mind.'

Kunzu moved his papers about on the lacquered table.

'When trouble appears,' the magistrate intoned softly, 'it is like thunder on a summer's day. The distant grumbles are ignored, the first clouds go unnoticed.'

Marco repressed his unease. Kunzu was a level-headed, hard-working man who very rarely brought cases to his attention. Something was deeply worrying him. Marco wondered if it had any connection with the secret crisis at court.

'Death is a matter of life in our city,' Kunzu continued. 'And there are as many demons in the city as there are human beings. Some people die unseen, like a snowflake which melts before it is even noticed.'

Marco held his silence. Such a poetic introduction meant that Kunzu was bringing something very serious to their attention.

'Your Excellency knows,' Kunzu raised his voice, 'how the Celestial One, the Son of Heaven has extended Cambaluc, building a new city called Taidu across the River Yu?'

Marco nodded. Kublai Khan loved nothing better than building. Cambaluc was important for strategic reasons: the Khan wished to impress on his subjects how the old city was not good enough for him, so his architects had built a new imperial city to the north of Cambaluc to house his palaces and administration.

'The cleanliness of both cities,' Kunzu pronounced, 'is a matter of supreme importance.'

His fellow magistrates agreed in whispers and nods.

'Those who clean the city,' Kunzu continued, 'the dung-collectors, the street-sweepers, the latrine emptiers, the scavengers and the sewermen, belong to the powerful Guild of the Pourers. They have a strict hierarchy. The Guild has a Dean who is assisted by his officers, and the city is broken into units, each with its own sub-Guild. The organisation is tightly controlled: rates of pay are fixed. Some of the pourers have become wealthy men. They make business agreements, selling manure to the farmers outside the city . . .'

'What is this leading to?' Marco asked.

'A number of violent deaths have occurred,' Kunzu snapped, annoyed at being interrupted. Then he remembered himself, put his hand to his chest and bowed an apology. 'At first the deaths were dismissed as accidents. One pourer fell into the canal: people thought he had been drinking. Another was crushed under a cart. Now these deaths took place amongst the lowly ones, the actual sweepers. As the days have passed, the number of fatalities has grown: it includes officers now, high-ranking members of the Guild who have all died in suspicious circumstances.'

'Give some examples,' Marco requested.

'Peng, an important official overseeing the area near the Bridge of Sighs, was found in his counting-house, head split by a machete. Another victim was Fang Lee, who worked in the Quarter of Perfumes: he was responsible for the streets and alleyways around the Court of Silken Perfection. Fang Lee was newly married. When the police broke into his house, someone had smashed his wife's face with a hammer and cut Fang Lee's throat as he sat in his bath. The police said there was more blood than water in the tub.'

'So, this is murder?' Marco said gravely.

'Yes, Excellency – indiscriminate murder. I can give you other examples from across the city. No one seems to be safe. And yet,' he lifted a finger, 'the police have been most vigilant.'

'And?' Marco leant forward and rapped his nails on the table.

'They thought the deaths were unconnected until one officer noticed, when he drew up the list of victims, that the latest victim was often linked with the previous murder.'

All etiquette was forgotten as the magistrates raised their eyebrows and stared at each other. Marco stirred in his chair and looked at Purple-Stain.

'Excellency,' the clerk intoned. 'We need clarification.'

'Are you saying, Kunzu, that, for example, Peng died before Fang Lee?'

The magistrate nodded.

'But that Fang Lee was somehow or other connected with Peng's death?'

'We have proof of it. Fang Lee actually was the last person to see Peng alive. He came across the city and asked neighbours for directions to Peng's house. He was seen going in. Shortly afterwards Peng's corpse was found.'

Marco was about to continue when the sound of gongs and drums echoed from the distant courtyard. He and the others sat in silence, until there was a patter of slippered feet in the passageway outside. The door was flung open, a servant rushed in, remembered himself, knelt and kowtowed.

'What is it?' Marco asked.

'Excellency, a courier has arrived from the Palace. Your presence is demanded!'

Chapter 5

A short while later, just as the Hour of the Sheep gave way to that of the Monkey, Tuhmo, second in the Guild of Pourers, chief scavenger near the River Prospect Gate, slipped along the narrow lanes of the old city, the air reeking of the fishy stench from the mud-spattered banks of the River Yu. Terrified, he padded over the unpaved surface between squalid bamboo-built houses. A group of tinkers, with mules so small they were nicknamed 'rabbit horses', forced him to one side. Tuhmo had to stand and let these pass as well as a group of burly porters, bamboo poles slung over their shoulders from which hung cloth bundles, wicker baskets, large earthenware pots and square wooden tubs. Whilst they squelched by, Tuhmo stared down at his torn, blood-stained gown. He truly did not know what was happening. He felt as if he had drunk heavily of rice wine: his mouth was dry as a stick, his stomach queasy, legs shaky beneath him. He looked at his feet, splattered with the dirt and ordure of the lanes then stared guiltily at the russet stains on his hands and wrists.

What a change! Tuhmo felt ill. He shook his head; at other times, more recently, he had felt he could climb up on to the roof of a temple and fly like a bird over the packed houses, fragrant gardens and spacious courtyards of the Khan's city. That exhilarating sense of power had gone now, and Tuhmo felt like a snail stuck in a muddy rut. His mind had become as mottled as greasy water: eerie memories pricked his consciousness. And what was he doing here? What was happening? He shouldn't be here at all. This was not his district. He should be across the River Yu with his wife and family, or celebrating with the Guild in one of the teahouses, enjoying the fragrance of their flowers or admiring the dwarf evergreens. His tongue shouldn't be dry but tasting jasmine tea or plum-flower wine whilst his ear was thrilled by the songs and playing of musicians. Tuhmo was respectable, admired. Didn't he lead the families of his Quarter out to the cemeteries to pay respects to their ancestors? He was always law-abiding. He paid his dues and taxes, he observed the Festival of the Moon and the other feasts, scrupulously following the ritual laid down by the Buddhist priests. So, what was he doing in this fetid alleyway, his clothes torn and ragged and stained with blood? Tuhmo vaguely remembered last night striding the streets as fearless as a demon – but afterwards? He had woken up shivering in the ruins of a burnt-out house.

Tuhmo put his face in his hands. He remembered leaving home, intent on visiting his friend and colleague Wen-Tiu. That's right! He had run into Shou-an who looked wild-eyed, his clothes disorderly. Shou-an wouldn't stop to talk. They'd clasped hands and the other man had hurried off. Tuhmo scratched his forehead. Or had he? Didn't he meet him later? Tuhmo shook his head. He could make no sense of it. He had intended to visit his colleague Wen-Tiu – but what exactly had happened?

Tuhmo stepped back into the street like a dreamwalker. He

reached the end of the alleyway and paused on a corner near the
door to a rough-looking cookhouse, no more than a crude shelter
fashioned out of bamboo trellis with shabby curtains over the
window. He lifted the leather partition and stepped inside. It
smelt sour. The board inside displayed the crudest fare for sale:
beancurd soup, oysters, mussels, noodles stuffed with vegetables
or pork dumplings served in a beanshoot sauce with boiled rice.
At the far end, above the rear window, hung the gutted corpses
of a dog and two cats. Tuhmo's stomach curdled.

'What do you want?'

The one and only table-server shuffled forward. Tuhmo didn't
like the look of this surly, narrow-faced individual with his
greasy hair, lank moustache and scrawny beard. The table-server,
in his turn, looked Tuhmo over from head to toe.

'And you are no gift from Heaven either!' he spat out as if
he could read Tuhmo's mind. 'Who do you think you are – one
of the Immortals?' He gestured at Tuhmo's blood-soaked garb.
'Who are you?' he repeated. 'A butcher or a cross-eyed barber?
You are not a Tartar executioner, are you?'

'No, no.' Tuhmo touched his wallet: the jingle of coins
reassured both himself and the table-server, who ushered him
to sit at a grease-covered table. Tuhmo did not care. He had to
collect his thoughts.

'A bowl of noodles and some rice wine!' he ordered.

The table-server, now more concerned, grasped him by the
shoulder and pushed his face close, his narrow eyes studying
Tuhmo carefully.

'Are you all right?' he asked. 'You're not ill, are you?'

'I am fine,' Tuhmo replied. 'I drank a little too much and got
into a fight.'

And then he felt it, just for a few seconds, as if he was two
persons, not one. His blood sang with the power, his heart

skipped a beat then the feeling left him, as if he had been touched by a sun and now its warmth was gone. The table-server, Kwei-Lin, tapped him on the shoulder reassuringly.

'A little bit of hot grub and some wine,' he advised, 'and you'll soon feel better.'

When Kwei-Lin padded off to the kitchen, Tuhmo looked around. The place was empty except for an old beggar sitting just within the doorway, staring at him suspiciously. When the beggar got up and came across, Tuhmo realised he was a wandering Buddhist priest, one of those crazy, holy men who went out round the city offering to say prayers or exorcise demons. He was dirty, his robe stank, and his face was badly shaved and cut, his steel-grey hair pulled back in a lank queue. He grasped his cane and stared at Tuhmo carefully.

'What is it, old father?' the pourer asked. 'Do you want a drink?'

The beggar-priest stood, eyes wide, mouth gaping. He whispered something under his breath, fingers flailing as if he wanted to drive Tuhmo away.

'What's the matter?' the pourer demanded.

The Buddhist was now gibbering with fright. He stared at Tuhmo, then at the kitchen door and, spinning on his heel, he fled the shabby cookshop.

Tuhmo had the place to himself now. He leant back against the beam and closed his eyes wearily. A sound startled him. He opened his eyes: a rat, sleek and brown, scurried across the floor. As it did, the table-server rushed back in, a cleaver in his hand. Startled, the rat scurried in another direction, but the table-server was faster. He leapt forward. Tuhmo glimpsed the cleaver slicing the air, then heard it fall with a resounding crunch. Tuhmo closed his eyes again. He had heard of places like this: rat and cat cookshops where the meat was highly cured.

What day is it? he thought. How long had he been away from his comfortable house near the Lake of Perfumed Tranquillity? He had gone to meet his colleague, that's right! Afterwards he remembered meeting Kei Mun, a Prefect in his Guild: they were to discuss the terrible murders occurring amongst the pourers of Cambaluc. Abruptly all things were clearer. Tuhmo recalled walking through the passageways of Kei Mun's house. The Prefect was sitting upright in a chair; his small chamber was, as usual, fragrant. He had risen to greet Tuhmo, offered to walk with him in the gardens behind the house but Tuhmo had felt different from usual: angry and powerful. Was there a quarrel? He remembered the garrotte string in his hands, Kei Mun's face turning a mottled hue. Was it all a dream, a nightmare? Or had he, Tuhmo, killed Kei Mun?

The table-server returned and slammed down the small cup of rice wine. Tuhmo drank it greedily. He sighed and felt better.

'Are you ready for your food?' The table-server was looking at him strangely.

'In a little while,' Tuhmo said. 'The wine is making me relax.' He put the cup back on the floor and gestured at the table. 'And before you serve my food, couldn't you clean this?'

'I'll do that now, sir.' The table-server smirked. 'I'll just get a cloth and some hot water.'

Tuhmo preened himself: that was the way to deal with these people. He heard the patter of feet coming from the kitchen and bent down to pick up the cup. As he did so, the table-server came striding across and, with the same cleaver with which he had killed the rat, struck Tuhmo expertly in the nape of the neck. With one blow, he sheared the pourer's head clean from his shoulders.

Marco Polo eased himself onto the purple, gold-starred sedan chair and lifted the stiffened silk curtains. He had prepared himself as well as possible. No one would go with him, not even Purple-Skin. The imperial summons had said he must come alone. Marco accepted the invitation as a great honour: to look on the Dragon's face was a rare privilege but, secretly, he was agitated. Kublai Khan was as friendly and supportive as ever but the Khan was growing old, more concerned about his different ailments. On two occasions Marco had tried to help, pointing out that the vast quantity of wine the Khan was drinking was doing his health no good. On both occasions the Khan had shown his temper and Marco had learnt his lesson. He was there to help and advise in matters of state, not to come between the Khan and his pleasures. But what if this dissatisfaction had spread? Every man's life was in the Khan's hands. The lifting of a finger, the raising of an eyebrow could mean a hideous death for whoever had offended the Dragon's throne. Was he being summoned to be questioned? He sat back in the sedan chair. Or had something happened to his uncles? He just wished they were here to advise him.

Marco lifted the curtain again and stared across the Courtyard of Lasting Peace. Mai-da, his lovely concubine, clad in oyster-coloured silks, her beautiful face grave under its white mask of make-up, was standing just within the doorway, a green silk shawl draped over her shoulders. Hands clasped, she stared across at him. Marco accepted that she was not pleased. Mai-da had a heightened sense of her own importance and worth, and he had been forced to promise that the next time he visited the court, she would accompany him and sit at his right hand in a place of honour. But what could he do? The imperial summons had not mentioned her, so she would just have to stay. He forced a smile, raised his hand then bowed. No one could see him in the darkness of the sedan chair. If they had, they would have judged that the foreigner had lost face. Mai-da, however, remained still as a statue. Marco stuck his tongue out, winked and let the curtain fall.

Around him the imperial foot soldiers were ready to leave. Dressed in their long red robes fringed with gold, black soft caps on their heads, blue slippers on their feet, they shouldered their broad-bladed axes and gathered round the sedan chair. Behind them, the cavalry massed in the clip of hooves and neigh of horses. There was a rapping on the side of the sedan chair. Marco sighed in exasperation and lifted the silk curtain. The officer there was dressed in sky-blue riveted armour, a pointed helmet on his head, a chainmail coif around his face.

'Your Excellency is ready to leave?'

Marco looked over the officer's shoulder at Mai-da still glowering at him.

'His Excellency,' Marco replied politely, 'is only too willing to leave.'

The officer looked puzzled at the sarcastic tinge.

'I am impatient to stand in Heaven's shadow,' Marco explained. 'And bathe in the smile of the Celestial One.'

He let the curtain fall. The cortège, with its gorgeous banners depicting white tigers, green dragons, red birds and black horses, left the House of Serenity to the crash of gongs and the clash of drums. Marco felt the sedan chair rise: the bearers moved swiftly and expertly so their precious burden would not feel a jolt, and his harmony would be maintained. Marco relaxed. The gongs and drums stopped: the heralds were now running ahead, loudly proclaiming Marco's importance and ordering all to stand aside. The Venetian wondered how Uncle Raffeo and Nicolo were doing: their business in the Hunan Province would take some time. Marco himself was alone in the House of Serenity, busy with his duties as Chief Magistrate. How many years had he been in Cambaluc, enjoying the confidence of the Great Khan? Marco smiled to himself – but who was using whom? Kublai, a Mongol, a foreigner himself, loved to employ other foreigners to help him rule his far-flung empire. First there had been Ahmed . . .

Marco stiffened. Now there was an example to beware of! Ahmed the Muslim had been murdered by courtiers. At first, the Great Khan had been furious and dealt out summary and cruel justice, then a jewel from Kublai's crown had been mysteriously found in the disgraced minister's house. The pendulum of imperial anger had swung in the other direction. Ahmed's body had been exhumed and hung in the principal marketplace of Cambaluc before being crushed under the heavy wheels of carts and fed to the city dogs. In due course, Ahmed's place had been taken by another foreigner – Sanghra. Was he Mongolian or Tibetan? Marco never knew. Sanghra certainly had to be watched. Sly, vicious, totally committed to the Khan's rule, Sanghra would brook no opposition. Ah well. Marco tapped his feet on the floor of the sedan chair. What was the use of worrying? He would find out soon enough why the court had summoned him, then he'd return to have words with Mai-da, wipe that angry frown from her face.

Marco lifted the curtain again and peered out at the vista of rolling green hills, bamboo groves, a blue, cloud-tinted sky; in the distance, a pagoda stretched up from the brow of a terraced hill. Peasants, in their thatched straw coats and peaked straw hats, armed with mattocks and hoes, were busy in the fields. They trotted behind a huge water buffalo ponderously pulling a great iron-rimmed plough.

Marco let the scene relax him. He always enjoyed the short journey between his own house and the city gates. Soon they would be in the sprawling suburb of Cambaluc. Marco felt trapped there. He much preferred the open countryside where etiquette was not so strict and he could feel the sun and wind on his face. He watched a group of old men in a nearby field, carrying cages; they were hunting for crickets to feed their songbirds. One of the heralds called out and, before Marco could intervene, the old men prostrated themselves, kowtowing in obedience. Marco ordered the peasants be left alone and the cortège moved on.

The Venetian watched a group of farmers who'd organised the ritual spring procession; their capped torches were lit, according to the rite, by fire taken direct from the sun through a small concave piece of glass. The seeds, laid out on silk paper, were being carried by boys whilst girls bore the dew collected in white jade bowls. Drums beat to summon the spirits of the water, earth and sky. Despite the noise, it was a peaceful, restful scene. Marco let the curtain fall and stared at the plate of meditation fixed on the far wall of the sedan: beautiful girls in pastel pinks collecting flowers from beneath a willow tree. Marco's eyes grew heavy and he smiled. He had been taught how to meditate and yet, every time, he fell asleep.

He was woken just as the imperial cortège reached the huge tower of the Gan Chin Gate which guarded the Vermillion Path to the Great Khan's palaces in the new city of Taidu. To Marco's right rose the northern gate of the old city of Cambaluc. Both entrances were closely guarded by crack units of the *Keshican*, troops who took a special oath of loyalty to the Khan. They were dressed in powder-blue armour with red-furred, sleeveless coats, spiked helmets boasting golden tips, whilst broad scimitars and daggers hung from brocaded belts and sheaths.

When the cortège was let through, Marco decided to look out at the city. The spring weather had brought forth the crowds. The court fops were resplendent in their amber beads, lambskin cloaks and embroidered shawls or gowns of the finest silk in magnificent, eye-catching colours. The womenfolk were just as finely dressed, the married ones distinguished by their hair, pulled back and kept in place by hollow combs with flowers pushed through them. Their brocaded robes of various hues with stiffened collars, were worn over silken trousers studded with gems.

Marco loved these sights, so different from the street scenes of Venice or Rome. Strange smells, exotic colours, the high-pitched voices: prisoners being led through the streets with wooden collars round their necks, public humiliation for their petty crimes. Tradesmen flocked to the markets and bazaars – blacksmiths, umbrella-repairers and barbers fighting for space with fortune-tellers, herbiavists and booksellers; money-changers setting up their small tables which could be so easily dismantled at the approach of the market police. The latter, self-important officials each with their retinue, umbrellas, flags, lanterns, heralds, all the strange insignia of office, proclaimed their approach with that love of status so peculiar to the Cathayens. The air rang with laughter and shouts, mixed with cries of lamentation from the funeral cortèges as well as that squally, strident music, so peculiar to the city, which Marco could never tolerate. Houses of stone, with their decorations and upturned eaves painted in varying colours, stood on either side of the thoroughfare, each protected by magic characters emblazoned to attract good luck and repel demons.

As Marco's retinue wound deeper into the city, following the Vermillion Path to the palace gates, the crowds thinned out; those who were unable to move out of the way had no choice but to bow and kowtow to this lord of the Great Khan's court. There were no exceptions: high-ranking officials, military commanders, the sellers of decorative chessmen or those who traded in oiled papers for windows or offered fumigating powder against mosquitoes, the sellers of red and fallow deer, venison, calf meat, rabbits and partridges – all had to come from behind their stalls and kneel. The word spread. Other sedan chairs disappeared from the avenue. Porters were led away. The wealthy closed windows and doors. The teahouses with their red and green balustrades, purple and green blinds, crimson and gilt lanterns, all fell strangely silent under the sharp gaze of the Mongol officers. These were quick to look for insult from the secretive, black-haired people whose cities they had conquered. The gong-carriers and drum-beaters, the heralds and the criers became more bold as the pool of silence spread.

They reached the Path of Perfection, the direct route into the palace. People clustered to the side, kneeling or, if they were old, allowed just to bow from the waist. All except one. Marco sat forward. A scrawny individual, dressed in dirty robes and blood-stained apron, who looked like some incarnation of a demon with his sunken face, jutting teeth, straggly hair and half-balding head, was staring directly at Marco as he walked, hands swinging by his side. The Venetian stared back. The impertinent stranger looked like a table-server from one of the squalid cookhouses down near the river, yet he walked with a swagger and his face, twisted to one side, leered at Marco. He was like a hunter calmly stalking an animal through the trees.

The more the Venetian stared, the deeper his unease grew. There was something sinister about the man's supreme confidence in himself. The table-server, as Marco now termed him, kept level with his sedan chair and began to make gestures with his hand, grinning at Marco in a menacing way. One of the Mongol officers saw this and turned threateningly, hand going to the hilt of his sword. The table-server waved his fingers impudently and disappeared down some steps.

'Who is that?' Marco whispered to himself as he sat back.

Some criminal he had met in court? He'd looked at Marco as if he was studying a victim and waved goodbye as if they would meet again. Then the Venetian's train of thought was broken as the gongs and drums of his escort were greeted by those atop the long crenellated walls of the palace, white-washed and loop-holed, which stretched to the sky before him. The walls were interspersed by imposing watch-towers over great yawning gateways. One of these now swung open and Marco's escort swept through.

They were soon moving across parkland, a striking contrast to the busy, teeming city they'd just left, past artificial lakes, toy pagodas and silver-grey fountains amongst trees which stayed evergreen. The Great Khan had insisted on this, bringing from the far-distant edges of his empire, herbs and plants which kept their greenness the whole year through. Nicknamed Green Mount, the parkland was a veritable paradise. Pavilions peeped out above the treeline: artificial canals, spanned by rainbow bridges, wound their way haphazardly to provide water for the white stags, fallow deer, gazelle and roebuck which grazed there.

The procession now passed through a second wall and into the palace proper, with its sloping roof of gold and silver, its upturned edges adorned with statues of unicorns and tigers whilst the fronting brickwork shone like crystal in shades of red, yellow, green and blue.

Marco's cortège stopped at the foot of broad, marble steps. Keeping his face impassive, the Venetian climbed out. He thanked the officer in charge and went up the steps, through the doors of pure cedarwood and along marble corridors. Imperial guards stood in the shadows. It was a place of silence, of eye-catching beauty with its gilt screens, beautiful hangings, fragrant flower baskets and gold-edged mirrors. Marco was careful never to step on a threshold, an act of ill-luck for his hosts.

Eventually he left the entrance corridor and went deeper into the palace. On his left and right stretched a series of chambers. One, decorated completely in silver, from which the moonlight could be admired: another, rose-coloured, for music-making. A third had its walls covered in scenes of snow and ice so that courtiers could cool down when the weather grew hot. The lintels, doors and windows were of precious sandalwood, the inlaid bricks on the floor of purest silver.

Marco walked alone, though every step he took was watched. He kept a calm demeanour, his face composed. He must not betray any fear or the unease fretting his nerves. He must also show admiration for the Khan's gorgeous palace. So, now and again, he stopped to stare through windows at sumptuously laid-out courtyards with their splashing fountains, artificial gardens, little man-made hills, winding streams, waterfalls and lily-covered ponds where gold and silver fish swam. Rare flowers blossomed beneath pine trees with white gnarled trunks and twisting branches which stretched over those little grottos so beloved of the black-haired people.

The deeper Marco went into the palace the more ostentatious, yet more silent, it became. Finally he reached the apartments of Eternal Spring. Guards came out of the shadows and ringed him as he continued his journey across a courtyard where urns containing jasmine orchards, pink flowering bananas, cinnamon and other exotic plants grew. The air was fanned by a small windmill so the fragrance would penetrate into the Hall of Heaven, the official chamber of the Great Khan.

Marco Polo stopped in a vestibule whilst guards in gold chain armour, silver helmets over headcloths of crimson and gold, searched him from head to toe. He had to wash his hands in perfumed water and change into a silken purple robe with slippers of silver. He rubbed perfume into his cheeks and neck and sipped from the snow-filled vases containing jugs of fruit and sugared juice to purify his mouth. He was then led along a rather dark corridor, the sandalwood doors at the end decorated with sunbursts of gold. The veterans on guard once again searched him. The officer beat a gong, the doors swung open and Marco crossed into the Hall of Heaven. Its walls were decorated with exquisitely painted scrolls depicting landscapes in the finest calligraphy. The marble floor shimmered in light from lanterns specially imported from Soochow and fashioned out of five different colours of glass. These competed with the pure light from jade vases set in niches from floor to ceiling which exuded a rich jasmine smell. Marco kept his eyes down.

A voice from the shadows called out: 'Bow and adore the Khan of Khans, The Celestial One, Heaven's Beloved Son!'

Marco Polo fell to his knees and touched the floor with his forehead. He glanced under his eyebrows: the red lacquered screens had been removed. Marco quickly looked away, hiding his astonishment. The Great Khan sat sprawled on a bed of cushions, dressed in a purple silken robe, a small table before him. To his right sat Chief Minister Sanghra, but it was the two figures to his left who astounded Marco. He was sure one was a Franciscan, dressed in the customary brown robe, white girdle and sandals. What on earth was a friar doing in the Hall of Heaven? And the other, clothed in slate-grey robes was, surely, a young Buddhist nun? Marco kept his head down. Kublai Khan was noted for his deep respect of priests of any religion. If Marco was correct, and this *was* a friar and nun, they would not have been searched by the court chamberlain but ushered into the Khan's presence as if they were old friends. Kublai never failed to astonish the Venetian. At times the Khan was the living incarnation of Heaven's will, insisting on every right and privilege, but with his friends, favoured officers and, above all, holy men, he would sit, relaxed as a tea merchant, and gossip like a fishwife.

Marco hid his smile. In truth he loved Kublai, a great ruler, sharp-witted, with a profound hunger for knowledge. A Mongol from the Steppes who had fallen deeply in love with the culture of the Middle Kingdom: a ruler who was constantly searching for the truth and who spent his days planning and improving the government of his empire. If only he didn't drink so much wine! Kublai had given up the *Kumiss*, the fermented mares' milk so beloved by his Mongol kinsmen, only to acquire an unquenchable thirst for imported wines. It was the sole matter of contention between the Emperor and the Venetian.

'Look on the Face of Heaven!' the voice demanded.

Marco sat back on his heels. Kublai smiled at him, his rounded, pink-skinned face creased into good humour. The Khan winked, as Marco had taught him and raised one hand, fluttering his lacquered fingernails, an extraordinary gesture of familiarity and friendship.

'It is good to look on your face, o Celestial One!' Marco intoned.

'I've had enough of that.' Kublai waved his hand. 'We've been waiting, Marco.' He gestured to the silken cushions in front of him.

Marco smiled and moved forward though he felt a chill of fear at the intimate privacy of this meeting. No councillors, clerks, scribes were present – none of the Khan's usual coterie. Kublai looked in good health: his face was not flushed from wine and his luxuriant beard and moustache were combed and oiled, whilst his large black eyes were not ringed with shadows, the usual sign that he had been on one of his drinking sprees.

Marco made himself comfortable on the cushions and kept quiet. Some people claimed the Great Khan could read minds: he certainly liked to sit and study his guests. He was now staring fully at Marco, who bowed his head slightly and looked to the far right. If Kublai appeared in good health so, unfortunately, did Sanghra, President of the Secretariat, responsible for the government of the left and the right, with his shaven head and blank face of the inscrutable Buddha. A serene-looking man, though his mind teemed like a snakepit, Sanghra was dressed in purple and gold, and he seemed more interested in the scroll laid out before him on a small table than in Marco's arrival. That's because, Marco thought, Sanghra does not see me as a threat, a rival. Just then, the Chief Minister looked up and caught Marco's gaze; his eyes creased into a smile then he went back to his reading.

The Venetian studied the two figures on the Khan's left. The Franciscan was young, nondescript: his boyish face olive-skinned and cleanly shaved, but the Buddhist nun made Marco's heart skip a beat. Dressed simply in her travelling robes, her head shaven, her face was one of the most beautiful Marco had ever seen: butterfly eyes, high cheekbones, a face in complete harmony and exuding an inner peace. She glanced shyly at Marco, eyes and lips betraying a smile. Marco forgot where he was and breathed out noisily.

'You are well?' Kublai Khan asked softly.

Marco smiled; the Khan had learnt this salutation from him.

'I am well, Celestial One.' Marco kept to the court etiquette. 'I am pleased and deeply honoured to look upon the Dragon's face: my life is complete, my happiness fulfilled.'

Kublai chuckled deeply in his throat.

'Here in my pavilion,' he declared, 'we are only dust in the eyes of God. I have not brought you here for flattery, Venetian, but for wise counsel.' He paused. 'The gates to the Underworld have been opened. The doors to the kingdoms of the Eight Hells have swung wide!'

Chapter 6

The table-server Kwei-Lin, whom Marco Polo had seen striding so insolently beside his sedan chair, had slid through the crowds, across Golden Fish Bridge and back into the old city of Cambaluc. Never had Kwei-Lin felt so powerful. He felt like a cloud-strider, a walker in the skies, one of the Eight Immortals. He, Kwei-Lin, of indeterminate origin, former bandit, killer of Tuhmo and, until recently, a poor cook of offal and other sweepings of the meat market, now grew in stature as if he had chewed the most powerful opiate. All things were subject to him. What did he care about Mongol guards, highly decorated officers or powerful officials with their banners, pennants and lanterns? He had scaled the Pearly Mountain. He had, like a Red Llama, that powerful body of sorcerers, sat on the table of the world. He was truly a peacock strutting amongst the sparrows. Everyone had to give way before him.

Kwei-Lin had looked fearlessly on the face of the foreign devil with his strange white eyes, and skin the colour of leather. How dare that popinjay have himself conveyed as if he was a powerful demon? Kwei-Lin would soon show them all! His normal aches and pains had gone; there were no more hot arrows shooting up his back – none of those terrible headaches which had forced him to give up his life as an outlaw. The ulcer on his leg, which used to bleed and weep, had now closed, healed and disappeared. If he wanted, Kwei-Lin could spread his arms and fly amongst the white blossom clouds. He could storm the gates of Heaven or stride the shadowed demon paths across the fiery lakes of the Underworld to hold court in the very Halls of Hell. However, right this minute, Kwei-Lin reminded himself, he must hurry. When he arrived here, his friend Lin-Po would expect to find everything ready. Kwei-Lin paused and stared blankly at a barber who gestured him to a stool as if Kwei-Lin was a most favoured customer. The table-server scowled and shook his head.

What was happening to him? He felt as if he was two people, not one. Who on earth was Lin-Po? And the woman Wei-Ning? He closed his eyes. Of course, Lin-Po was the sorcerer, the Demon Father of the Water Lily Society. Kwei-Lin had been a member of the same society, or had he? As for Wei-Ning . . . Sweet memories pricked his mind. Wei-Ning on top of him, her beautiful body coated in sweat as she worked lustily, exclaiming loudly with pleasure. He had enjoyed that. So, why did he doubt himself? And what was he doing here? Suddenly, the table-server didn't feel so powerful any more. Shouldn't he be back in his cookshop? he thought, confused. Who would be looking after the oven? The furniture? The kitchen utensils?

'I must go back,' he murmured, feeling frightened. 'I shouldn't be here.' Then: 'Shut up, you loathsome little snake!' The words were out of his mouth before he could stop them. Flinching, the barber turned away.

So he should be scared, Kwei-Lin preened himself. Was he not a Lord of Hell? Had he not fallen like lightning and were not his enemies in Cambaluc? Would he not meet them again as he had, hundreds of years ago?

The Demon Lord, the Baron of Hell known to the Buddhists as *Wen Yi Kwei*, and to the Franciscans as Azrael, secured his hold more firmly on Kwei-Lin's soul. Any token of resistance was weakened in a will already steeped in evil, shattered by the sins of the past.

The table-server paused outside a shop where its owner was angrily pointing to the gourd, the symbol of the Guild of Beggars, painted above the door. He was arguing with a burly, dirty oaf who carried the beggar's matted wallet. The beggar's ugly face was contorted in anger. He wanted to beg outside, create a nuisance until the poor shopowner bribed him to move on.

'I have already paid your headman,' the trader roared. 'I'll not pay again!'

The oaf was now joined by a blind beggar, whose scrawny body was covered in rags; white hair hung down to his shoulders, his eyeballs mere dark, empty sockets. He, too, joined the argument.

Kwei-Lin decided to intervene. Were not these his servants, the creatures who did his bidding? Emptying his purse, he threw the coins at the feet of both the beggar and blind man. Immediately other beggars came out of the alleyways, a motley collection of garishly dressed vagabonds: men and women with ulcerated limbs, legs and arms. Lepers, their faces marred and blotched. A few were genuinely sick, though Kwei-Lin knew that many of their sores and wounds were more the result of clever artifice and paint. He was soon surrounded but not afraid.

'Get you gone!' he growled deep in his throat. 'Till I need you!'

The beggars stopped. The burly oaf pushed his way forward, his face full of insolence.

'We want more!' he shouted, hand extended.

Immediately Kwei-Lin began to speak. He didn't even recognise himself or the tongue he was speaking until he realised he was talking the patois of the beggars, using their slang to warn and threaten them. Frightened, the beggars backed off. Kwei-Lin took the bloody cleaver which swung on his belt beneath his tattered cloak, held it up like a champion would a sword and the beggars disappeared.

'Do you know what you said?'

Kwei-Lin turned: an old scholar, standing in the porch, came shuffling forward.

'What's all this about?' the old fellow asked. 'What *are* the terrors which are to come?'

Then he shrank back in terror as Kwei-Lin's angry eyes flashed at his.

'I am sorry,' the scholar muttered and scuttled back into the darkness of the shop.

Kwei-Lin continued along the narrow street, past windowless shops, doors flung wide open, next to blocks of private houses with their walls blind to the street, no doorways, no windows. Kwei-Lin smiled at such petty superstition. How could the position of a door or window protect any of them from a demon like himself?

He crossed a small square. A seller of sweets and fruit had laid open his baskets beneath a dying fir tree, displaying candied arbutus, Tientsin apples drenched in sugar and peanuts fried in fat till they turned a light-brown. Next to them lay bunches of ripe bananas and succulent pineapples cut in slices, portions of water-melon with their black skin and crimson heart, and mangoes, their green skins turning yellow. Kwei-Lin stopped and bought some: the trader took one look at his eyes and refused his money or to touch his hand.

A storyteller was sitting beneath the tree, surrounded by a group of urchins listening to him read from a dingy, dog-eared book. He, too, looked up and refused to continue until Kwei-Lin had moved on; even then he made the sign against the Evil One. The yellow, coarse-haired, high-tailed dogs who usually challenged the approach of any stranger, growled deep in their throats at him and slunk away.

Kwei-Lin continued his march through the city. He knew where he was going, the Temple of the Red Horse, a crumbling Buddhist shrine on the edge of the old city. He turned a corner, and a prostitute stepped out, dark almond-shaped eyes glaring in her light-coloured face. A stiffened robe was clasped round her shoulders; if she wished, she could open it to show her favours to any customer. Kwei-Lin hired her, pushing her into the small cubicle just inside the doorway. He took her roughly, slapped her face and threw a coin on the ground. Mocking her with jeering laughter, he returned to the street.

At last, just as a drum from a nearby tower proclaimed the Hour of the Monkey, Kwei-Lin entered the dusty, lonely park which surrounded the old Buddhist temple of the Red Horse. Huge boulders lay scattered about, carved by the weather into fantastic shapes which resembled sleeping dragons. It was a sinister place, not much visited, its grass sparse and dry under lofty pines which cast fingerlike shadows over the path. Kwei-Lin walked over the old bridge which spanned the canal. On its shabby, cracked balustrades stood chipped effigies of lions, tigers and griffins. He paused and stared over the side into the canal, which was filled with dirt and ordure and gave off a reeking stench. He looked up at the fretted stonework.

'The Temple of the Red Horse,' he said, and smirked.

It looked what it was, derelict and unused, its would-be worshippers driven away by the canal turned sewer which ran under the bridge and polluted both temple and park. As he entered the darkened doorway, an old attendant shuffled forward offering incense sticks. Kwei-Lin grabbed some of these and pushed him away. He gestured at the half-open door.

'How many priest-mumblers are inside, old man?'

'Just two,' the man whined fearfully. 'And myself makes three.'

'Soon there will be none!'

Kwei-Lin drew the cleaver from beneath his cloak and caught the old man a killing blow to the side of his neck. He then walked inside. The old Buddhist priest sitting on a cushion before the altar died even before he recognised the danger. The second one, sleeping on the matting beside the large smiling statue of the Goddess of Mercy, was awake only for a few seconds and glimpsed what he thought was a demon standing above him, blood-soaked cleaver raised.

In the Hall of Heaven, Kublai Khan had fallen silent after making his dramatic announcement. He was staring moodily at the floor as if trying to work out the intricate gold and silver pattern carved there. Sanghra clapped his hands and a servant came out of the shadows and served cups from a tray. Marco sipped from his and felt a pang of homesickness. This was not rice wine but an import from the vineyards of the West. It tasted sweet and cloying, and evoked memories of cool terraces and shady walks in the Italian countryside. He sipped and watched the Khan. He was not in Italy but in the private chamber of the Celestial One, the *Shun-tin-foo*, the Place Obedient to Heaven, and the Great Khan was about to reveal what had caused the comings and goings at court during the last few days.

Marco felt a slight thrill churning his stomach. Sanghra lifted a finger to his lips, a sign for Marco to keep silent. The Venetian repressed his fear. He glanced sideways at the carved *Men-Shen* in brilliant coloured robes and orange faces, the great guardians of the doorway. These were painted on the costliest paper and hung either side of the lintel. Was the Great Khan truly frightened? Had he lost faith in the *Men-Shen*? Or the mighty door-handles, specially carved to repel evil spirits? Marco fingered the piece of pure jade hanging next to the cross on the silver chain round his neck. Something dreadful had happened, or was about to happen, he felt sure. Both the Khan and Sanghra were wearing red silk scarves around their necks, one of the well-accepted symbols to repel evil. He longed to speak up and demand an explanation, but the Khan often lapsed into these silences and then spoke bluntly.

When Kublai finally lifted his head, his eyes were brimming with tears.

'I have been given Heaven's mandate,' he intoned huskily, 'but Heaven may take it away.' He gestured at Sanghra to explain.

'You may recall,' and here the Chief Minister's crafty face creased into a cold smile, 'the fall of the reprobate Ahmed.'

Marco nodded wisely, glancing quickly at the Buddhist nun and Franciscan monk. They seemed totally unperturbed by these events. What were they doing here? If this was a spiritual matter, were there not sorcerers and wizards Kublai could call on?

'I will explain in due time,' Sanghra murmured as if reading Marco's thoughts.

The Venetian bowed in apology. He had committed an indiscretion, looking away when Sanghra was talking to him.

'The accursed Ahmed, whose soul is now with the demons, was both a traitor and a rebel,' Sanghra continued. 'The roots of his wickedness spread far and deep. He had as an accomplice, the sorcerer Lin-Po.'

Sanghra paused and Marco kept his face schooled. He and

his uncles kept out of court intrigue yet everyone had heard of Lin-Po, conjurer, magician, a man who prayed to the *Kwei*, those evil spirits, elementals, or demons, who dominated the life and culture of the black-haired people.

'You may remember Lin-Po.' Sanghra leant forward slightly, eyebrows raised. 'Think now, my lord.'

Marco vaguely recalled the sorcerer's face. The man had been favoured by Ahmed the fallen minister: he also remembered that blood-stained, sinister figure who had stalked his cortège on the way to the imperial palace.

'What about Lin-Po?' he asked.

'Lin-Po led the Water Lily Sect,' Sanghra answered, a secret society of magicians who paid special devotion to the *Wen Yi Kwei*, the Demon Lord of Epidemics. The Water Lily Sect is of ancient origin. It began in the Province of Fukien, spread through the Prefecture of Wen Chou and along the coast of southern Chekiang. It crossed the Yangtse and affected many cities and villages along the Yellow River. The sect is like the water lily itself; it blossoms, it fades and apparently dies – but it always comes back. It is mentioned by the great classical scholars . . .'

'And their powers?' Kublai intervened. 'Tell our friend what powers they possess.'

'Oh yes.' Sanghra obeyed. 'The sect was weak until it was taken over by Lin-Po and his wife Shunko, who assumed the titles of Demon Father and Demon Mother. They were assisted by Wei-Ning, a courtesan and concubine of the cursed Ahmed. Together they practised human sacrifice and communicated with the Great Khan of Demons. Such practices are graphically described in *The Book of Changes* and *The Book of Rights*. They explain how these sacrifices, and the power they invoke, cannot be challenged by amulets, mirrors, almanacs, the *Pa Kwai*, the Eight Trigrams, the depiction of the characters of Perfect

Goodness or reference to the Holy Mountain.' Sanghra shook his head. 'All those count as nothing.' He gestured sadly towards the doorway. 'As do the *Men-Shen*, the burning of incense, and fire crackers.' He tugged at his red silk scarf. 'Or any colour under Heaven. The power of the Water Lily, or rather the power of the demon they worship, is impervious to all these.'

Marco gazed quickly at the Khan.

'Is this really true?' he asked. 'Do not *The Jades* say' (and here Marco quoted from a famous Chinese work on exorcism): '"By fear alone are the forms of demons wrought, and phantoms are the brood of thought"?'

Sanghra smiled at Marco's quotation of the couplet then breathed out noisily, a sign that he took issue with him on this point, though he was secretly pleased to be able to put this clever foreigner in his place.

'It is also written,' Sanghra retorted, 'that the approaches of the spirits cannot be surmised. So how can you treat them with indifference?'

'Continue,' the Khan said impatiently.

'Ahmed was a traitor and a conspirator,' the First Minister declared, 'with close ties to the Water Lily Society. His link with them was his concubine Wei-Ning. We do not know what he planned but we have discovered that he intended to send Lin-Po and his wife into Saanxi Province.'

'For what reason?' Marco asked.

'We do not know.'

'And what did Ahmed want?'

'Again, there is no evidence except that he was plotting against the Celestial One, being full of fury, eager to frustrate the will of Heaven.'

Marco stared at the floor. As a foreigner at court, he had to deal with a succession of ministers. Ahmed had been no better, or worse, than others: an arrogant, power-hungry man, the former First Minister had regarded Marco and his two uncles with complete indifference. They were favoured by the Khan so he deigned to tolerate them. In turn, the Venetians had done their very best never to threaten, or appear to threaten, any court faction, as rivalries in the imperial palace ran deep and bitter. Ahmed and Sanghra, however, had been confederates, sharing power. That's the way the Khan wanted it: *divide et impera* ran the Latin tag: *divide and rule*. The Khan deliberately encouraged his nobles to watch each other whilst he, like some benevolent Buddha, overlooked and arbitrated in their squabbles. In doing so, the Khan ensured he was given the best advice and each minister strove his best to sit in the warmth of his celestial smile.

'Why wasn't Lin-Po killed?' Marco asked, although he half-suspected the answer. Kublai, for all his wisdom and sophistication, was still a Mongol with all the superstitions of the Steppes. This was reinforced by Cathay culture, which enhanced the status of warlocks and wizards and made the imminent attack by demons a very real danger.

'Answer that.' Kublai's voice was scarcely a whisper.

'Lin-Po was put on trial,' Sanghra told Marco heavily. 'Both he and his wife Shunko were tried by secret court.' He ran a lacquer-nailed finger along his nose. 'Indeed, at one time the Celestial One thought of asking you to try the case.' He smiled craftily. 'But you had other duties so the Celestial One decided otherwise.'

Kublai spoke quickly. 'Lin-Po was tried by secret court but the evidence against both him and his wife was not as damning as it should have been. Lin-Po has one gift: in most cases he can read people's minds. Do you believe that, Marco?'

'Of course, Celestial One. I have been in your court for years.

I have seen feats of conjury, tricks and magic, unheard or unseen in the West.'

'Lin-Po used his gift to great advantage,' Kublai nodded, 'against both judges and prosecutors. The case went round and round like a dog chasing its tail. In the end I could not have the blood of such a man on my hands. He and his wife were exiled to Sachiu, a faraway place on the edge of the Great Desert.'

Marco pulled a face. Both his uncles and himself had crossed that same desert on their journey to Cathay; it was a frightening, forbidding place with rocks and trees, and secret, dusty hollows where demons and evil spirits dwelt.

'Now, in the normal course of events,' here Sanghra took up the story again, 'Lin-Po and his wife should have died, if not from homesickness at least from boredom. However, during the period of *Ta Han*, which you would call the beginning of spring . . .'

Marco realised the Chief Minister was referring to the beginning of February, almost three months ago.

'. . . According to reports, Lin-Po and his wife were invited to a festival at one of the ancient cemeteries. The local headman put a sleeping potion in their wine and they were buried alive in passageways and caverns beneath the cemetery. A short while later, a beautiful, mysterious woman entered the village: we believe this to be Wei-Ning. She seduced the village elder and learnt where Lin-Po and Shunko had been incarcerated. The man was found with his throat cut. The villagers hastened out but Wei-Ning had moved more quickly than they thought. The caverns were reopened. Shunko's corpse was found stabbed through the heart. It appears Lin-Po had sacrificed her to the Plague Lord. Of himself or Wei-Ning there was not a trace. The villagers confessed as much to the local commander. They have been punished for their crimes whilst the imperial secretariat has issued proclamations and warrants for the arrest and summary execution of both Lin-Po and Wei-Ning.'

'But no trace of them has been found?'

'Only vague rumour. They may have been going towards the Province of Saanxi, though for what reason, we don't know. Lin-Po,' Sanghra emphasised, 'is a very dangerous man. Wei-Ning has now probably taken the place of the dead Shunko. The Demon Father and the Demon Mother of the Water Lily Society are free once again.'

'How are members of this sect or society known?'

Sanghra spead his hands. 'They have secret signs, passwords. However, when they are initiated into the society, a strange emblem is carved on their left shoulder.'

'A water lily?'

Sanghra shook his head. 'No, that would be much too obvious. Each member of the society is given a letter of the alphabet: that's the only record kept.'

Marco nodded wisely. He just hoped his own reaction did not show – a quickening of the heart, a sudden spurt of fear. He glanced across at the Franciscan and Buddhist nun sitting as immobile and serene as temple statues. Marco was used to such detachment. The Cathayens practised it but these two seemed more engrossed in each other. The friar would, now and again, glance at the Buddhist: she was gazing at him as if in one of her trances. Marco noticed how, now and again, her lips would move as if she was muttering a mantra. Were they aware of what was going on here? And was Sanghra conscious of the turbulence in Marco's mind? For didn't Mai-da, his beautiful concubine, also have on her left shoulder, slightly faded or deliberately covered, a letter of the Chinese alphabet? Was his concubine a member of the Water Lily Society?

Or was it some other mark – a legacy of Mai-da's former life.

'You seem perturbed?'

'I was thinking about what Your Excellency said,' Marco replied; he moved restlessly on the cushion. 'I cannot see why the escape of a sorcerer and his lady friend, now being pursued by imperial troops, can pose any threat to the harmony of the Celestial One or his empire. If Lin-Po is so powerful, why did he not succeed in the first place?' Marco shrugged one shoulder. 'Here is a man, a great sorcerer, trapped by villagers and rescued by a woman. What danger does he pose? He will be caught and both he and the woman executed.'

'Lin-Po is a man like you and me, Marco,' Kublai interrupted harshly, lifting one hand and staring at the diamond rings which flashed there. 'He has his weaknesses.' The Khan smiled to himself. 'He loves the taste of wine and he can't always exercise his great gift. However,' and now Kublai bowed his head, left hand still raised, a sign that he was not to be interrupted or contradicted, 'I believe that Lin-Po and his sect, at the behest of Ahmed the traitor, was seeking the help of the Plague Lord, the *Wen Yi Kwei*. We do not know whether they were successful or not.' He gestured at the Buddhist and Franciscan. 'Reports to the Imperial Chancery have mentioned how, over the last few months, a number of visionaries and mystics in our empire, north, south, east and west, have experienced hideous and horrifying visions of the Plague Lord devastating the Middle Kingdom and spreading his dark shadow over the face of the earth. Do not doubt me, Marco. The history of Cathay is long and stretches back thousands of years. In the sacred scrolls and chronicles there are times when the Plague Lord has appeared and spread devastation such as we have never seen, bringing pestilences which devastate the earth and turn whole cities into charnel-houses.'

'But . . .' Marco paused and searched for words. 'Such epidemics come and go. They are like the seasons. God knows where they come from or why.'

'They are a punishment of God.' The Buddhist nun was looking directly at him. 'My name is Su-Ling,' she added. 'I am from the Buddhist Nunnery of the White Dove on the outskirts of Cambaluc. I have seen visions which are not phantasms of the night. A great terror is to come. A powerful demon will walk the face of the earth and no soul under Heaven will be left. If you do not believe me, ask Brother Raphael.' She gestured at the Franciscan.

Sanghra was about to intervene but Kublai raised his hand once more.

'We have not only heard such stories in our own empire,' he said. 'The leader of your holy men, who calls himself the Pope, the Bishop of Rome, has also sent me letters.' Kublai picked up his cup as if seeking warmth and sipped from it. 'The Pope says this demon will begin in my kingdom: he sends his prayers as well as his messenger to help me combat it.'

The Khan fell silent. So this was the origin of the comings and goings at court over the last few days, Marco thought. Kublai could be suspicious, but something in this seriously worried the Great Khan. Marco himself only believed what he saw or heard, yet he, too, felt his confidence crumble. Sitting in this darkened hall, listening to these dreadful revelations, he almost had to pinch himself and reflect that he was Marco Polo, a Venetian, a merchant, an adventurer, who had come to this kingdom and made himself a powerful lord.

Now Sanghra spoke again. 'It is best,' he said, 'if we hear from our visitor Brother Raphael.' He stretched across and grasped the young Franciscan's hand.

'Can he speak the heavenly language?' Marco asked.

'I can, *signor*,' the Franciscan answered fluently. He grinned shyly at Marco's astonishment.

Kublai laughed openly. Sanghra chuckled behind his hand.

'I apologise.' Marco bowed. 'Brother, it is good to see someone from my own country – although I am very happy here,' he added hastily. 'Which Pope has sent you?'

'By the grace of God, Nicholas IV, a member of our own Order.'

'So, your Order goes from strength to strength?' Before he had left Venice, Marco had seen these brown-robed friars become a powerful force in the Church.

'We are only strong because God wishes it,' Raphael replied. 'I was born Aeneas Piccolomini. My father was a lawyer in Rome. However, from an early age, I had a vocation to be a Franciscan.'

'And the flowery language?' Marco asked.

'In all things, *signor*,' the Franciscan replied, 'I was curious. In our house in Rome is Brother Joachim – a friar who entered the Middle Kingdom many years ago. Joachim became very skilled in its language, customs and religion. He brought back manuscripts, gifts of their learned men. Thirteen years ago, when I entered the novitiate, Brother Joachim would tell me of the marvels he had seen and he started a thirst in me that could not be satisfied. He taught me the flowery tongue, described to me the wonders of the Middle Kingdom, the Silk Road, the great Wall in the north, the glories of the Sung Empire and the rise of Genghis Khan and the Mongol Dynasty,' he bowed towards the Khan, 'which has had its highest, most supreme manifestation in the Lord Kublai, may God bless and protect him.'

Kublai, deeply flattered by this benediction, raised both hands in a gesture of humility.

'For thirteen years,' Raphael continued, 'I was taught all

Joachim knew. My superiors gave me dispensation. I am not learned in theology or philosophy but I have a love of all that Joachim taught me.'

'When did you arrive?' Marco asked curiously.

'Five days ago,' Raphael replied. 'But, unlike you, I came by sea rather than overland. I was armed with letters of introduction. I know from Brother Joachim how the Great Khan is always interested in messengers from the West.'

'A safe journey?' Marco asked.

Raphael's face became sad. 'There were two of us. My brother Gabriel died on board ship.'

'And do you have visions too?' Marco asked wryly.

Brother Raphael stared askance at him.

'Is that why you are here?' Marco asked.

'*Signor*, I do not have visions. I am skilled in the tongue and customs of these people: that was why I have been sent.'

Marco turned to the Khan.

'O Celestial One, it is good to see a fellow countryman. May I have your gracious permission to speak in my own tongue?'

Kublai nodded his assent.

'I cannot understand this.' Marco spoke rapidly in the *lingua franca* of his own countrymen. 'Brother Raphael, I beg you to be honest with me. You are an envoy of the Holy Father? Please,' Marco smiled, 'do not show alarm or any distress and, if you reply, talk quickly. Have you had visions?'

'I am what I have said,' the Franciscan told him stolidly. 'A disciple of Brother Joachim and an envoy of the Holy Father. I did not have visions, but Brother Joachim did – hideous and ghastly ones! Dreadful phantasms of the night, foretelling of a great death sweeping the face of the earth. I have studied the Buddhist and Taoist beliefs. I believe what the Great Khan has said.'

'You are a fully professed Franciscan priest?'

Brother Raphael nodded.

'Then why does the Buddhist nun Su-Ling clutch your hand so affectionately?'

Raphael blushed and withdrew his hand. Su-Ling now looked closely at both Marco and Raphael.

'For the first few days in Cambaluc,' Raphael went on, 'I did nothing but sleep. After that Su-Ling was brought to meet me, and she described what she had seen. In many ways, *signor*, there is a close resemblance between her visions and Brother Joachim's. I believe the very Gates of Hell are about to be opened. The Beast of the Apocalypse is ready to stalk the paths of man.'

'Enough!' Kublai made a cutting motion with his hand. 'Brother Raphael, I will explain. Perhaps,' he added slyly, 'the *signor* will then understand.'

Chapter 7

'Does the *signor* believe in Satan?'

Marco pulled a face. 'I'll be honest, Brother, I very rarely think of matters spiritual but I have seen enough to believe.'

'In the beginning,' Raphael continued as if Marco hadn't answered, a dreamy look in his eyes, 'all things were in harmony.' He joined his hands together. 'The visible and the invisible were one. There was no barrier or wall; beings physical and metaphysical, natural and supernatural, passed from one to the other. Two worlds in one. In our belief, and there are similar stories in the Buddhist and Taoist tradition, a great revolt was led by the spirit Lucifer, the Lord of Light. A terrible war erupted in the Heavens: all creation fell and, with it, Lucifer's army. The spirits of the air now live in the Kingdom of Hell, a state of complete hostility to God and man. Just as in our earthly armies there are different ranks, so it is in the Lord Lucifer's, whom we call Satan. One spirit in particular before the Fall, had been beautiful – Lord Lucifer's lieutenant. We call him Azrael: he became the Lord of Sickness and Death. It is his duty to pollute God's creation, to raise up pestilence.'

'Why?' Marco interrupted, uneasy at this sermon. 'Pestilences come from rotting corpses, filthy alleyways, the unclean.'

'That's true,' Raphael agreed, 'but their origin is Azrael. You see, Lucifer's rebellion was caused by God's plan for man to fill the earth and the Heavens beyond, to become Lords of Creation. Each demon has its task to prevent this. Azrael, one of the principal Barons of Hell, is to raise up sickness and pestilence. His great dream is to turn every man living on the face of God's earth to a corpse. So a time will come when no human heart beats, no breath is drawn, no image is thought.'

'And one demon is responsible for this?'

'Read the Gospels.' Raphael's voice was insistent. 'Have you noticed how many times, when Jesus cures a man, He drives out demons? How much of the sickness He encountered was caused more by the spiritual than the physical?'

'So, why is Azrael not successful?' Marco wanted to know.

'Again, look at Scripture, *signor*. The demons, like men, are limited. When the Lord Christ exorcised the Gadarene demoniac, the evil spirit asked to move from the possessed man to a herd of pigs. Azrael is similar. Since the beginning of time, when the revolt first broke out, he was bound up in the affairs of men and has stayed here ever since. He looks to cause mischief, be it petty or be it on a scale only imagined in our worst nightmares. In other words, *signor*, he is dependent upon man as much as upon his own strength. The only way he can exist in our world is by possession of a human being.'

'And if he doesn't?'

'Then Azrael must return to Hell, at the other end of Eternity. The journey there and back, even for a spirit, requires time and strength.' Raphael saw the disbelief in the Venetian's face and spread his hands apologetically. 'I can only tell you what Brother Joachim told me. We know little of the world of demons and spirits.'

'And you believe this?' Marco glanced at Su-Ling.

'Why not? I am not a Christian but I recognise your Christ as the Lord of Light. You must believe what Brother Raphael says to you.'

She chose her words carefully. Marco had never heard such a beautiful voice: calm, tinged with laughter.

'Spiritual truths are like human truths: they can be manifest in many ways, take many forms – but that does not mean they are not the truth. Surely you agree with that, *signor*?' She'd understood Raphael's use of the Italian title. 'Would you not agree that the sky at night is beautiful? A lily in full bloom beautiful? A galloping mare beautiful? Snow on the mountain peaks beautiful? So it is with truth. I do not fully understand some of the terms Brother Raphael uses but I recognise the truth he speaks.'

Feeling slightly chastened, Marco bowed in acknowledgement. Sanghra smiled, Kublai chuckled deep in his throat. He was looking at both the Buddhist nun and the Franciscan as if they were a favourite son and daughter. Marco's heart warmed to the Great Khan: a ruler of power, of great personal majesty and charisma, yet there was something childlike about him. The Supreme Lord of Cathay sat like a small boy fascinated by a storyteller. The Khan took out a pearl-encrusted fan and gently wafted it, inhaling the perfume it exuded.

'Continue, Brother Raphael. I have heard your story before but it's more fascinating in the retelling.'

'Azrael is limited,' the Franciscan continued obediently. 'He needs to be housed in a human soul, a human body. In such a way, Brother Joachim claimed, the Demons mock the incarnation of Christ or the spirit of Lord Buddha. Azrael needs a dwelling-place as do we. If the heart is evil and the will is turned against the light, Azrael can slip into a human soul as easily as a rat slithers beneath a door.'

'How?' Marco asked.

'Simply by touch.'

'But he cannot enter everyone?'

'Of course not. The human soul is like a house. If the doors and windows are closed and the will is on guard, no evil can enter. Is that not true of all of us? I can choose to love or to hate, to steal or be honest, to kill or protect, to envy or to praise. In most cases Azrael simply dwells like a poor man in an attic but he constantly looks for opportunities. He studies the affairs of men and, like a hunting panther, pounces when he thinks fit.'

'And this is to happen now?' Marco mused.

He would have rejected what the Franciscan was telling him except he kept remembering that blood-soaked, bedraggled figure with the insolent eyes and smirking mouth.

'You must remember the first revolt against God,' Raphael said. 'Satan and mankind in complete alliance. Azrael can, and will do damage like a spiteful child, but if he is approached directly, deliberately invited in, then think of the words of Scripture: "With Hell they have made a compact, with the grave they have come to an understanding".'

'And this is happening in Cambaluc?' Marco asked.

'We have reason to believe so.' Sanghra spoke up. 'When we seized Ahmed's papers we found evidence of how Lin-Po had carried out human sacrifice in a bid to call up Azrael to seal such a compact.'

'And what was the purpose of that?'

'Each lies to the other. Ahmed and Lin-Po for power, Azrael for a way into men's affairs.'

'And now?' Marco asked.

Sanghra sipped from his wine cup.

'Every religion has a celebrant. Lin-Po and the woman Wei-Ning are Azrael's high priest and priestess. He needs them here in Cambaluc.'

'Why?'

'We don't know.'

'If Azrael is such a powerful spirit,' Marco kept his voice steady, 'why doesn't he just travel through the air, meet Lin-Po and bring him here?'

'Don't mock these things.' Su-Ling's voice was harsh, her eyes flashed angrily. Marco quickly bowed lest he give offence.

'I am sorry,' he said. 'I am trying to understand.'

'Azrael is confined to human flesh,' the Buddhist nun declared. 'He must find possession. He can move but, if he leaves one person and does not find a dwelling-place, he becomes weak, dwindles back into his own spirit realm. If he is bereft of such habitation, even for a few hours, he is drawn back to Hell. Oh, he has certain powers – he can send malevolent thought, stir up hatred – but he is dependent upon man as the Lord Buddha is dependent upon me to do his will and the Lord Jesus on Brother Raphael. The Celestial One,' Su-Ling bowed towards the Great Khan, 'is Lord of the Earth but does he not depend upon the likes of you, Sanghra?'

Marco glanced sharply at her. Had he caught a note of dislike in the nun's voice?

Sanghra ignored her and leant forward, addressing Marco. 'I understand that this morning, when you met your fellow magistrates, you discussed murders amongst the pourers, the scavengers of Cambaluc.'

'I heard a fantastical story,' Marco replied, 'of indiscriminate, mysterious murders: how the victim of one murder was often the cause of a previous one. I confess I was as puzzled as the magistrate who reported it.'

'Azrael is a killer,' Su-Ling declared.

'Are you saying these murders are caused by a demon?'

'The pourers of Cambaluc are not noted for the sanctity of their lives,' she retorted. 'They live in a closely organised Guild. They eat and drink to their hearts' desire. They take bribes, they chase each other's wives. I do not wish to condemn, but Azrael would easily find a home in many of their Guild members.'

'And you have proof of this?'

'May I bring in the perfume-seller Chang?' Sanghra asked.

Kublai agreed. The Chief Minister turned and lifted his hand. A dark-garbed servant padded softly out of the shadows. Sanghra murmured to him and the man left. Marco sipped from the wine. He felt his unease grow. These were not childish stories about demons who were frightened by fire crackers or lanterns. Something very sinister had entered Kublai's city. If the Khan believed it, then so must he.

When the servant returned, the man who had accompanied him prostrated himself, tapping his forehead on the marble floor. He was dressed in the usual purple robe and special slippers provided by the guard. He was also trembling with fright. Sanghra had to tell him three times to get up and take a seat on one of the cushions. A young man, with a drooping moustache and beard, his black hair swept back and gathered by a comb, he sat cross-legged, head down, beads of sweat coursing along his face.

'He has been given a slight opium,' Sanghra murmured. 'He is so full of the terrors.'

'Look at me, Chang.' Kublai leant slightly forward. 'Raise your head and look on the Dragon's face.'

The young man did so.

'You have nothing to fear,' Kublai reassured him. 'You are my friend, my guest. You will leave my palace with gift heaped upon gift. Tonight you shall hold a party and tell all your friends of the great honour shown you. You have sons?'

Chang swallowed hard.

'You have sons?' Kublai repeated.

'Three, o Celestial One.' The words came out in a strangled gasp.

'They will all be allowed to enter the academy,' Kublai continued soothingly. 'If they show merit, they could rise to high office. This is what comes, perfume-seller, of looking on the Dragon's face. Now, tell me your story.'

'I am Chang.' The words came out in a rush. 'I am a perfume-seller in the Court of a Thousand Fragrances near the south gate of the new city.' He hung his head. 'I am humble,' he continued, recalling where he was. 'I am the Celestial One's most wretched servant.'

'We will be the best judge of that,' Kublai intervened. 'Tell your story, but after you leave here, tell no one else.'

'I have a wife,' the perfume-seller gabbled on. 'She is beautiful and as comely as a summer's day. My courtyard is cleaned by a pourer, an official high in the Guild. His name is, or his name was,' he corrected himself, 'Huyan. Now my wife is a good cook: in spring she makes us onions with minced meat. When the weather turns warm, she brews the tastiest of fragrant drinks from plums and peaches. Boiled fish is her speciality.'

'And the pourer Huyan?' Sanghra intervened.

'At first I considered him a friend. He would clean our cesspool, arrange for the latrine pit to smell fragrant and the rubbish from my shop was promptly cleared away. I paid him well and gave him gifts at New Year.'

'But he liked your wife?' the First Minister prompted.

'I became suspicious,' Chang confessed. 'The pourer Huyan was often in my home, particularly when I was not. I remonstrated with my most wretched wife but she assured me she was as faithful as the willow.' Chang shook his head, relaxing as he became immersed in a story he must have thought about many times.

'The most Celestial One's most wretched of perfume-sellers,' Chang continued, 'became convinced that Huyan was making love to his wife. So I followed him. I left my shop and made excuses so as to discover whether Huyan was renting an apartment – anything, I suppose, to quell my suspicions. One day, late in the afternoon, about the Hour of the Monkey, Huyan left the tavern where he had been drinking with other members of his Guild. Oh, I thought, his belly is full of rice wine, my shop is empty, will he visit my wife? Instead, something strange happened. Huyan went to a shabby eating-house. I thought it was a place of assignation and crept nearer. I felt like a mouse watching a cat.'

'And what did you see then?'

'I expected a woman to join Huyan but it was another member of his Guild. They left the eating-house and headed in the direction of my shop. Curious, I followed but they went through the gate and along the banks of the Yu. Huyan was acting as if his companion was a great friend. He slipped his arm through his, they were talking, laughing, much the worse for drink. They walked until we were in the countryside. Huyan stopped, pointing to a pagoda on a hill some distance away. His companion was becoming angry, as if Huyan had promised something and not given it.' Chang's fingers went to his lips.

'Tell your story,' Sanghra commanded.

'It happened so quickly.' The perfume-seller's fingers fluttered. 'And on such a fine spring day, too. Huyan was talking to his friend then he stepped behind him. I stared open-mouthed as a knife appeared.' Chang clicked his fingers. 'Cut his throat in a trice. All I saw was the sun flashing on the blade and that hideous gurgling as the man choked on his own blood. I was so terrified I hid. Huyan just wiped his dagger and sauntered back along the towpath. Oh, Excellencies, believe me, I was so frightened, my bowels turned to water, my legs couldn't stop trembling. I ran home. I didn't even tell my wife.' He looked down at his hands. 'I'm not a brave man.' He began to sob, shoulders shaking.

'Finish your story, most law-abiding of perfume-sellers,' Kublai urged.

'I could not get the scene out of my mind. I was terrified. Was Huyan a murderer? An assassin? He had eaten in my house, we had shared moments together. After three days of thinking, I went back to watching him again. I noticed he was very strange. He had stopped washing himself or changing his clothes. Sometimes I'd catch him staggering in the streets like a man drunk, at other times he would be striding purposefully. Then I stopped seeing him. I made enquiries of a neighbour. "Ah," they replied. "Huyan is ill. He is very sick. He lies in his bed and looks at the moon painting on the wall." I neglected my own business. My wife became curious. She also became suspicious and wondered if I was visiting a singing girl.' Chang smiled through his tears. 'A singing girl!' He laughed nervously.

'One day,' he went on, 'I was outside Huyan's house. By now I was keeping a virtual vigil. I noticed he was being visited by another member of his Guild. I could tell that from the insignia of a horse bucket on the parasol he carried. There was something in the man's walk, the smile on his face . . . well, it reminded me of Huyan walking along the towpath the day he killed his friend. I became alarmed. I entered Huyan's house.' Chang waved his hand. 'Faugh, it smelt like a midden heap. The floor hadn't been swept, buckets and bowls not emptied. I went along the passageway . . .' Now his lower lip began to tremble. 'The smell from the bedchamber was offensive. Huyan's corpse lay sprawled on the floor. His throat had been sliced from ear to ear. I could take no more. I ran from Huyan's house, vowing I would have nothing more to do with the pourers.'

'When was this?' Marco asked.

'At the beginning of *Ching Che* when the insects awake. I remember it was still cold. I thought a blood feud had broken out amongst the Guild of Pourers, so it was none of my business. However, as the days passed, I began to hear of other deaths, terrible murders. People are talking, you know? Anyway, I have a kinsman. I sell perfume to some of the ladies of the court . . .'

'You did well.' Kublai cut him short. 'And your honesty and directness are to be praised. You may withdraw.'

Bowing and kowtowing, the perfume-seller, keeping his face towards the Celestial One, retreated into the shadows. Marco heard the door open and close behind him.

'So you see,' Sanghra broke the silence. 'Terrible deaths, horrible murders.'

'And what makes you think these are connected with Lin-Po, Azrael or any other demon?' Marco asked.

'There is a connection,' Sanghra told him. 'It would appear that a pourer first becomes a murderer then a victim: Chang's tale proves this.'

'Only the Plague Lord explains these deaths,' Su-Ling added. 'He is now moving from one man to another.'

'The logic of it is quite simple,' Sanghra said. 'If these deaths continue, the pourers of Cambaluc will be massacred. It is now spring but soon the sun will grow strong, and the time of the small heat will be upon us. Can you imagine what will happen in Cambaluc at the height of summer, be it the old city or the new? Sewers, cesspools, canals and latrines will no longer be purged or cleansed. Refuse will mount up in the streets. We have already received so many complaints from certain quarters, soldiers are being drafted in to help.'

'There are plagues and pestilences every summer,' Marco pointed out.

'True,' Sanghra nodded. 'But if these murders do continue, Cambaluc will reek to the heavens and become as polluted as any battlefield. Whatever we do, this Plague Lord will continue his slaying.'

'And yet?' Kublai intervened.

'And yet,' Sanghra took his cue, 'that will be only the beginning of the horrors. Cambaluc is being prepared for Lin-Po: the brushwood and kindling are being collected. It's only a matter of time before he puts a torch to it and the flame becomes a raging inferno. I have been studying the calendars and almanacs. Hundreds of years ago, a deadly pestilence swept the Middle Kingdom. Is that what Azrael intends this time? To let the fires of Hell break through and the contagion grow, like a deadly mist through all of Cathay, north to the Great Desert, along the Silk Road and the sea routes into the West?'

'Do you believe in astrology?' Su-Ling asked. 'The study of the stars?'

Marco gazed blankly back.

'You believe in very little, *signor*,' she reproached him gently. 'Then let me take another example. You travelled overland into this heavenly place, did you not? Well, think of five or six roads stretching across the desert but all meeting in one place.'

'You are saying that is going to happen here?' Marco queried. 'We have the deaths amongst the pourers, the consequent chaos in the city, the coming of summer and the plague season and, finally, the arrival of Lin-Po?'

'Yes,' she replied.

'But what can Lin-Po be bringing?'

'I don't know.' She shook her head. 'Perhaps he is the carrier of the disease? A hideous new contagion?'

'So, what can we do?' Marco moved restlessly. 'Are we to sit here and wait? Can't this Lin-Po be hunted down and, in trapping him, entrap Azrael himself? Brother Raphael, you are a Franciscan priest: we have Buddhist monks, our own exorcists.'

'We could try that,' Su-Ling agreed, 'but Azrael is cunning. Remember, he can move simply by touch. Think of a bat trapped in a house. You close one door, he flits to another. Yes.' She rocked gently backwards and forwards. 'That is what Azrael is: some great evil shadow scurrying away from the sun.'

'Could he possess you?'

'I hope not.' She smiled. 'Nor you, *signor*.'

'We can do little about Azrael except trap him,' Sanghra intervened. 'But I have issued urgent messages, sent the fastest couriers along every road in the empire. They have Lin-Po and Wei-Ning's descriptions. My orders are quite explicit: Lin-Po, and any taken with him, are to be executed immediately.'

Marco stared down at the marble floor. 'And in the meantime?'

'In the meantime,' Sanghra said, 'we shall do what we can in Cambaluc. The deaths will be investigated, mercenaries employed to keep the city free of contagion. Su-Ling and Brother Raphael will also help.'

'If Azrael is a spirit,' Marco said, 'then he possesses a will and intelligence of his own. Does he know what we are plotting?'

He then quickly described what had happened on his journey to the palace: the bloodstained, arrogant stranger stalking his cortège.

'You should have told us earlier,' Su-Ling said briskly. '*Signor*, you have been more fortunate than we are. Azrael has looked upon you. To answer your question, yes, he *will* know, he *will* sense it; he can send images, thoughts and phantasms. True,' she waved her fingers, 'Azrael must be confined to human flesh. He must find a home in one of God's creatures. But think of him as a fire trapped in a hearth: its warmth and smoke can still travel beyond it. Indeed, the closer Azrael is to us, the more powerful he becomes. We must all tread warily, be careful as we move around the city. Our sleep will be plagued by nightmares, particularly at dawn and dusk, when the body is weak and the fire in our souls burns low. Azrael will strike, he will protect whatever he has to. We must pray that Lin-Po and he never meet.'

Marco was about to ask more but Kublai clapped his hands softly.

'You know what I want you to do, Marco. Sacrifices will be made. You will investigate the deaths amongst the pourers. With the help of Brother Raphael,' Kublai stumbled on the man's name and smiled apologetically, 'and our good sister Su-Ling, you must try to capture Azrael. Undoubtedly, great murder is planned – the slaying of mankind. In the end, the demons are what they were in the beginning, assassins, in total rebellion against God!'

In the Temple of the Red Horse, the table-setter Kwei-Lin had now finished his bloody work. He dragged the three corpses across and left them as a mockery at the base of the Goddess of Mercy, who soared above him.

'Bricks and mortar! Bricks and mortar!'

Kwei-Lin chanted the phrase as if he was a child playing in the marketplace. He opened the matted wallet on his belt and took out a piece of chalk specially brought for the purpose. He went round the temple walls and, in shadowy corners, etched certain signs and symbols. When he had finished, he came back, squatted by one of the corpses and, dipping his fingers in the blood, flicked it to the north, south, east and west, muttering a formal curse.

'All must be ready,' he whispered.

Kwei-Lin knew what was happening. He had seen the foreign devil in his sumptuous sedan chair. He could already imagine the couriers, in that marvellous system of the Great Khan, riding from five-mile house to five-mile house getting fresh horses, passing the message on. However, Wei-Ning would do her task. She had been instructed most carefully. The servant Lin-Po had to be free. He still had his uses; his time had not yet come. Both would be protected by others here in Cambaluc. Kwei-Lin dreamt on. The Demon Lord within him now pictured the great underground vaults in the Province of Saanxi, the traps, the pools of acid, the armed crossbows, the sacrificial victims, their skeletons mouldering, the army of jade statues and, at the centre, the jade coffin with its precious crown. More importantly, oh yes, those small, sleek, black-coated couriers. They'd be brought to Cambaluc . . .

Kwei-Lin opened his eyes. He was no longer a table-server. All that had disappeared. Azrael was thinking of former times, of other homes he had dwelt in. He stared up at the Goddess of Mercy and bit his lip.

'But the race is not won yet,' he cautioned himself. 'The prize is not seized, my enemies are still here.' He thought about that foreign devil. Oh, the Venetian might be sharp-eyed and sly as a fox, but he was only the sheath. More dangerous was the dagger, a two-edged weapon: the virgin nun Su-Ling and that brown-robed foreigner with his shaven pate and long, olive-skinned face. So they were all back! They had returned again. Their faces came before him, soft and weak. He moved angrily. No, no, they were not soft and weak. They were the ones to be watched! As he hunted, so they would hunt him.

Kwei-Lin got to his feet and moved round the temple, studying the paving stones very carefully. Every one of these mausoleums, so-called Houses of the Gods, had its hiding-place. And he was determined to find this one.

At last he did. A paving stone, behind the statue next to the wall, concealed a trap door. Kwei-Lin opened it up and went down. A torch had been lit though it was spluttering weakly. He walked around; it seemed to be no more than a storeroom. He checked its contents carefully: sacks of rice, a jug of wine, bowls of dried spices.

'Not enough!' he whispered. 'The flesh needs more than that!'

He glimpsed the bow and quiver of arrows, picked these up and went back up into the temple. Placing them against the door, he took the key from one of the corpses and left, locking the door behind him. The day was drawing on. Humming under his breath, Kwei-Lin left the dusty silent park and hastened along the narrow alleyway into the small market beyond. He moved quickly, buying this and that: dried meats, more rice, sealed jars of fruit drink and a large pannikin. Happy with his purchases, Kwei-Lin hurried back to the temple. He placed what he had bought in the storeroom and, taking the pannikin outside, found a small fountain, the water clear and pure. After washing himself hastily, he filled the pannikin and made his way back. Too late. He was at the door of the temple when he heard the horses' hooves and spun round. Two mounted archers had entered the small park: they stopped on the other side of the bridge and stared curiously at him.

'Who are you?' one of them called out. The man took off his spiked helmet, placed it carefully on the saddle horn and wiped the sweat from his brow.

'I am a visitor,' Kwei-Lin replied courteously. 'I have come to pay my devotions.'

'Where is the old porter?' the archer asked. He craned his neck as if trying to see round Kwei-Lin. 'And the priests, where are they?' He was now studying the table-server curiously, especially his blood-stained, ragged gown.

'Oh, they are in here, sleeping.' Kwei-Lin smiled. 'And the porter is in a shed at the back.'

'I don't believe you,' the first archer grunted.

He and his companion broke into a canter. Both riders were on the bridge. Kwei-Lin picked up the bow and notched an arrow. He felt a surge of pleasure: he would teach these idiots to interfere. He took careful aim: the first arrow hit the leader in the face. The second archer tried to turn but Kwei-Lin's aim was true. The arrow whirled through the air and struck the soldier in the side of his exposed neck. Kwei-Lin dropped the bow.

'All in a day's work! All in a day's work!' he chortled.

He caught the two horses, unbuckled their saddles and harness and tossed these beneath a bush; then, with his bow, he smacked both animals on the rump, sending them galloping across the park. After which, sweating and cursing, Kwei-Lin lugged the corpses inside the temple and locked the door.

'A time for killing,' he muttered to himself. 'And now a time for eating and drinking.'

So it was that Kwei-Lin, in the midst of all this death, sat down, pushing handfuls of rice into his mouth. He prayed his own demonic chant, eyes closed, exuding his hatred, a fierce opposition against Su-Ling, the foreign priest and their host in the House of Serenity.

Chapter 8

Around dusk, the beginning of the Hour of the Dog, Kwei-Lin picked up his quiver and bow and stared round the Temple of the Red Horse. He took pleasure in the bloody mayhem he had caused. The corpses of the soldiers had now joined those of the priests. The temple had been polluted and the secret storeroom filled; he had done his task well.

On leaving the temple, he crossed the bridge and quickly passed through the slums of the old city. He'd just hurried over one of the canals when a sound distracted him. He paused and looked at a man sitting on a stool, staring into a solitary white glazed bowl: a professional gambler trying his luck. Others had clustered about, their dull heavy faces throbbing with expectation: black eyes gleaming with avarice as they watched the gambler throw the dice into the bowl. Kwei-Lin's lip curled; that was life, a game of chance – if his luck held, he would win every throw. An itinerant barber, distracted by the gambling, had left his stall, and two urchins were attempting to rifle the small drawers of his portable table.

Kwei-Lin blinked as vague memories stirred. Shouldn't he be back at his cookshop? No, no, more important business required his attention.

After striding along a narrow lane, he stopped by a temple where a fortune-teller sat on the steps loudly inviting customers to use his services. A hard-looking man in his shabby gown, his long, dirt-filled fingernails clawed the air as he tried to draw potential customers closer. On glancing up, he seemed to recognise Kwei-Lin, and his expression turned from impatience to terror.

The fortune-teller jumped to his feet, snatched up his tawdry possessions and fled through the door of the temple.

Kwei-Lin deliberately dawdled: he didn't know why. Perhaps he wanted to savour, for the last time before he died, the ordinary sounds and smells of the city. Soon all this would be gone from his life. Kwei-Lin paused, rocking backwards and forwards on his feet, as his soul, for the last time, made a pathetic attempt to break free.

'Is there something wrong with your mouth? Can I help?'

Kwei-Lin opened his eyes and looked to his right. A dentist was waving him forward, the stall beside him strewn with teeth: huge molars marked and discoloured, battered eye-teeth and other items which the dentist could insert into anyone's mouth for a fee.

Kwei-Lin bared his mouth in a snarl and imitated the barking of a dog. The dentist scurried back. Kwei-Lin was now near the new city. He entered the execution ground by the Golden Stalk Bridge. The sandy area was deserted except for one condemned man standing in a huge, vat-like tub. The prisoner's head protruded through a hole in the lid, held fast by clasps. Kwei-Lin stopped as if he was interested. The prisoner's face was contorted with pain: at the bottom of the vat were bricks resting on a deep pool of lime. The sheer agony of standing with his neck trapped was exacerbated by the executioner returning every so often to pour in water. The lime was then activated, its fumes rising to sting the prisoner's mouth and nostrils. At the same time, one of the bricks would be removed. When they were all taken away, the prisoner's feet would burn while he choked on the sharp wooden rim around his throat.

Kwei-Lin made a sympathetic noise and stretched out his hand as if he felt a pang of compassion. It was evening time. Apart from a lazy-eyed guard, no one was near. As Kwei-Lin touched the prisoner's cheek, he felt the power surge within him. He, a table-server, was now as strong and fierce as a tiger. He could fly like an eagle above this city in a blink of an eye. Life and death, what were these?

'Brother.' Kwei-Lin ignored the guard. 'You are in deep pain?'

The prisoner, grey-faced, eyes protruding, could only gasp. Three of the bricks had already been removed and he could feel the scorching lime around his feet.

'Move on!' the Mongol guard snapped. 'Go on, you – get about your own business!'

As the guard came closer, so his alarm grew. He did not like the look of this shaggy-haired, dirty man with his flat face and brooding eyes. And were they not bloodstains on his filthy gown? And why was he carrying a cleaver as well as a bow and arrow? The guard panicked. Perhaps he should sound the horn, raise the alarm? Kwei-Lin, however, smiled cringingly, head forward, hands extended in a stance of supplication. The guard relaxed. Kwei-Lin greedily examined the horn bow and quiver of arrows the soldier carried.

'Do you want peace, Brother?' Kwei-Lin asked.

The prisoner stared beseechingly back.

Kwei-Lin immediately drew the cleaver and hacked it deep into the unfortunate's head, killing him immediately.

The guard was fumbling for his sword but Kwei-Lin, who felt invincible, struck again, driving the cleaver in at the line of exposed flesh between the soldier's neck and shoulder. The man collapsed, falling to his knees. Kwei-Lin made the last killing blow, took the horn bow and quiver and left the execution ground. He crossed the Golden Rose Bridge and entered the new city of Taidu, emerging onto its broad-ribbed, paved roads with gulleys of gravel running down the middle. Kwei-Lin studied these carefully. They were not as clean as they should be. The deaths amongst the pourers and scavengers were having their effect. He sniffed at the putrid tang which polluted the air, savouring it as if it were a fragrant perfume.

The city, however, unaware of such pending horror, was settling down to enjoy itself for the evening. Houseboats, elegantly furnished with kitchens, tables and chairs out on their dining decks, made their way along the different canals. On the roads, carriages covered with gorgeous hangings and containing silken cushions for their passengers, passed languorously by. The day's work now done, citizens were leaving their houses to take the air and stroll in the parks. Tea and wine kitchens were busy preparing banquets. On their upper storeys, singing girls were getting ready for an evening's entertainment. Criers, clustered in the doorways of restaurants and banqueting houses, loudly advertised silkworm pies, shrimp pies, pork pies and other delicacies.

Kwei-Lin passed them all. He had now taken off his ragged cloak, using it to carry the stolen bows and quiver. He smiled cynically. Soon all this would be deserted. There'd be no more feasting, no more revelry on silken couches with brimming wine cups. The fat bodies of these citizens would be the breeding ground for mice and maggots. He revelled at how the gorgeous displays of this wealthy Quarter would soon be brought as low as Hell. Gateways and windows, protected by screens, were filled with baskets of flowers. Chunks of meat, pig and mutton, hung next to these to be cured before being brought into the kitchens. In the courtyards jugglers, shadow players, storytellers and acrobats gathered to entertain their customers in the light of brilliantly coloured lanterns.

Kwei-Lin, however, hastened on. He was already attracting the glances of passers-by with his wild, tangled hair, furtive eyes and gore-streaked gown. Near Rice Market Bridge, he paused to check that the news he had learnt earlier was correct. A market porter told him it was: the principal officers of the Guild of Pourers had gathered for an important banquet in one of the pavilions across the lake.

The table-server hired passage on a pleasure boat, *The Hundred Flutes*, ornate and bright with its marvellous carvings. The boatman had never taken such a disreputable-looking customer before but Kwei-Lin paid him well then told him to shut up and row. Once they reached the mooring place, Kwei-Lin, infused with a renewed vigour, followed the lantern-festooned path up to the pavilion. Coloured banners and pennants fluttered outside. The pavilion itself, built of teak and sandalwood, was bright with lights, its doors and windows flung open. Kwei-Lin entered as quietly as a rat and climbed the staircase to the small gallery which overlooked the main eating-hall.

At the top Kwei-Lin bolted the door behind him, then he went to the balustrade and looked over. The dining room was a blaze of light and colour which gleamed in the black lacquered tables and the precious dishes and ornaments. The banquet was nearly finished. The officers of the Guild of Pourers, resting on cushions, were now toasting each other. Kwei-Lin studied the scene carefully. The main door had been closed; the Guild apparently wished to discuss their matters in secret. The table-server undid his bundle without making a sound. He checked both bows, plucking at the strings.

'All is ready!' he whispered. 'The banqueting is over. The revelry is finished. Death will be your guest.' Kwei-Lin notched an arrow to the bow, chose his target and took aim . . .

In the House of Serenity Marco Polo leant back on his cushions. According to the time stick burning in its special dish, the Hour of the Pig was well under way. He wiped the corners of his mouth. His cooks had served him well. He and his guests had spoken in the *Hwa Yen*, the flowery language, discussing this and that, whilst outside the swallows squabbled in the eaves of the upturned roofs. Poets of the Western Lake Society had recited verses whilst Marco and the others had dined on sweet soya, soup, pork cooked in cubes, shellfish in wine, goose with apricots. The red lacquered tables of his Room of Fulfilment were covered with cups of silver, glass platters and jade chopsticks. On the broad terrace outside, blind musicians regaled them with the softest notes.

Marco was pleased. He clapped his hands softly and Purple-Skin ushered the servants out, quietened the musicians and closed the shutters. Marco glanced to his right. Su-Ling was sitting erect, calm and poised. The Venetian sipped a little of the rice wine and kept his face impassive. If Mai-da sensed his inner turbulence, she would immediately become suspicious and demand to know what was happening. In truth Marco was fascinated by the Buddhist nun. She was so beautiful! Every time he looked at her his heart skipped a beat. Her face was light-skinned, her eyes, slightly upturned, were almond-shaped. They looked so pure, like the fire glimpsed in the heart of a precious jewel. Marco secretly wondered what she would be like naked, a coral necklace round that comely throat, her velvet skin drenched in perfume. He immediately felt guilty about these thoughts and, at the same time, angry for feeling guilty. Su-Ling had no eyes for him. During the journey from the city, their preparations and the banquet itself, she had been completely taken up with Brother Raphael: the young Franciscan simply stared dewy-eyed back. Marco wished he could order him away, leave some space for he himself to try his charm, or at least get to know this exquisite, enigmatic woman. Marco closed his eyes. He was getting soft and arrogant, more like a mandarin every day! Just because he wanted something didn't mean he had to have it.

Just then, Mai-da coughed, and he opened his eyes. His concubine was sitting on his left, Purple-Skin beside her. The scribe had a knowing look, Mai-da one of reproach. You idiot, Marco thought. She can tell what you are thinking! He smiled at her. Mai-da still glowered.

'You're as alluring,' he murmured ardently, 'as the heavenly lotus!'

Mai-da's face didn't change. She did look beautiful, Marco thought. She wore a gorgeously brocaded oyster-pink jacket, embroidered with golden dragons; its stiffened collar opened at the throat to display an amethyst on a silver chain – a gift from Marco the previous New Year.

'I am pleased that the Master is pleased,' Mai-da replied, but her eyes flashed with annoyance and her voice was heavy with sarcasm.

'And I am pleased too,' Purple-Skin now joined in the baiting, 'that our great master has returned and imparted to his wretched servants what the Celestial One has deigned to discuss with him.'

Marco bit back his annoyance. Purple-Skin was teasing him again. Before they had left the palace, both Kublai and Sanghra had agreed that Marco could discuss the matter with those he trusted. He had hurriedly done so. Mai-da had been more interested in the Buddhist nun whilst Purple-Skin, full of wonder, had grown importunate with his list of questions. Marco, already tired from his visit to the palace, had answered sharply. Purple-Skin had refused to be abashed.

'If the Celestial One,' the scribe concluded mournfully, 'believes the Gates of Hell are open, then, Master, we are all in terrible danger.'

Purple-Skin had wanted to hire sorcerers and conjurers to weave spells as well as hang up magical drawings to protect the House of Serenity.

'We have enough protection!' Marco had snapped, eager to get back to Raphael and Su-Ling.

Purple-Skin had only become more insistent, at which Marco had rebuked him so the scribe still nursed a deep sense of injury.

Marco sighed and leant across Mai-da.

'Purple-Skin, the Celestial One trusts you. I will reward you and, when this is over, I promise, both of you will come to the palace. I shall beg the Celestial One to turn his face towards you and smile.'

Both became slightly mollified. Marco sipped from his wine and brought his cup down rather noisily, attracting the attention of both Su-Ling and the Franciscan.

'Friar Raphael,' Marco began more harshly than he intended. 'You are most welcome. I thank you for bringing me news of the West. I have discussed with my friends here what we learnt at the palace. Can I ask you again? You are sincere in your belief?'

'I am,' the young Franciscan said, and tried hard to stay polite.

He had travelled far. In truth, he was overcome, not only by exhaustion but this beautiful Buddhist nun staring at him so intently. At times Raphael felt as if he was dreaming or had entered a painting of strange sights and sounds. The awful power of the Great Khan: the city with its gorgeous palaces, broad streets, its coloured banners and pennants such a contrast to the dark trees and wild open countryside with its lonely pagodas and drum towers. Even though he was experienced in their tongue and customs, the very sight and sound of these people disconcerted Raphael. He remembered Prior Joachim's advice.

'The black-haired people are not barbarians, young Raphael. *We* are the barbarians. They regard their land as the Place of Heaven, the centre of God's creation. Their cities were civilised before Rome was even built on the Tiber. In all things, remember, they expect you to keep face and not force them to lose theirs.'

'And what is face?' Raphael had asked.

'We call it honour. At no time, even if you are angry, must you take their dignity away.'

On reflection Brother Raphael found this hard. He had dreamt of this fabulous kingdom but the reality was more exotic than his wildest imaginings. Now he had to face this smooth-faced Venetian who, snake-like, could coil his way round the Great Khan's heart, bridge cultures, and openly wear a crucifix next to a piece of magical jade. Perhaps if he had slept properly, Raphael thought, he would feel better, more composed.

'In which case we have two problems,' Marco declared briskly, deciding to ignore Mai-da's hostile looks; in fact, he wondered whether she should be there at all. He recalled the insignia of the Water Lily Society and the mark he had seen on Mai-da's beautiful shoulder. Was she a member of that secret sect? Is that why she had sought him out, insinuated herself into both his heart and home?

'The first problem,' he continued, brushing that sinister thought aside for the moment, 'is the demon Azrael or the Plague Lord. According to the evidence we have,' and here Marco sounded as if he fully believed what he had been told, 'he is responsible for the deaths amongst the pourers. He is also preparing the ground for Lin-Po's return to Cambaluc. What the enemy intends we do not know. Agreed?'

They all murmured their assent.

'The second problem is Lin-Po and Wei-Ning. If fortune favours us, they could be trapped and killed before they ever arrive here. If fortune favours them, that will be our task.'

He glanced sideways. Mai-da and Purple-Skin sat, heads down, as if they were listening carefully. However, he felt sure they were communicating with each other. Or were they quietly mocking him? Marco shifted his gaze to Su-Ling and Raphael.

'Whatever way this matter goes,' he went on, 'we will have killing. Are you reconciled to that?'

'I am reconciled to nothing,' Su-Ling retorted. 'My faith is that of Raphael's.'

Marco noticed how she referred to him almost as if he was a brother or lover.

'We are committed to non-violence. However, if Heaven has turned its face against us, we are left to our own devices. A field must be weeded before the sowing can take place.'

Marco stifled his annoyance. One thing he never accepted about these people was their constant hiding behind enigmatic, ambiguous sayings.

'So, you *will* kill?' he said harshly.

'"Fear not those who kill the body",' Raphael answered for her, quoting the Scriptures, '"but rather those who kill the soul".'

Su-Ling held up her rosary beads, moving the hardened shells along the piece of string. 'We must find the place,' she said, 'cut and do so quickly.'

'And what protection can you offer?' Marco asked.

'Prayer? Fasting?'

'Our religions are not so different after all,' he told her, gently mocking.

'Are we safe here?' Purple-Skin asked.

Marco stared round the dining-hall, at its decorated walls, polished teak floor, the warmth coming up from the flues beneath, the baskets of jasmine and red periwinkle, the gold and silver ornaments, the sensuous cats, yellow and white, which lounged around. Could all this be threatened? Sanghra had intimated how soldiers and cavalry could be despatched to bivouac in the fields round the house. Marco realised then that his life was truly changing; its serenity had shattered. Outside, the gardens would be ripe and splendid under a silvery moon and a sky dotted with stars. He should be there composing a poem by the waterfall.

'If Your Excellency,' Purple-Skin's voice was tinged with sarcasm, 'could arrange protection?'

'What can we do?' Marco threw the question back.

'We can put up banners, display the characters NUH and SHAU?' Purple-Skin quoted the signs for happiness and longevity. 'We can light lamps, say our prayers, wear amulets and charms.'

'Child's play!' Su-Ling retorted. 'Azrael must be seen for what he is: a great Lord of Hell with all forms of power at his disposal. We will experience phenomena. We may even have to withstand physical attack. In the end, Lin-Po must be killed and Azrael's plans foiled. This great Baron of Hell must be thwarted and sent back to the fiery pit where he belongs.'

As if in answer, a dog howled; the sound swept through the

room, hollow and eerie. Shadows raced across the ceiling as if some giant bat had flown in and blocked out the light. Lamps guttered and died whilst the perfumed breeze flowing through the shutters turned rank and fetid. Marco jumped up at the shrill screams which came from other parts of the house. There was the sound of running feet, and Infinite Joy, Mai-da's principal maid, burst through the door, hair dishevelled, a cloak wrapped about her.

'Master!' Her face was a mask of fear. 'You'd best come! You'd best come!'

They followed her along the passageway into the Courtyard of Moon-filled Happiness, which stretched out to the Gate of the World, the main entrance to the house. This had now been locked and barred for the night, but the watchman's booth beside it was empty. Inside, his small table and stools had been overturned. Lanterns had been cut down, streamers slashed. Purple-Skin exclaimed and pointed to the tablets on either side of the porch: the *Shen Yui*, the guardians of the portal, had been ripped off. A servant came running up with shield and sword which he thrust into his master's hands. The Venetian did not like what was happening. This was his courtyard, yet it had changed. It was no longer moon-filled but dark, dingy, full of threat. Moving cautiously forward, he flinched at the blast of heat that met him, then gagged at the smell of ordure, as if a sewer had been opened, its vapours pouring towards him. From somewhere beyond the walls, a gong boomed, mixing with the jarring clash of cymbals. Voices were raised, curses hurled. Marco felt as if he was on a battlefield with some fierce enemy moving menacingly towards him.

Suddenly, the clashing and gonging stopped. A war drum rattled, followed by the discordant notes of a *pipa*, a balloon-shaped guitar, which was echoed by the harsh sound of the *Ti Kem*, the crowing lute. Deciding to ignore this, Marco walked towards the large ornamental pond in the centre of the courtyard. He heard a sound behind him and spun round. Su-Ling and Raphael were approaching. For some reason, Marco recalled that ghastly, blood-soaked figure walking beside his sedan chair. He gripped his sword and shield more tightly.

'Go back! Go back!' he shouted.

They both ignored him. Marco reached the pond with its small rockery and dwarf trees. These had now been viciously hacked down whilst, in the dim light, he could see the golden and silver carp, belly up, floating amidst a bloody froth. The Gate to the World began to shake. Grey wisps of mist swirled over the wall. The raucous music drew nearer.

'It is the *Kwei*, the ghosts of the dead,' Su-Ling whispered.

Raphael was now praying softly under his breath. Marco recognised the quotations of the Latin Mass of the Dead. Su-Ling joined him with verses from the *Ta Tsiau*, the Buddhist rite to appease hungry ghosts. The phenomena subsided then began again. The water in the pool gushed up over the rim and splashed about their feet. A small table and stool near the wall burst into flames. The servants, clustered in the doorway, screamed and fled.

'*Shau I! Shau I!*' Purple-Skin yelled, referring to the Buddhist rite of burning clothes and paper money to appease the dead.

'You have made a covenant with the grave and with Hell have reached an agreement!'

The voice rang, bell-like, across the courtyard, cutting through the cacophony of sound. An arrow, or what seemed to be one, whistled through the air. The grey tendrils of mist curling round the courtyard formed faint figures, ghoulish shapes: some had skeletal features, others no heads at all. Marco stared. He had seen the work of Chinese magicians and illusionists. Was that happening now? Some of the shapes grew more material. A few wore the *cangue* or wooden collar of criminals.

'Brother Marco,' Su-Ling whispered. 'We should ignore this. We must go back into the house.'

But Marco stood his ground as the shapes drew nearer. He could make out individual features. They were substantial yet, at the same time, transparent, eyes and mouths filling with blood. The creatures wore tattered clothes, carried rusty weapons.

'They are the dead,' Su-Ling breathed, 'the souls of those who have been executed.'

Marco recalled the legends about the fields around the House of Serenity: how once they had been the execution ground and burial-place of criminals from the old city of Cambaluc.

'Let us return,' the nun insisted.

Marco looked over his shoulder.

'We must go and pray,' she urged him. 'We can do no good here.'

The ghoulish shapes stayed still. Marco realised discretion was the better part of valour and agreed. The rest of the servants had scattered but Purple-Skin and a few hardy souls had armed themselves. Marco laughed at their conical helmets, shields and swords.

'They are no use here,' he commented.

'Close all the doors!' Su-Ling ordered. 'Brother Marco . . .'

The Venetian felt pleased: for the first time he had caught a note of kindness in her voice.

'Brother Marco,' she repeated, 'Raphael and I should pray.'

Marco led them into the Hall of Moonlight, an exquisite chamber with a large window facing east. This was now barred and shuttered: at this time of the year it usually stayed open all night so he could come in here and watch the sky. At Su-Ling's suggestion, they sat down on the cushions placed round a small table. Mai-da and Purple-Skin joined them though Su-Ling looked at them askance. The sounds of disturbance from outside had grown.

'What is it?' Marco asked. 'An illusion?'

'Yes and no,' the nun answered. 'More simply, it is the work of Lord Azrael. He sends us warning. He knows we are here: those restless ghosts are his envoys.'

'Are they real?' Marco wanted to know.

'What is real?' she teased him. 'Were they distinct from us or part of our own lives? I don't know.' She smiled dazzlingly. 'But you are brave and, by the way, you don't need a sword and shield in here.'

Embarrassed, Marco put the weapons in a corner. He couldn't forget that awful voice and the macabre quotation from the Bible about a compact with Hell, an understanding with the grave.

'We should pray,' Su-Ling urged. 'Let your mind float, meditate.'

Marco found this very difficult. Mai-da abruptly rose and left the chamber with Purple-Skin, who was muttering under his breath about more practical measures. Marco, however, was curious; he did try to say the *Requiem*, allowing his body to relax, bring some control to his breathing. However, instead of praying, he felt warm and sleepy as if the chamber was bathed in sunlight: when he opened his eyes, it was dark, except for the flickering lamp in the corner. Raphael and Su-Ling were lost in their own world of prayer. Marco shifted. It wasn't an illusion: the room was warm and perfumed like the costliest bathwater with crushed flowers and precious oils mixed in. He felt as if he was floating and closed his eyes. He was walking along a road trying to catch up with two figures but the faster he walked, the more distant they became. He woke with a start. The lamplight had burnt much lower; had he been asleep? The house was silent; Su-Ling and Raphael were still lost in their meditation. Then suddenly, the Buddhist nun lifted her face, eyes wide open.

'Leave us,' she whispered. 'Mai-da is waiting for you in the Chamber of Spilling Joy.'

Marco felt he had no choice but to obey. He got up and went out along the deserted passageway. At the end of it, he unbarred the door, entered the courtyard and stared at the Gate to the World. All was silent. Purple-Skin had organised the servants: the mess had been cleaned up, the fish removed from the pond. The night air was soft and balmy. Myriads of burning night moths fluttered about. Even from where he stood, Marco could hear the crickets in the field beyond.

'But it's night-time,' he murmured, still a little confused by Su-Ling's abrupt dismissal.

A bird began to sing. The door behind him slammed shut. Marco, fearful, stared at the top of the wall. He almost expected black garbed figures to come flowing across like some death-bearing water. The courtyard was transforming itself before his eyes. He shook his head. Was he dreaming? He turned and pushed down hard on the door handle, but it refused to open. A chill clawed at his sweaty back. He whirled round. Someone was in the courtyard, surely? Marco stared into the darkening corners. Was that a sharp hiss of breath?

'Marco!' The voice came soft. 'Marco Polo, the teller of tall tales.'

The Venetian's legs trembled. He recognised that voice, but it couldn't be her, could it? He glimpsed a shadowy form in the far corner garbed completely in white. Marco's mouth went dry. Wasn't white the funeral colour of this country?

'Who are you?' he called out.

'Why, Marco, you are so forgetful!'

A young woman stepped out of the shadows, and Marco's heart skipped a beat.

'Lucrezia!' he whispered. 'Lucrezia Sforza!'

He stared in terror. There she was, yet he could remember the day Uncle had taken him down to the piazza to watch this witch be executed. A seller of potions, a dabbler in the Black Arts, all of Venice had seen Sforza hang, her body consumed by fire. Marco had never forgotten the scene: a beautiful, tall, auburn-haired woman being carted to execution whilst the mob howled and she shouted back curses. His uncle later admitted that their presence there had been a mistake; his young nephew had suffered nightmares for weeks.

'You are dead,' he breathed.

'Am I?' The woman drew closer, her face a ghastly, bluish-white, dark-red rings under her eyes. 'All will be dead soon, Marco Polo – bodies bequeathed to the Kingdom of the Worms.'

Despite himself, Marco backed to the door, his bravado forgotten. The witch swaggered closer, laughing deep in her throat. Just then, Marco stumbled against a spear the servants had left propped against a wall. He tripped and fell but, moving like a cat, immediately sprang to his feet, only to find the courtyard empty once more. Above him the moon rode the starlit skies, with no sign of his visitor from Hell.

Chapter 9

In their silk-strewn bed in the Chamber of Spilling Joy, Marco
and Mai-da, bodies soaked in perfume, moved, locked together in
the dance of love. Marco stared down at Mai-da's face, beautiful
in the lamplight, the black hair framing her lovely face, eyes
glittering with passion as she writhed and twisted, refusing to
take off the pleasure ring she'd expertly fixed over his penis. Her
long nails scraped his skin and the soles of her feet massaged
the back of his legs. She moved and caressed him until Marco
exclaimed in pleasure at the voluptuousness. She was no longer a
woman but a velvet serpent coiling herself about him. He tried to
control her, press her down. She came back, moving aside, then
she lay still: her fingers gently removed the ring. Then, pulling
him towards her, she cried out in high-pitched exclamations of
pleasure.

Afterwards, Marco stared across at the lamp on the other side
of the bed. Mai-da lay quietly. Although he felt drained, the
Venetian could not forget the face of the Buddhist nun, nor the
way she kept looking at Brother Raphael. His heart lurched. If

only she would look at him like that! He turned on his side; the light from the lamps was not very strong. Mai-da appeared asleep. He eased himself up on his elbow and peered at the mark high on her left shoulder. He could not clearly make out the faint tattoo. Had some attempt been made to cover it? Mai-da was an expert in the use of creams and cosmetics.

Marco rolled over on his back and stared up at the teakwood ceiling. Was Mai-da a sorceress? He grinned. She certainly was in bed. What did he really know of her? She, like Purple-Skin, had fled from the Sung city of Hangchow just before the fall of that Dynasty, when Kublai Khan had finally asserted his power over the whole of the Middle Kingdom. The last Sung Emperor, a mere boy, had committed suicide by jumping off a ship and drowning himself – the signal for the end of all resistance. Marco moved restlessly. Mai-da, like Purple-Skin, had travelled to Cambaluc and, with the money she earned, made herself as comfortable as possible. She'd caught Marco's eye at a tea-tasting festival at the Pavilion of the Brilliant Spring.

Marco ran his tongue around his teeth; his mouth still tasted of rice wine. Secret societies in Cambaluc were as numerous as weeds in an untended garden. Some were hostile, others mere confraternities, no more dangerous than the Guilds of the city. But the Water Lily Society? Had Mai-da been a member when she had lived in the city of Hangchow – and then given it up? Was it a mere accident they had met – or was it deliberate? Marco wanted to question her but, from the start, they had had an agreement, which formed the bedrock of their relationship: his private life, and hers, were a closed book, never to be opened.

Try as he might, Marco was unable to settle himself to sleep: he could not banish the face of Su-Ling. Throwing back the coverlets, he slipped off the bed and donned a silken robe. From a small coffer he took out a thin curving dagger in its jewelled sheath. He was at the door when Mai-da spoke.

'You cannot forget her face, can you? I saw it in your eyes.'

Marco did not answer but slipped through the door. The House of Serenity now lived up to its name. All was peaceful. Night-lights gleamed and, through a window, he glimpsed the brilliant nightlight nocturnal moths attracted by the flames. Purple-Skin had ensured that everything was safe: the doors were locked, the skylights firmly fastened down. Marco reached the antechamber to the Hall of Moonlight and crept quietly across. Removing the ornate drawing on the wall, he stood on tiptoe and stared through the small eye-opening specially placed there so the owner might secretly observe any guests who'd gathered to admire the moonbeams. Su-Ling and Brother Raphael still sat opposite each other, two lamps on the shining floor between them. Someone had served them a dish of fruit and small cups of jasmine tea.

Marco watched, intrigued. The Buddhist and the Franciscan were debating, discussing their respective theologies but they were in harmony, looking for similarities rather than differences. Marco listened carefully: despite their reputation as mystics and as holy ones, both were eminently practical. Marco had never met two people so unlike in many ways, yet so peaceful in each other's presence. He could make out the Franciscan's face but it was Su-Ling's eyes which attracted him. Never had he seen a beautiful woman look on anyone as she did Raphael. Her very eyes seemed to breathe into his soul. Why was this? Marco felt like a petulant child. Why did this Buddhist nun attract him so much? And why was she so drawn to the shabby, young Franciscan priest? The two had hardly met, they were separated by culture, yet they sat and chatted as if they had known each other for years.

Marco stiffened. The conversation was changing. He had expected them to discuss the dangers which confronted them, but Su-Ling was openly teasing the Franciscan about his own country. He shyly defended it but, joining Su-Ling in her soft laughter, he explained the different customs and traditions of both his Church and the Eternal City. When he described the infamous ladies of Rome, their dress, their perfume, their cosmetics, Su-Ling clapped her hands like a child and chuckled, a heart-catching laugh which lit up her face. Apparently flattered by this, Raphael sprang to his feet and mimicked the women's swaying walk, the tilt of their heads, their gesticulating hands and rapid, high-pitched voices. Su-Ling, holding her sides with laughter, lay down on the cushions and, raising her hand, begged him to stop. Still chuckling, Raphael re-took his seat.

As the conversation continued, Marco became aware of how much each knew of the other's culture and country. He realised he had made a mistake: neither the Franciscan nor the Buddhist were as simple-minded as he had thought. In fact, Raphael seemed to know as much about the Middle Kingdom as he did. Marco did not know if Su-Ling had studied the customs and traditions of the West, or whether she had just learnt quickly from what Raphael had told her. No attempt was made to assert the supremacy of one above the other. Christ and Buddha were One whilst the world manifested the glory of God despite the evil of men and the presence of demons.

Marco felt no guilt for spying on the couple; he was glad he had come. He was aware that both were moving towards something; he had to stay and see what it was. The spy-hole was expertly built, not only to give a good view of the room but also to catch every sound; although his guests spoke softly, each word carried.

'Why did you become a Buddhist?' Raphael asked.

'I had no choice,' Su-Ling told him. 'I don't know where I come from. My parents must have been poor. In the Middle Kingdom, if there are too many mouths to feed, baby girls are left outside and exposed to the elements.' She did not show any pain or anger at this. 'My parents must have been very poor,' she continued. 'According to the Buddhist priest who found me, I was almost naked except for a ragged cloth; a small cup of wine and a bowl of rice had been left beside me.' She laughed. 'The Buddhist priest was hungry. He ate the rice and drank the wine so he was obliged to help me. He picked me up – it was outside one of the villages near Cambaluc – and took me to the Temple of the White Dove.' She spread her hands. 'That has been my home ever since.'

'You could have left?' the Franciscan prompted gently.

'Yes – once my blood courses had begun, I was free to go, but I wanted to stay. I had grown to love the temple, the old priests and nuns. I was shown the libraries, and I received an education any candidate in the Hall of Examinations would have envied. I also experienced visions: the coming of a storm, a terrible shaking of the earth, or some great disaster, like the collapse of the Temple of the Silver Mulberry in Cambaluc.'

She stared across at the wall: Marco wondered if she knew he was there.

'But there were other visions,' she said quietly. 'At first it was like looking across the countryside when a mist hangs heavy and you can see nothing except indeterminate shapes. In each succeeding dream, that curtain of mist began to lift and hideous visions emerged. They had the same theme: the Plague Lord stalking the face of the earth, spreading devastation and terror wherever he went. I saw cities . . .' her voice became passionate, 'where the dead lay piled in heaps, higher than the span of a man. I saw visions of a countryside where the trees were blackened and

125

the earth was burnt. Not a stalk of rice grew, nor did any bird chirp or cricket click. Above me the sky was a lowering grey, edged with fire: the wind was hot like the blast from a furnace. At other times, the countryside lay under a black snow. I saw cities, Raphael, empty of life: corpses mouldering in the streets. Rivers, lakes and pools dried and shrivelled.' The nun paused, her head down. 'And there were other visions.'

Marco barely caught her words.

'What?' Raphael asked.

'In my nightmares,' Su-Ling whispered, 'I saw the Plague Lord himself. His face was hidden but I sensed it was ghastly. Two figures stood either side of him, a man and a woman. Occasionally they were human with all their features and limbs. At other times they assumed the form of a huge rat.' She smoothed the side of her face with her hand. 'I always woke screaming.'

Marco tensed: of the two of them, Su-Ling had assumed the leadership. She had been a virtual recluse in the Buddhist temple but her mind was razor-sharp, strong-willed and incisive. He was convinced she was leading Raphael along a certain, predestined path.

'You had other visions?' the Franciscan asked her.

'I cannot explain these fully.' She relaxed a little and laughed girlishly behind her hand. Then she bit her lower lip. 'I lack the words to describe what I saw: I was in cities, far, far away from here. I recognised myself but I was dressed in different robes. My hair, my face, were different.' She laughed again. 'Do you know, sometimes I was male, other times female. These dreams came in drops like water from a pipe.'

'Describe some of them,' Raphael urged.

'One time I was standing on steps. The steps led up to a temple. The sky was blue, much bluer than ours, and the sun very strong. Soldiers were ranged on either side of me. They had armour over

126

their chests, scarlet cloaks, strange helmets.' She described these with her hands. 'Plumes which ran from the front of the helmet right down to the back; their shields were round, emblazoned with strange devices. Another time I was in a city with marble houses and narrow, winding streets. This, too, was a city of the dead. Corpses lay in doorways and, above the lintel, red crosses had been daubed. The air was black with raging smoke. Funeral pyres had been lit and the stench . . .' She wrinkled her nose in distaste. 'I remember a beautiful church, its gleaming dome stretched up above the city. Brother Raphael, do you know such a place?'

The Franciscan moved restlessly. He pressed Su-Ling to repeat her description, particularly of the church.

'Do you know such a place, Brother Raphael?' she asked again.

'Santa Sophia,' he replied.

She tried to imitate the words then gave up. 'What is it?' she asked.

'Many years ago, Brother Joachim took me on an embassy, a delegation to the Byzantine city of Constantinople,' the young monk told her. The city stands on a great waterway hundreds of miles to the north-west of the Middle Kingdom. It sounds very similar to your description. Its main cathedral, in their tongue, is "Santa Sophia", the Church of Holy Wisdom. I may be wrong, but it's the only city I can think of where a church dome dominates the sky.'

'In all my dreams,' and now Su-Ling was choosing her words carefully, 'I was aware of great evil. However, someone often stood beside me, a friend, a lover, a companion. When I turned I could not see him or her, as if the mist had come down again. Yet, I caught glimpses.' Her voice faltered. 'And you?' she asked, changing the subject abruptly. 'Brother Raphael of the Franciscan Order, where do you come from?'

'I was born of rich parentage,' he replied. 'My father was a merchant in Rome. He sold wine and other foodstuffs to the nobles. I went to school – my father tried to educate me. He claimed I had a good mind and wanted to send me to the University at Bologna. Rome is a very dangerous place; its yellow-bricked houses are fortified as the great lords are often at each other's throats. Fighting and killing are a commonplace occurrence. Even the Pope has to hide behind high walls and guards.'

Raphael folded back the sleeves of his gown. 'Of course, like any other hot-blooded young man, I ignored my father's advice. I drank, I ran riot, I fought with dagger and sword. I also fell in love with a young courtesan. One summer, a terrible pestilence raged through the city. My beloved died and I attended her funeral. Even there the guests were drunk, talking and whispering throughout the service. I volunteered to carry her coffin. One of my companions was so befuddled he slipped and fell. The casket crashed onto the cobbles and the corpse rolled out.'

He shuddered. 'It was disgusting. Already the comely face, the shapely body, were beginning to rot in the heat of Rome. I placed her remains back in the coffin and shouted at my companions to show some respect. Afterwards, I was no longer the same person; those few minutes had changed me for ever. Was this, I thought, the end of all glory? The promise of the world? I withdrew from my companions, went back home and, slowly, I returned to God. At that time I was attending a Franciscan church, where I met Father Joachim. I can only have been around eighteen.'

Brother Raphael looked up and met Su-Ling's eyes. 'The rest followed like the seasons, one after the other. I became a novice, a student. My parents died and Joachim became my father in every sense of the word. He taught me about your country: once, I'd had a hunger for wine and good food, then I acquired an unabiding hunger and thirst for everything he could teach me.' Raphael grinned. 'In all things, I believe I was a better scholar than I was a Franciscan.'

'And he had visions?' Su-Ling asked.

'Oh yes. Joachim had terrible visions. As he grew older, he asked for me to sleep in the cell next to his: I would often be roused in the early hours by his heartrending cries. At first he wouldn't tell me about them but, like yours, his visions became clearer, more precise. A terrible evil was to be loosed on the world, he told me.'

'And your visions?'

'I don't have them.'

'But you have dreams?'

'Yes,' Raphael replied. 'I have dreams, very similar to the ones you described. I am a soldier. I am in a house. I am armed with a bow and arrow. I look behind me and see a town in flames but the buildings are not burning. The fires are huge funeral pyres.'

'And how are you dressed?'

'Like one of the soldiers in your dream. I have taken my helmet off; the plume is horse-hair, dyed scarlet. I feel weak, unwell. I am waiting for someone. No—' He paused. 'I am going to kill someone who deserves to die . . .' His voice trailed away.

'So, we meet again,' Su-Ling said softly.

Marco bit back his gasp.

'You know that, Brother Raphael? We meet again.'

The Franciscan sat, head bowed. Marco watched intently. Was this the cause of the attraction? Did these two really believe that they had met in a former life? Marco had studied Buddhism and other religions of Cathay. People here accepted reincarnation as a matter of fact, as his own countrymen believed that Christ had died and risen. People organised their lives, both material and spiritual, in anticipation of the next time their soul was allowed onto the Wheel of Life. If one lived honourably, a superior status

status would be the reward of the Goddess of Mercy. It was a firmly held tenet of Buddhist belief that each soul journeyed through the Underworld to receive rewards and punishment. It then drank from the cup of oblivion which wiped out all memories of former lives.

Marco gently eased himself away from the spy-hole. There were those who claimed they had not drunk fully of the cup, or that spiritual forces could draw back the veil. Did not the Red Lamas of Tibet profess to such a wisdom? Was not their ruler reincarnated within forty days?

Marco looked back through the spy-hole. The Franciscan hadn't moved but Su-Ling had drawn closer, sitting opposite, her knees touching his: she'd clasped his hands in hers, stroking them gently.

'I remember glimpses,' she murmured, 'of marble halls, of gardens where flowers blossomed all the year round.'

'I cannot believe in reincarnation,' Raphael declared sombrely. 'Over seventy years ago, the Catholic Church held a great council in our Pope's Church of St John of Lateran, during which reincarnation, the theory of having more than one life, was solemnly condemned.'

Su-Ling threw her head back and laughed.

'And if the council had ruled that the sun didn't shine or the moon didn't rise – would you have believed them? We have both been on the Wheel of Life. We are like dice, Brother Raphael, thrown from a cup. We may lie differently, but each time we lie with the same dice.'

The Franciscan looked puzzled.

'I believe that when we are reincarnated, we all come back,' Su-Ling explained, 'one with each other, sometimes richer, sometimes poorer, one time male, another female.'

'And for the same reason?' Brother Raphael asked.

'And for the same reason,' she confirmed. 'This is not the first time we have confronted Azrael and only God knows if it will be the last.'

'And the Venetian?' Raphael asked. 'Was he with us last time?'

Su-Ling turned and stared directly at the wall where Marco was standing. He stepped hurriedly away, replaced the painting with shaking hands and tiptoed out of the antechamber.

The moon had risen full and bright above the pavilion on the Island of Eternal Greenness but this was no longer a place of pleasure. Kwei-Lin's massacre of the Guild of Pourers had spread as swiftly as a rushing breeze, causing a stampede by people desperate to get off the island. Men and women who had drunk too much rushed down to the quayside offering huge bribes to the boatmen to take them to the other side. The shrieks from the pavilion, where the killing was still taking place, only intensified their efforts. In the light from torches fixed on poles along the ill-named Quayside of Quietude, revellers were offering jewellery and money for a safe passage, and some of the young women even offered themselves to escape this place of terror. Some hardy souls tried to swim; only a few were successful. Boats became overcrowded and capsized. Partygoers who, only a short while earlier, had been filling their bellies with every delicacy and cups of rice wine, were drowning in the cold waters of the lake. When the alarm reached the far shore, gongs and drums were sounded. Other boats were soon making their way across, whilst officials had sent couriers speeding to the Imperial Palace, demanding that war junks be brought along the canals and into the huge lake.

The deaths caused by the stampede were unnecessary. Kwei-Lin had no intention of leaving the Pavilion. He had loosed at least two dozen arrows. Twenty of the guests now lay in widening pools of blood, sprawled on the cushions or across tables. One corpse lay half-hung through a window: he had almost escaped before Kwei-Lin's arrow thudded deep into his spine. A few fortunate souls had fled the massacre, running headlong from the eating-hall which only a short while earlier had been filled with soft light and savoury smells. Now it was no better than a battlefield. Kwei-Lin smiled proudly as he heard the screams and yells outside. He stared over the balustrade.

'All dead!' he called out jovially. 'None of you will hunger or thirst again!'

He walked noisily away but then tiptoed back. One of the guests, who had pretended to be dead, was crawling as fast as he could towards the door.

'Good day!' Kwei-Lin shouted.

The man turned in terror, clutching at his blood-stained robes. Kwei-Lin was still smiling as he pulled back the bow, sending a barbed arrow straight into the man's face. He watched the body jerk then lie still, and calmly went down the stairs into the eating-hall. He closed and barred the side door he had come through, then, walking round the eating-hall, he shuttered the windows and the main door through which a few guests had escaped. He tore down the *Shu Yen*.

'So-called guardians!' he jibed, and ground them underfoot.

He then removed painted scrolls from the walls, tossing them aside as if to show his contempt for these messengers of good fortune, magical spells to ward off demons.

Hearing a moan, and going across, he found one of the pourers, his face buried in a cushion, beginning to move. Kwei-Lin took his cleaver and immediately despatched him and then, going to the top table, he pulled away the corpse of the Principal

Official of the Guild, the first man he had killed. Ignoring the pools of blood, Kwei-Lin helped himself to some food and drink: rice, shellfish, slices of goose and pork. He relished every piece, dipping his dirty fingers into the sauce he liked, whilst what he disliked, he threw across the room. Seizing a porcelain vase of the rice wine, he drank greedily, as if his mouth and throat were on fire.

'Very well. Very well.' Kwei-Lin belched, and put the vase back on the table. 'I would like to call this meeting of the Guild of Pourers to order.' He stared round at the corpses lying in various grotesque positions. 'Do you have any objections?' He sniggered behind his hands. 'Am I, Kwei-Lin, elected your Chief? I am? Excellent! That's what I like to see. Unanimity and consent. Very well, gentlemen, what do we have here?'

He pulled from beneath the table a costly leather satchel full of pens, pencils, brushes made from the hair of dog or tiger, pots of ink, scrolls, and books sewn together with reinforced silk. He looked at these.

'I am very clever,' Kwei-Lin murmured.

As a table-server he could barely read or write but now he understood everything he saw: minutes of meetings, stores, orders, festivals planned, celebrations, letters: he went through everything very carefully.

'So they know,' he declared, lifting his head. 'The fat Mongol knows I am here. The bunch of numbskulls have seen a pattern in the deaths.'

He picked up a scroll tied with a blue ribbon and undid it, stretching it out on the table, ignoring the blotches of wine, food and blood sent racing across the costly parchment. It included a list of the pourers killed in Cambaluc. Kwei-Lin read it quickly and tossed it aside. In mocking imitation of scolding himself, he smacked the back of his hand.

'Twenty-one in all. Dear me.' He counted the corpses. 'There are many more now. Well I never, what a night's work!'

Outside, the sounds of screaming and yelling had subsided.

'I don't know what they are so frightened of,' he shrugged. 'I will settle with them all later. Oh yes, they can all go into the dark. But, Kwei-Lin, one thing at a time.'

He stared moodily down the chamber.

'This shall be renamed,' he intoned. 'From now on, it will be known as the Hall of Hell in the Pavilion of Perpetual Pain. We'll stay here for the meantime, but we've got work to do.'

He now cleared one table, kicking aside corpses, sweeping cups, chopsticks, platters and plates onto the floor. He then piled up all the records plucked from the dead men's satchels, stacking them high.

'Now that's good. That's very good.'

He got to his feet and walked into the kitchen, which was now deserted. The cooks and servants had fled through a side door.

'That was silly of me,' he chided himself. 'I had forgotten about you. That's what comes of drinking too much.'

Kwei-Lin kicked the kitchen door shut and brought the bar down. He pulled across one of the movable stoves to reinforce the door, then glanced back over his shoulder at the main eating-hall and sniggered. 'Time for another little job.'

He searched the place carefully and found a jug of cooking oil. He sniffed at this and smacked his lips appreciatively. Then Kwei-Lin went back into the main hall and surveyed his handiwork all over again. He was delighted to have turned this place of pleasure into nothing more than a ghastly charnel-house.

'Time passes! Time passes!' Kwei-Lin muttered, cocking his head like a guard dog. 'Soon the soldiers will arrive.'

He tossed the oil over the records of the Guild of Pourers, drenching the parchment and vellum scrolls, the sheafs of papers, the books and ledgers. Selecting a lamp, he carried it carefully across before smashing it against the stacked papers. The glass shattered, the flame inside caught the oil. Kwei-Lin hurriedly retreated as the fire danced.

'Now for a little help.'

He opened a window. The evening breeze swept in and turned the table and the oil-drenched books into a raging fire. Kwei-Lin watched fascinated, stretching out his hands.

'They'll think it's New Year,' he chuckled. Outside, the parks and gardens around the pavilion were deserted. He was about to shut the window when, faintly on the night breeze, he heard shouted orders.

'Is that the clink of armour?' he asked the air. 'Have they come to kill poor Kwei-Lin?'

He slammed the shutters closed and retreated from the raging fire. The flames were already beginning to die. Kwei-Lin hurried back into the kitchen and brought in buckets of sand stored in case of fire. He began to smother the flames with the sand. The air filled with black ash and grey smoke which made him cough. Kwei-Lin dropped the buckets and retreated down the hall. He waited for the smoke to clear a little before opening two of the windows. The sound of approaching soldiers was now very close. Kwei-Lin began to arm himself: going around, he collected his arrows, using his booted foot to pull the killing shafts from the corpses as well as those which had missed their targets. He helped himself to more food and wine then, taking a cushion, sat down with his back to the wall of the pavilion, humming softly to himself.

At the deserted quayside the war junks, their tiger and dragon banners fluttering in the breeze, were now debouching troops who clambered along the wooden platform onto the grass where officers, in the light of torchbearers, organised them into groups. The General in charge, a Mongol from the Great Khan's personal retinue, supervised the arrangements. When all was ready, he called out to the cloaked figure standing in the shadows of a juniper tree.

'Your Excellency, shall I give the order to move?'

'Take him alive!' The Great Khan's First Minister Sanghra came out of the shadows. He let his cloak fall away, revealing costly armour beneath. 'He is to be taken alive and questioned!' Sensing the General's uncertainty, he added, 'The Great Khan himself has ordered this.'

'It would be easier, Your Excellency, for us to fire the pavilion. It would drive him out.'

'You have your orders!' Sanghra snapped. 'The assassin, who-ever he is, must be taken alive!'

The officer bowed. Scouts were despatched ahead; they crawled through the darkness and glimpsed the smoke billowing out of the two open windows. Meanwhile, the General studied the line of the building and glimpsed the small door to the kitchen.

'We will attack on all three fronts!' he ordered. 'The main door round the other side, the side one leading to the balcony and the kitchen door!'

The different squads broke up, in a clink of metal and a gleam of armour.

Again the scouts raced forward: this time they heard the whirr of an arrow. One of the scouts seemed to jump in the air, hands going out before collapsing, spluttering on his blood. The officers hurriedly urged the others forward. Each of the three squads were carrying a makeshift battering ram, a heavy log. Those on the kitchen door side suffered casualties and had to be replaced.

'Whoever he is,' the General acknowledged, 'he's a master bowman.'

'No,' Sanghra corrected him. 'The man inside him is a demon!'
The officer looked startled. 'The men do not know this.'

'The men do not need to.' Sanghra smiled.

He heard a shout: the side door had buckled and given way.
Soldiers were now pouring into the pavilion. Kwei-Lin, standing
by the window, turned and loosed his last arrows. A number of
men fell. He searched for another shaft, but both quivers were
empty. Picking up the cleaver, he advanced threateningly, but
the soldiers had their orders: running forward, they cast the
weighted net. It went up into the air then fell, catching Kwei-Lin
in its tangled embrace.

Chapter 10

Early the next morning, Marco rose and sat out on his verandah. He watched the sun rise, sipped his tea then said his prayers, more of a routine than a rite. At the other side of the house Raphael had set up a makeshift altar. Su-Ling had eagerly agreed to attend Mass but Marco was too embarrassed to take the sacrament. He washed, changed and went into the Room of Tranquillity where his cooks, specially hired from the south-east Province of Kainsu, had prepared bowls of steaming rice, fruit dishes of pears and apricots, and platters of salted pork, goose and honeyed fritters. Marco always supervised the cooks, being unable to accept certain dishes such as edible dogmeat and other so-called delicacies. Raphael and Su-Ling joined him. Mai-da had not left her chamber and no one had seen Purple-Skin. Marco was about to ask what they should do, when he heard the noise and commotion outside – raised voices, people running. Marco sighed, threw a cloak round himself and went out into the courtyard.

The Gate to the World stood open. Purple-Skin, surrounded by servants, was watching three men. Marco pushed his way through. The three were strangers: their leader had his head and face shaved. He wore no footwear or clothes other than a pair of dirt-stained trousers. His naked muscular chest and puggish face gleamed with sweat. He was thick-lipped, coarsened with wine. Marco recognised one of the travelling sorcerers, wizards or conjurors who travelled the roads of the Middle Kingdom, hiring out their services. The sorcerer was standing, feet apart, holding a curved scimitar up towards the rising sun. His two ragged, dirty-faced attendants stood on either side, grasping canes. Tanglefoot, the local beggar, with his damaged feet wrapped in sacking, was jumping about: his wizened face and one good eye were bright with excitement.

'A great sorcerer is here! A great sorcerer is here!'

Marco glared at Purple-Skin.

'I did it for you, Master,' the scribe whined. 'I paid him well. He'll protect us against the demons.'

Before Marco could intervene, a bedraggled urchin, another member of the sorcerer's entourage, started to beat a drum. The sorcerer jumped about then stood still.

'I summon you,' he bellowed in a loud voice, 'to come from the north!' He changed direction. 'East, south and west to guard this house!'

The drumbeat grew louder. The sorcerer moved as if in a trance, faster and faster. As he did so, he whirled his sword up and around, bringing it dangerously back over his head. Marco considered it a miracle he didn't gash his own flesh: his two attendants with the bamboo canes moved with him. At last the sorcerer collapsed in a sweaty heap at Marco's feet. Then he glanced up slyly.

'The Protectors have come,' he whispered. 'Because of their intervention,' his voice grew stronger so everybody could hear, 'I did not cut my own flesh.'

140

Purple-Skin, his lips pursed, nodded sagely. The assembled servants clapped, expressing their admiration in 'oohs' and 'aahs'.

'I am sure you have provided great protection,' Su-Ling remarked drily, coming forward.

She held the Franciscan by the wrist. They stood like a young boy and girl getting ready to go to school. The sorcerer clambered to his feet, watching her suspiciously.

'However,' the Buddhist continued, 'I wonder if you could do the same dance without your attendants participating? I mean, if you have won Heaven's protection, nothing will happen.'

The sorcerer dramatically thrust out his sword. Marco knocked it aside.

'Purple-Skin, pay him and send him on his way. If we need protection like that, I will decide.' He led Su-Ling and Raphael back to the courtyard.

'That was very clever!' Raphael exclaimed. 'But why did he become angry?'

'A fairground trick,' Su-Ling replied. 'If you study the sorcerer's dance very carefully, when he brought the scimitar back, his two attendants intervened, placing their bamboo rods between the edge of the sword and the sorcerer's flesh.'

'I didn't see that!' Raphael exclaimed.

'An illusion,' Su-Ling laughed. 'I've seen Buddhist monks do the same.'

She stood, feet apart, and pretended she had a sword in her hand.

'You bring the sword back over your head; it looks as if the blade is going to bite deep into your flesh but your two attendants very cleverly use the bamboo poles to block the cut. Oh, it's quite skilled, like a dance. You must learn the moves and steps. If you rehearse long enough, it will work. You do yourself no harm and earn a little money.'

They returned to the Room of Tranquillity and continued their meal. Marco felt heavy-headed, annoyed at Purple-Skin's pathetic attempt to protect the house against what had happened the previous night. He also felt like a stranger in his own home. Su-Ling and Raphael were friendly enough but he felt excluded. Indeed, the Buddhist nun was exercising an authority and power with which Marco felt uncomfortable. He ate slowly but then admitted to himself that he was never at his best in the morning. Su-Ling had cleverly intervened and sent the imposter packing, so why should he object? When he glanced up, the Buddhist nun was watching him.

'I am sorry,' she apologised. 'This is your house: Purple-Skin is your scribe. I am sure you could have taken care of the sorcerer yourself.'

Marco shook his head and cleared his throat. 'What you did was necessary but the problem still remains. How *do* we protect ourselves?'

'I don't know.' She shook her head. 'I truly don't. Of one thing I am convinced – tricks and amulets will be no protection against Azrael. Prayer and fasting will.'

Marco was about to tell her of his own vision when there was a further commotion. Sighing with exasperation, he threw his chopsticks on the table. Going out, he was surprised to find all his servants down on their knees in the courtyard, foreheads touching the ground. Imperial soldiers carrying banners were marching through the gate, followed by other officials wearing the black caps and coloured robes of the Imperial Secretariat. Gong-beaters and drummers, more flunkeys and liveried servants appeared next. Marco groaned as the purple and gold sedan chair finally made its way through the gates. The servants and soldiers were now kneeling in a sea of colour across the courtyard, leaving only a small space near the ornamental pool.

Marco immediately grabbed the purple, gold-edged carpet from its small recess near the door, and he himself rolled this out, not caring whether soldiers and servants had to move quickly aside. The sedan chair was lowered. Marco knew enough about court protocol also to bring a scarlet cushion embroidered with silver thread. He placed this to one side of the sedan and muttered the words of welcome. The silk curtains were summarily pushed aside and Sanghra leant out.

'My heart leaps with joy . . .' Marco began.

'I am sure it does,' the minister replied drily. He was standing on the cushion; he extended his hands for Marco to rise.

'My house is now happy . . .'

'I think we've heard enough.' Sanghra plucked Marco by the sleeve. 'Come into the house, I bring urgent despatches from the Great Khan.'

'Will your servants need hospitality?'

'They have eaten and drunk enough,' Sanghra said dismissively. 'Let them kneel. It's good for their humility.'

Marco took him to the Sunrise Chamber which overlooked the gardens to the east of the house, and was specially reserved for important visitors.

Purple-Skin came hurrying in, all of a bother.

'I didn't know, Master, who was coming,' he gabbled.

Marco glared at him while Purple-Skin bustled around, preparing the cushions. Marco took Sanghra's parasol, black felt cap and the oyster-pink over-robe. Beneath it, the First Minister was dressed in a purple silk, gold-edged gown. Dispensing with the usual formalities, he plumped himself down on the cushions, rubbing his hands, pleased that he had put this foreigner into such a turmoil at his arrival.

'Some fruit juice, if you please,' he requested. 'The road is dusty.'

Marco snapped his fingers at Purple-Skin.

'Is the foreign priest and Su-Ling here?' Sanghra continued. 'I would like them to join us and your scribe. Oh, we'll have the shutters closed, the same for the door. Keep the servants well away.' He glared at Purple-Skin. 'If I catch any of them eavesdropping, they'll be wearing a wooden collar till the next full moon!'

For a while Marco was distracted, issuing instructions. He was relieved when Su-Ling and Raphael joined them. Sanghra didn't stand on ceremony with them either, but indicated the cushions next to him before enquiring about their welfare. At last all was ready. Sanghra's servants in the courtyard were now allowed to relax. Purple-Skin himself served the First Minister, who drank the chilled plum juice slowly. Sanghra smacked his lips and recited a short poem at his pleasure in this unexpected visit to the House of Serenity. The Venetian, his guests and Purple-Skin politely heard him out and expressed their congratulations. Sanghra's deep black eyes studied each carefully.

'So much has happened,' he began. 'So many deaths.'

'Another murder?' Marco queried. 'Amongst the pourers?'

'Murder!' Sanghra exclaimed. 'Ah – of course, your servants reside here. They don't get abroad to hear all the news. It is all over Cambaluc. Last night, there was a massacre.' The listeners gasped. 'The principal officials of the pourers gathered in one of the Lake Pavilions to celebrate as well as discuss the murders which had taken place amongst them.' Sanghra paused. 'It was supposed to be an important Guild function until Kwei-Lin arrived. No, you don't know him. Kwei-Lin is, or was, a table-server in the slums of Cambaluc. He owned a small eating-house, one of those cooking-shops which serve all forms of rancid meat to the poor. There was also gossip that Kwei-Lin had formerly been a brigand; when his youth, or his courage, began to fail him, he bought this cookshop and settled into a squalid life. He was well-known to the raddled whores and prostitutes in the area, whilst his cooking left a great deal to be desired. Last night his shabby shop was searched after his neighbours complained about the offensive smell. Inside, the police found the corpse of a pourer called Tuhmo who had been missing for several days. He had been hacked up and hung on skewers: his decapitated head was half-cooked in a mobile oven. The place stank like a charnel-house. It was so disgusting the police simply burnt it to the ground.'

Marco sat in horror. Now and again in his judicial duties he had to do business with the denizens of the slums and their nightmarish lives.

'This Tuhmo was also under suspicion?' Su-Ling asked.

'Yes, yes,' Sanghra agreed. 'He had been seen around in one of the houses where another pourer had been killed. Before you ask, Reverend Sister, it would appear that the demon Azrael passed from Tuhmo to Kwei-Lin. In a sense it was a good choice. If Kwei-Lin had any scruples before, he certainly lost them after meeting Tuhmo. He abandoned his shop and continued Tuhmo's bloody work but this time with a difference. Strangely enough, he did not immediately attack members of the Guild but went to the Temple of the Red Horse on the outskirts of Cambaluc.'

'I know it,' Su-Ling said. 'It is a rather decayed, lonely Buddhist temple. It stands in a dusty parkland near a canal with a hump-backed bridge over it.'

'Why did he go there?' Marco asked.

'We don't know,' Sanghra said, 'but he killed the porter and two old Buddhist priests. Later in the evening, two cavalry mounts were found wandering loose by a patrol: the temple and the park were in their jurisdiction so a careful search was made. The doors to the Red Horse Temple were forced, and all five corpses, including those of the soldiers, were found within. The priests had been killed with a cleaver, the two cavalrymen by well-placed arrows. Now Kwei-Lin is a brigand, used to murder, but he could never be described as a master bowman. However, he soon acquired the skill. Last night he crossed to a pavilion on the Island of Eternal Greenness. On his way there he perpetrated two more murders: he executed a prisoner in the punishment ground as well as the Mongol guard.'

'That's a lonely place.' Purple-Skin spoke up.

'At night it certainly is,' Sanghra replied. 'Only Heaven knows why he showed compassion to the prisoner and gave him an easy death. Perhaps he wanted to provoke the Mongol? Kwei-Lin not only murdered him but took his bow and arrows as well. At the pavilion he continued his bloody work. He must have killed at least twelve men.' Sanghra sipped from the juice cup again and smacked his lips appreciatively. 'The rest, including the servants, managed to escape. The news of the massacre caused hysteria and stampede: six people drowned trying to swim from the island. Kwei-Lin, however, made no attempt to flee. He locked himself into the pavilion, finished off the wounded, then dined and wined amongst the corpses. He then gathered all the records of the Guild of Pourers and created a huge bonfire. Of course, when the news reached the palace, war junks were despatched along the canals. The pavilion was stormed and Kwei-Lin was taken.'

'Captured?' Marco asked, surprised.

'Oh, he resisted,' Sanghra explained. 'The soldiers were under orders to take him alive so that's what they did. The Great Khan,' Sanghra bowed his head, 'has issued a decree under the Purple Wax: Kwei-Lin is to die later today by *Ling chi*.'

'What is that?' Raphael asked fearfully.

'A slow, bloody death,' Marco told him. 'He'll be crucified.' He saw the Franciscan flinch. 'Then the executioner will cut at his body with a sword: it is literally a death by a thousand cuts.'

'The Great Khan is determined on this,' Sanghra said.

'And has Kwei-Lin been interrogated?' Marco asked.

'Well, he certainly hasn't been put up in one of the imperial chambers!' Sanghra snapped. 'He's in the principal prison of Cambaluc. He has been threatened, he has been hung up by his fingers, but he just laughs. He says if he wanted to, he could fly out of his cell.'

'But he wants to meet us, doesn't he?' Su-Ling said.

Sanghra gaped in surprise.

'He refuses to answer your questions, doesn't he?' she guessed accurately. 'He mocks and jibes at you. He says that he will speak to no one except the foreign devil's priest and the Buddhist nun.'

'Yes, yes.' Sanghra recovered from his surprise.

'He has made that request. But,' he lifted one shoulder elegantly, 'it's whether you agree?'

'How did you know that?' Marco asked the nun.

Su-Ling blinked. 'Azrael the Plague Lord has decided to move, though only Heaven knows his reasons for doing it.'

'Explain,' Marco demanded.

After his experiences the previous evening, Marco's doubts about the real danger they faced were fast disappearing. Su-Ling smiled at him, and Marco coloured slightly. She can read my thoughts, he concluded. She knows I doubted her but now I don't.

'It is hard to describe, and it is even more difficult to believe.' Su-Ling winked at him. 'I have read your Scriptures, or some of them. The Lord Jesus describes demons wandering the face of the earth looking for habitation. Azrael is one of these, for although he ranks high in the hierarchy of Hell, he is bound by certain laws and limitations, as are we. However, he is pure spirit so he can send images, thoughts, emotions like flashes of light through the air but, in truth, he is bound by flesh. Through human wickedness he can achieve great evil. Sometimes he waits for what the astronomers would term a convergence of the stars, a time in the affairs of man when certain forces come together. Then he ceases his prowling and lurks like a tiger in the thicket.'

'But why now?' Marco asked.

'Because he has been summoned, possibly, or because he wants to seize an opportunity. Lin-Po . . .' She paused and stared down at the floor, lost in her own reverie. 'Yes, Lin-Po and Wei-Ning must have summoned him, along with this table-server Kwei-Lin and, perhaps, someone else here in Cambaluc? Now Kwei-Lin has done his duty. He has perpetrated more murders amongst the pourers as well as destroying their records.'

'Why do such a thing?' Sanghra asked, perplexed.

'To cause chaos, my lord,' she answered simply. 'He has caused chaos?'

'Ministers are already meeting,' Sanghra confirmed. 'Summer is approaching: the lanes and canals, the sewers and the cesspools of both the old and new city must be cleansed.'

'So, why the records?' Raphael still didn't understand.

Sanghra spread his hands. 'The Guild of Pourers is an ancient one. Such documents would list the needs of the city; places to be cleaned, merchandise to be bought. Only the weeks ahead will truly reveal the real chaos Kwei-Lin caused.'

'But why the massacres at the temple?' Marco asked.

'Kwei-Lin needed a place to hide. The priests would have opposed this and so they were executed. The same is true of the Mongol guards. For the rest, I don't know. That is why I would like you to go to Cambaluc and speak to this demon in human flesh.'

'But listen.' The Franciscan had had great difficulty in following this conversation. All apart from Su-Ling had spoken quickly, unlike the measured tones used in the court of the Great Khan.

'We listen, Brother,' Marco replied.

The Franciscan ignored the sarcasm in his host's voice. 'If Azrael can move from one body to another, like you and I would rooms in a house, why not keep him separate now? After Kwei-Lin's execution, according to your theory, Azrael must travel back to Hell, if he has no habitation ready to receive him.'

'If that were true,' Su-Ling replied, 'it would all be so simple. However, Kwei-Lin has only to touch someone before his death to gain possession. Azrael cannot inhabit just anyone. He must seek a will as evil as his: if Kwei-Lin has already touched such a person, keeping him separate will provide no remedy.'

'Then it could be one of us?' Purple-Skin, who had been sitting open-mouthed, now intervened. 'Master,' he cleared his throat noisily, 'I have studied for the *Sui Tsau*, the first degree in the Hall of Examinations as well as my *Ku-jin*.'

Marco looked surprised.

'Oh yes, Master. If it wasn't for my deformity,' and here the scribe looked bleakly at Sanghra, 'I would be clothed in purple and not just have it across my face. I would have the good fortune to smile on the Dragon's face.'

'And?' Sanghra prompted him.

'I have never heard of this, yet I believe everything our Reverend Sister has told us. One remedy does offer itself, and it may come to this.' He fell silent.

'We wait,' said Sanghra.

'Anyone this demon touches,' Purple-Skin replied, 'should be executed – I realise that now,' he continued hurriedly. 'And your humble servant apologises for hiring conjurers and putting his faith in petty charms and amulets. We really need to purify ourselves. It is only a matter of time, is it not, Reverend Sister, before Azrael, the *Wen Yi Kwei*, this Plague Lord, a Great Khan of Hell, secures a place in one of us?'

'It could happen,' Su-Ling confirmed.

'Then let us meet our enemy.' Marco got to his feet.

'I will not come with you,' Sanghra declared.

'We will travel as we are.' Marco grasped his scribe's shoulder. 'Purple-Skin, stay here and guard the House of Serenity. Excellency,' he bowed towards Sanghra, 'if I could borrow two of your guards?'

The principal Prison of Hell of Cambaluc was like a huge fortified stable: concentric rings of walls and watch-towers with entrance through heavily fortified gates. Marco, Raphael and Su-Ling, escorted by two imperial officers, gathered in the first smelly gatehouse. The Venetian had visited these prisons only once before and, as he whispered to Raphael, it had been an experience he would never forget. The chief turnkey kowtowed, bowing and scraping, insisting on delivering a flowery speech of welcome to his honoured guests. Marco had no choice but to endure this ritual of protocol and etiquette. Afterwards they processed into the Court of Torture where prisoners were put to the question.

It was a gruesome, bloody place. Prisoners lay around on the cobbles; sharp-edged boards with specially carved grooves clamped legs, heads, hands or necks. Every so often the torturers would walk around tightening these clasps or imposing greater weights.

'They are so silent,' Raphael whispered. The Franciscan's face had paled, and he looked rather unsteady on his feet. Marco could only agree.

'The silence makes it all the more ghastly,' he murmured.

He watched as the shabbily dressed torturers moved around, inspecting one victim after another like a gardener would a flower or vegetable patch. Only the slap of sandals on the cobbles and the occasional muffled moan betrayed the horrors being perpetrated.

'They are a brave people,' Marco said quietly. 'Even in death the most unfortunate criminal will not lose face.' He glanced at the turnkey. 'Has Kwei-Lin been questioned?'

The man's fat, greasy face broke into a smile.

'We did what we could do, Your Excellency, but he is obdurate. We were also under orders to go so far and no further.'

'And he said nothing?'

'Apart from curses and threats. We tried everything. His hands were tied to a bar behind his knees, the wooden collar around his neck, then we made him kneel on pounded glass sand mixed with salt.'

The turnkey chewed his lip in disappointment. 'Kwei-Lin is impervious to pain. Be it his ears nailed to a board or being suspended by his thumbs, it made no difference.'

'Can we move on?' Su-Ling demanded, dabbing at the sweat at her neck.

The turnkey looked at her curiously. 'A Buddhist nun here?' He tried to make it sound less like a jibe. 'We rarely see your kind.'

'Keep a civil tongue in your head!' one of the escorts snapped. 'If the Reverend Lady wishes to move on, then we should do so.'

They crossed the courtyard and went through another set of gates into an enclosure where horse-box cells looked out over a central yard. The smell was offensive, the noise hideous as prisoners shouted and screamed abuse at each other or sustained their courage by mocking their guards. The turnkey opened the door to one of the boxes. At Marco's request the guard stood aside. He, accompanied by Raphael and Su-Ling, stepped into the pitch blackness. The turnkey brought an oil torch and placed it high in a wall-bracket. Marco narrowed his eyes, pinching his nostrils at the pungent smell.

'Felicitations and salutations!' the mocking voice sang out. 'Welcome to my humble abode, Foreigner. And I see you've brought other guests. Tell that fat turnkey to go back to his sty!'

The gaoler hurriedly brought three stools and placed them just within the entrance.

'That's right, now roll away, you piece of dung!'

Marco could make out a dark shape squatting in the corner. He and his companions took their seats, slightly unsteady on the coarse, bamboo shards which served as matting. The figure in the corner crept forward in a rattle of chains. Raphael murmured in astonishment. Su-Ling sat transfixed. Marco quietly admitted that he had never seen such an evil face: the high cheekbones and pitted skin, the straggling greasy hair and those almond-shaped eyes full of malicious intelligence. The man lifted his arms in a rattle of chains; he moved them from side to side, mimicking a child singing.

'Do you like the smell?' he chanted. 'Oh, what a delicious stench! Muck and blood – eh, Foreigner? What are you doing here, baiting poor Kwei-Lin, a humble table-server? You should have come to my eating-house.' He glowered at Raphael. 'I'd have chopped *that* little delicacy into soft pieces of meat, then fried them in oil until they turned brown and crisp.'

'Shut up!' Marco ordered.

'Shut up? I *am* shut up and, in a short while, I am going to die.' Kwei-Lin smacked his lips. 'I would love some bean soup, hot and tasty with morsels of fish and a nice cup of wine. You missed a good banquet last night, Foreigner.' He flung his arms up again and threw himself on his back, kicking his legs in the air. 'That's how they died! That's how they died! One minute guzzling like a styful of pigs, the next jumping up and down as Kwei-Lin's arrows took them in the throat or heart.'

The prisoner returned to squatting on his haunches.

'Ah well.' His voice became deeper. 'And what have we here, the foreign devil's priest? Look at him now – what a pretty bumboy. He'd fetch a good price in the slave-market.'

Raphael didn't move.

'What are you going to do, priest? Make a magical sign so old Kwei-Lin will jump up and disappear in a puff of smoke? But I mean no offence.' He stretched out a clawlike hand. 'So, like you do in Rome, clasp my wrist and say you are my friend.'

'What do you want?' Marco demanded.

'What do I want?' Kwei-Lin mimicked. 'Look at you, with your costly robe and velvet buskins.' He sniffed. 'I can smell Mai-da on you from here. I'd love to give her one.' He smiled, clicking his tongue against his broken teeth. 'And the lily-white ones?' He clasped his hands together in mock piety. 'Look at them, eyes only for each other.'

Kwei-Lin crept forward, wicked face grimacing. He clawed at his straggling beard and moustache; those staring, livid eyes inspected Marco from head to toe. The Venetian realised that this monster hardly ever looked at Su-Ling. Perhaps Kwei-Lin, or the demon who possessed him, was frightened of her.

'You are the table-server, Kwei-Lin?' he asked.

'True, *signor*.'

Marco started in surprise as the prisoner lapsed into coarse Venetian.

'The menu is yours for the taking: minced cats' flesh, grilled snakes or just Tuhmo's entrails on a nice bed of rice. Or perhaps you would prefer something more delicate. Venison? Succulent pig?' Kwei-Lin's voice had now changed to fluent Italian.

'He's mad,' Raphael muttered.

'Am I now, Friar? Am I mad?' Kwei-Lin was now speaking in clear incisive Latin. *'In nomine Patris et Filii, et Spiritus Sancti.'* Kwei-Lin began to sing. 'Am I mad or am I just resting?'

'What do you want?' Su-Ling interrupted.

'Oh, the pretty shaven-headed one has a tongue! Open your mouth!' Kwei-Lin clawed between his legs. 'And I'll put something in it!' He pointed at Marco. 'He likes you, you know. He'd like to do to you what I'd like to do!'

Marco shuffled his feet in embarrassment.

'What do you want?' Su-Ling asked again, ignoring his coarse jest. Then she lapsed into a tongue Marco did not recognise. At this, Kwei-Lin's demeanour changed. He became watchful, tense, now and again scratching his left ear. Marco listened intently. He suspected she was speaking a language long forgotten, using a powerful exorcism taught her by the masters of the Buddhist faith. She paused and looked across at Raphael.

'Don't be frightened, Brother,' she said. 'It's what he wants. You have not prayed since you came in here, have you?'

Raphael shook his head.

'While I talk, just call on your Christ.'

'What are you doing?' Marco demanded.

'She is trying to seduce me,' Kwei-Lin sniggered. 'She wants to gobble me up, take me into her private garden.'

'Be silent!'

Su-Ling's face was angry. She again lapsed into the tongue, holding out her hand, fingers splayed.

'Be silent or we go! And you do not want that, Kwei-Lin, do you?'

The table-server bared his teeth and snarled like a dog. He moved restlessly up and down in a clatter of chains: he turned his head, watching Su-Ling from the corner of his eye.

'It is the last thing he wants us to do,' Su-Ling murmured. 'He wants to frighten us, to show his contempt. This is a war fought not with sword and shield but with mind and soul. He wants to beat us down, render us soft and vulnerable for the next attack.'

'Ah, shut your hole, you nasty bitch!' Kwei-Lin had now lapsed back into Venetian. 'Do you really think I'd want you with your stupid face and bald head!' He sniggered. 'Kissing that would be like sucking an eggshell!'

'I think we've heard enough.' Su-Ling winked at Marco. 'I can take you to a tavern nearby where the wit is sharper and the language more colourful.'

Kwei-Lin lunged forward to attack but he could not reach them; his dirty long nails scythed the air.

'Just wait till my friend Lin-Po gets here!' he spat.

'Ah.' Su-Ling smiled. 'So you *do* want to talk!'

Chapter 11

'What do you know of Lin-Po?' Su-Ling asked the prisoner.

'He's my friend.' Kwei-Lin began to hum under his breath. 'And he's coming! Oh yes, he's coming!'

'But you are not Kwei-Lin, are you?' the Buddhist nun demanded. 'You are Azrael, known in the Middle Kingdom as the *Wen Yi Kwei*. Kwei-Lin's soul is now completely in your control and Kwei-Lin is going to die.'

'About time,' came the scoffing reply. 'He's been a very, *very* wicked man!'

A cold shiver of fear pricked Marco's neck. Here they were, sitting in this smelly, ill-lit box: they were talking not to one, but to two, and they could only hear their real enemy.

'And when Kwei-Lin dies,' the Buddhist nun asked, 'where will you go to then?'

Kwei-Lin lunged forward. 'Maybe I'll come to *you*. Make myself snug in that soft, brown body of yours. Umm, that would be nice! I'll be able to smell and taste you.'

Su-Ling replied in the ancient tongue. Kwei-Lin glowered back.

'I was only joking! I was only joking!'

'Where will you go?'

'I can go wherever I want!' came the barked reply.

'But you can't,' Su-Ling retorted. 'You and I both know that. Not every door is open. Not every soul welcomes you.'

'I'll fly away,' Kwei-Lin boasted.

'But you won't. You've told us – you're waiting for Lin-Po to arrive. Why is that? Are you too frightened to tell us?'

Kwei-Lin began to chatter in a high-pitched tongue that Marco did not understand; nor, by the look on her face, did Su-Ling.

'I don't understand.' The Buddhist nun pushed back the stool as if to rise and leave.

Kwei-Lin replied quickly in one of the dialects. Marco could follow it a little, catch certain words, fragments. Su-Ling shifted uneasily.

'I command you!' she declared. 'Talk so we can all understand!'

Kwei-Lin's head went down as if he had fallen asleep.

'It's so long,' he replied wearily, then his head snapped up, eyes bright. 'We've met before. You, me, the foreign priest, even this devil here.' He clicked a hand in Marco's direction.

'I know we have,' Su-Ling replied. 'And what happened then?'

'A struggle, a fight. Don't you remember? Your name was Perdicca, then. That's right. Pretty Perdicca!'

'And what was his name?'

Kwei-Lin gestured at Raphael. 'Cleon.'

'And this one?' Su-Ling put her hands on Marco's shoulder.

'I don't know, I forget. At the time he wasn't important.'

Kwei-Lin crossed his arms and rocked backwards and forwards. He sang in a tongue which Marco recognised from his schooldays as Ancient Greek; he heard the word *kalos* meaning beautiful, *adelphos* for brother, *philos* for love. Marco sat astonished.

According to Kwei-Lin they had all met before in a different time, a different place. Su-Ling had referred to this the previous evening. Now the table-server was actually giving them a time and place – Ancient Greece, perhaps even Athens?

As they all sat listening to the sounds from the prison yard, the air was rent by a man's shout. Kwei-Lin sniffed and smiled.

'You can smell fear,' he murmured. 'It tickles the nostrils most delectably.'

'Ask him where,' Marco whispered. 'Where did we all meet before?'

'He's lying,' the Buddhist nun said shortly. 'Kwei-Lin knows nothing of Greece.'

The table-server crawled forward like a dog.

'Don't you remember?' he said. 'Haven't you dreamt of it time and again? The temple on the hill soaring up against the blue sky? Athena with her golden helmet and spear? The *pynx*, the *agora*, the long walls down to the Piraeus?'

'It's Athens!' Marco exclaimed. 'He's describing Ancient Athens.'

'Clever boy, foreign devil! Clever boy has learnt his work. The bitch remembers, all right. The war galleys out at sea, their sails red and white: the great triremes with their banks of oars. The Hoplites marching down. Oh, and the air, full of smoke, human flesh being nicely cooked.'

'And what happened?' Su-Ling asked. 'Why was human flesh being so nicely cooked?'

The table-server wagged a bony finger. 'Now, now. Naughty girl!' He sniffed. 'What do you think Kwei-Lin is, some silly goose, who'll squawk to order? I've told you enough!' He shuffled back.

'Why is Lin-Po coming?' Su-Ling asked.

'I must go soon. It is time to move on. I am to die at noon.'

'Why did you kill the priests at the old temple?' Su-Ling tried next.

'I wanted a place to hide. It was nice and quiet there. The old fools were in my way. So I had to kill them; chop, chop, like a bundle of faggots for the fire.'

'And Lin-Po?'

'The Rats' Great Flitting Day will soon be upon us, that's all I am going to say, so there now.' He blew a kiss at Su-Ling, did the same to Raphael and made an obscene gesture in Marco's direction.

'What's the Rats' Great Flitting Day?' Raphael asked, puzzled.

'Oh, go away! Kwei-Lin's tired.' The table-server lay down on the damp matting.

'We must go,' Su-Ling said softly. 'There is nothing more he can or will tell us.'

'See you soon!' Kwei-Lin sang out. 'And sooner than you think!'

They left the boxed prison. Marco was pleased even to breathe the fetid air of the courtyard. The turnkey was waiting outside, beside him the Tartar executioner, his sword drawn. He was dressed like a ghost, completely in white from head to toe. The masked hood over his face was capped by a spiked metal helmet: a black cord belt was tied round his waist. He took off his helmet and mask, revealing a flat face, eyes almost hidden in rolls of fat, a black wispy moustache and beard; his hair was oiled and pulled back in a queue. He put his hand inside his robe and pulled out a piece of parchment bearing the imperial seal.

'Excellencies.' He bowed again. 'Kwei-Lin is to die at noon.'

'Then take him out!' Marco ordered.

He led his companions, the military escort behind, out into the execution ground which stretched to one side of the prison. News of the impending punishment had already attracted the crowds.

160

There were plum-sellers, a considerable number of the Guild of Pourers, together with relatives of victims slain in the previous night's massacre. Beggars came too, looking for easy customers, along with fruit-juice vendors and wandering scholars ready to note the gory details for their stories when they left the city to visit the villages and hamlets round the capital.

The sun was growing stronger. The clatter of carts and the shuffling of feet raised small clouds of white dust. A group of Buddhist priests dressed in grey travelling robes, small bells in one hand, candles in the other, made their way across the ground. They glimpsed Su-Ling, stopped, bowed then passed on. Raphael stayed close to Su-Ling, like a younger brother would with an elder sister, his gaze drawn to the great scaffold which had been set up: a huge cross on a dirty white platform, a set of ladders leaning against the crossbeam. Steam billowed out of two huge brass cauldrons standing nearby.

The Hour of the Snake, the official time for executions, was halfway gone. The executioner's assistants, also garbed in white and wearing monkey masks, scampered about putting the finishing touches to their preparations. From the drum tower came a low solemn beat; the crowd fell silent. The gates to the prison opened to the clash of gongs, cymbals and the screech of pipes. Kwei-Lin, a wooden collar round his neck, was brought out onto the execution ground. The executioner pulled him by a rope as if he was a dog. On either side walked wardens carrying little spears and shields. The condemned man's arrival was greeted with an ominous silence: the most offensive insult which could be offered. The rattle of the drum now reverberated through the hot morning air, the gongs and cymbals answering.

Kwei-Lin was taken up onto a platform, the wooden collar still round his neck. He was forced to kneel on chains and had his eardrums painfully pierced, his eyes removed. The executioner dipped his knife into boiling hot water before making the fatal cut. Su-Ling was staring at the ground. Raphael turned his back, eyes closed and murmured a prayer. Kwei-Lin, his face streaming with blood, was now stripped of the wooden collar and the rags he wore. He was taken to the edge of the platform. A herald read out his list of crimes, or at least the official version; and sentence was pronounced how this ignominious man would be subject to death by *Ling chi*. The crowd breathed a collective sigh of approval. Kwei-Lin, who now looked like a demon from hell, opened his mouth to speak, and the crowd listened, fascinated. This was rare. Most condemned criminals went to their deaths without uttering a sound.

'I see the demons in the air!' Kwei-Lin shouted. 'Faces of green and bodies of red! Fierce they are, and they come for vengeance!'

'Kill him!' someone shouted. 'Silence his stinking mouth for good!'

Kwei-Lin was dragged up the ladder. His loincloth was removed and he was hoisted and bound to the makeshift cross. The assistants scurried away as the executioner dipped his two-handed, broad scimitar in one of the pots of boiling water and expertly sliced at Kwei-Lin's body: a cut to the abdomen, one to the leg, another to the thighs.

'The Rats' Great Flitting Day will soon be here!' Kwei-Lin shouted then fell silent as the executioner gashed his chest.

'I've seen enough,' Marco declared. 'He died the death he deserved.'

'Let's move away,' Raphael urged.

Marco led them out of the execution ground, walking quickly up a narrow lane and into a small park well shaded by trees. He looked over his shoulder; the military escort trailed behind. Marco went across and sat on a bench overlooking a pool. Su-Ling and Raphael joined him whilst the soldiers lounged on the grass. A street vendor came hurrying over. His tray of cups looked clean so Marco bought sugared wafers and porcelain cups of apricot juice from the small barrel strapped to the vendor's back.

'How will it end?' Raphael asked, slaking his thirst.

'*Ling chi* is a horrible death,' Marco replied. 'It's literally execution by a thousand cuts, after which his head will be severed. The people regard that as the most humiliating punishment. Kwei-Lin's ghost will have to wander headless; he will not be able to find his way through the Underworld.'

'I will burn incense sticks for him,' Su-Ling promised. 'Although his soul may have been wicked, those terrible deeds were the work of Azrael the Plague Lord.'

'I hope they burn his corpse,' Marco said. 'After an execution, the apothecaries and physicians fight for pieces of the corpse: they claim it possesses magical healing properties.'

'What did he mean by the Rats' Great Flitting Day?' Raphael wanted to know.

'It's a festival,' Marco explained. 'Held on the eighteenth day of the first moon. It's based on the legend of a cottager who was visited by a beautiful woman. She came into his kitchen whilst his wife was making *Chu Po Po* – dumplings,' he translated. 'The beautiful woman tried to steal one. The peasant took up an axe and cut off her hand. The woman disappeared and her severed hand turned into a giant rat's claw. She must have been a were-rat, a human being who can turn herself into the form of a rat. The peasant was later visited by ill-luck, so a tradition grew up: on the eighteenth day of the first moon, householders should clear the rats from their houses then put down *Chu Po Po* to welcome any new rats in the hope of placating them.'

'And what has that got to do with Lin-Po?' Raphael asked.

'I don't know.' Su-Ling laughed self-consciously. 'I need to return to the masters in my temple and consult our sacred writings. There is a pattern to what is happening. The Guild of Pourers has been decimated. This will cause chaos in cleaning and purging the filth of this city.' She gazed up at the sky. 'The sun will grow more powerful and the heat will turn the midden heaps into festering mounds. The city authorities will have to make sure the streets are kept clean and the water supply is not tainted.' She drained the apricot juice. 'I know very little about rats: however, some physicians believe they carry infection.'

'But that's no real danger, is it?' Marco commented. 'There are enough rat-catchers and rodent-killers in the city, and the warehouses stock plenty of poisons. Sewers and canals can be fumigated.'

He beckoned to the juice-seller, who was patiently waiting for his cups and handed them back.

'In my opinion, we have two more pressing problems,' he went on. 'First, how will Azrael now manifest himself? Secondly, what will happen when Lin-Po enters the city?'

'And thirdly,' Su-Ling added, 'what precautions and protection can we take?' She got to her feet, extending her hand to Raphael. 'But come, Brother, we are poor hosts. Enough of death and demons. Let us show you the city. We can talk as we stroll. Cleanse Kwei-Lin from our minds.'

Marco agreed and, with the escort behind them, the three left the park and crossed the Rainbow Bridge spanning the River Yu. Marco paused halfway across, pointing to the guards on the ramparts and the coloured flags they carried.

'It's a fire warning system,' he explained. 'The citizens have a great fear of it. The soldiers are instructed to keep a sharp lookout. If they see a pall of smoke, the slightest threat of fire, the drums are beaten and those different flags are raised. The different colours denote the seriousness of the blaze.'

Raphael, however, was looking over the bridge, watching a group of fishermen pay devotions to the Water Star, a local god.

'So much water.' He glanced at Marco. 'It should remind you of Venice?'

'Both the old city and the new are threaded by canals and sluices,' Marco told him. He pointed further down the river, and grinned. 'Notice the coloured balustrades, Brother. They are there to protect the drunks from falling in.'

They crossed the bridge and entered the city, pausing to admire a brightly decorated teahouse, its gardens fringed by trees in blossom, plum, peach and apricot. They sat on benches in the shade watching the barges slip by, drinking more juice and eating wafers of puffed pastry and sweet apple. The military escort, pleased at these light duties, sprawled on the grass. Marco pointed out a line of high-sided, black-painted barges, their decks covered by leather awnings. Braziers, full of charcoal, glowed in the prow and stern. These billowed perfumed smoke.

'That's what Kwei-Lin was interested in,' Marco said and he chuckled. 'Despite their bright colours and fragrant smells, those barges belong to the Guild of Pourers. They collect refuse and take it out into the countryside.'

'Will the deaths amongst the pourers affect us?' Raphael asked.

'Certainly.' Marco looked up to the entwining branches. 'The massacre last night will disarray the entire Guild. If only we knew what Azrael intends and why Lin-Po is so important.'

They left the teahouse and moved onto the broad boulevards. The crowd had come out, the sedan chairs and palanquins of the rich creating a gorgeous sea of colour. Raphael seemed fascinated by everything, hungrily drinking in the sights. He reminded Marco of himself as a child, when his uncles took him to a festival. The three visited the place of the Salubrious Six Wheels, the great reservoir of the city, then they went to the rice and pork markets. Marco pointed out to Raphael some of the most expensive eating-houses in the city, as well as the taverns and pickled pork shops where great painted boards displayed the wide range of delicacies available.

'Let's show him one of the lakes,' Su-Ling suggested.

Marco looked over his shoulder. The two soldiers were strolling behind, eyeing the girls, picking things up from the stalls, only returning them when their owners screeched abuse.

They entered a park and came to the Lake of Shimmering Purity which surrounded the Island of Heavenly Joy: a holy place for many of the citizens of Cambaluc with its shrine to the Goddess of Mercy. They hired one of the boats named *The Hidden Jewel*, and Marco told the escort to wait whilst they went across. The boatman pulled away. Marco, Su-Ling and Raphael sat in the stern. The Venetian pointed out the pleasure boats with their highly ornamented sides and deep blue sails, each carrying a small choir of singing girls in the prow. Fishermen were also busy, using their oars to beat fish into the extended nets; nearby, pious Buddhists were making sacrifice to the water gods.

Marco relaxed. The lake shimmered in the sunshine, whilst the island looked invitingly green and cool with its parklands and small groves. Above the treeline jutted the fretted cornices and decorated towers of the shrine. They disembarked and went up the pebble-dashed path. Gold and silver peacocks strutted on the grass: songbirds in gilded cages sweetened the air with their elusive notes. The crowds were streaming up to the pavilions which sold food and drink. Despite the sunlight, lanterns had been lit surrounded by colourful banners and pennants.

Marco was walking slightly in front. When he looked round, he exclaimed in annoyance. Su-Ling and Raphael were some distance away, hand in hand, admiring the flowerbeds. Marco was about to call out when he felt the first prickle of fear, a sense of danger. Something was wrong. He heard a humming and recognised Kwei-Lin's song in prison. Marco whirled round: he carried no arms, the soldiers were across the lake. Where was that sound coming from? Passers-by looked suspiciously at him. A father called his children away.

'Su-Ling! Raphael!' Marco called out.

The Franciscan and Buddhist monk looked up. Su-Ling was the first to show alarm. She grasped Raphael's hands tightly and pulled him away, walking quickly back to where Marco now stood on a stone plinth.

'What is it, Brother?'

'I heard a tune,' Marco answered breathlessly. 'The last time, Kwei-Lin was singing it.'

The Buddhist nun cocked her head, listening intently. Marco looked back down the path and glimpsed a figure near the ornamental fountain they'd just passed.

'What shall we do?' Raphael asked.

Marco stepped down and grasped him by the shoulder.

'Perhaps it's an illusion, meant to frighten us? Let's walk back to the lake. It's time we left, anyway.'

He urged them on, almost pushing his way through the crowds back down towards the noisy quayside. As they passed the fountain, a man dressed in white was there, staring at the fish swimming amongst the lotus pads. He looked up at them and grinned. Marco's stomach lurched: it was the Tartar executioner, still wearing his bloody apron.

'Good day,' the executioner whispered hoarsely. 'We meet again, eh?' He got to his feet, grasping the stout walking cane, and spread his arms. 'The sunlight, the flowers, the water! Look at everybody: the silken robes, the parasols!' He sniffed the air.

'The women's perfume. Won't you stop and buy your friend a drink?'

'You are not our friend,' Su-Ling said sharply.

'I thought I was.'

'Leave him!' Marco snapped.

They moved on along the path. A moment later, the executioner passed them and, as he did so, he touched a merchant, fat and portentous in his coloured robes, flat velvet cap and gaily coloured parasol. Marco was not too sure what happened next. The executioner grasped the man's wrist: the merchant, probably ambling up to one of the pavilions for his noonday rest, stopped in surprise. The executioner let go and staggered; apparently tired and confused, he left the path and slumped down on the grass. Marco and his companions stopped. The merchant looked at the executioner then stared boldly at the three of them before grinning and, swinging his parasol like a sword, marching forward to block their path. His fat face creased into a lascivious leer. He doffed his hat and studied Su-Ling from head to toe before blowing her a kiss.

'Still a virgin?' he whispered.

When Marco lunged forward, the man lifted the parasol and pushed him roughly in the chest. Raphael went to go around him but the merchant moved just as quickly to prevent him.

'Come on!' he growled. 'Buy me a drink. I'd love to lie in the cool grass and have the bitch's legs and arms wrapped around me.'

Marco panicked. He grabbed Su-Ling and Raphael, pulling them away.

'We'll go to the quayside on the other side,' he told them. Then, hurrying Raphael and Su-Ling before him, he went back the way they had come, up into the shelter of the trees. Marco glimpsed the merchant running after them and, as he did so, he touched different people. The ordeal quickly turned into a nightmare. Men and women came hurrying up. Sometimes they cursed in Latin, Italian, the *lingua franca* of the Venetian merchants, the language of Cathay and other tongues which neither Marco nor his two companions could comprehend. Merchants, soldiers, vendors and pedlars, even a Buddhist priest: faces thrust into theirs, hands clawing at their garments.

'He's passing quickly,' Su-Ling whispered. 'Moving from one person to another.'

When Marco realised their path was blocked, he pulled Su-Ling and Raphael into the shade of a nearby oak tree and looked back the way they had come. The presence of Azrael in the crowd was making itself felt. Those he had possessed, if only for a few seconds, now looked confused and staggered about. A few lay down on the grass. Others were helped by friends. Su-Ling watched carefully.

'They don't know what's happening,' she said. 'They probably think it's the heat, or something they have eaten or drunk.'

'What *is* happening?' Marco asked.

'Azrael is choosing his victims. He possesses for a while and then moves on. They think it's no more than a faint or a slight weariness.'

Just then, a barber ran up, a bloody razor in his hand. He lunged at Su-Ling, the sharp blade scything the air. Marco lashed out with his boot, giving the man a terrible kick to his stomach. He fell to his knees and rolled away clutching his belly. Then he clambered to his feet and staggered into the crowd. The nightmare continued. It reminded Marco of some ghastly dance, a parody of the parties he had attended in Venice where the dancers whirled and turned in a sea of masks. Different people detached themselves from the crowd.

A few came running up threateningly. Others swaggered. Each time the tongue was different: Venetian, Latin, French, the patois of the slums, the flowery language of Kublai's courtiers. Marco felt his legs grow heavy with tension. The passers-by, those who noticed, thought it was some form of pantomime. Only Marco and his two companions glimpsed the hate-filled eyes.

Marco looked longingly towards the lake shimmering in the afternoon sun.

'Are we in danger?' Raphael demanded.

'Yes and no,' Su-Ling replied. 'Azrael is frightening us. He's at war but this is not of the body but the mind and soul. If he can, he will terrify us. If the opportunity presents itself, he may inflict grave injury, even death.'

'How do we escape?' Marco asked.

Su-Ling smiled. 'I am praying. I do not wish to be proud, but I believe that's why we've had no more physical attacks. Brother Raphael, you must join me. Marco, you must get us to the lakeside but stay between me and Raphael.'

She extended a hand, and Marco grasped it. Unlike his own, it was cool and soft; he felt ashamed of the sweat coursing down his body.

'Don't be frightened,' Su-Ling reassured him. 'That's what Azrael wants. You are a soldier, Brother Marco, you have faced danger before. This is no different.'

They walked out from the shade of the trees back onto the path. Su-Ling and Raphael were lost in their prayers, impervious to the sights, smells and sounds around them. A beggarman ran up, his face contorted into a snarl; Marco ignored him. When a local juice-vendor offered to help, the beggar disappeared. As they approached the lake Marco heard footsteps running behind them. He whirled round to see the Tartar executioner, grinning from ear to ear, brandishing his staff in the air. People were shouting and screaming. He aimed the weapon directly at the back of Su-Ling's head. Marco let go of her hand and moved to intercept the blow but the Tartar was too quick. Marco felt a thud against his head: the pain sent him screaming to his knees. Before slipping into unconsciousness, he was dimly aware of Su-Ling bending over him.

Su-Ling turned and glared at the executioner now aiming a second blow at Marco, and beside her, Raphael heard her talk in that strange tongue again. Her assailant stopped, heavy-eyed. People were shouting and gathering round. Two soldiers, drawn by the clamour, now intervened. The executioner disappeared, running up the hill towards the trees.

'Help us! Help us!' Su-Ling commanded the soldiers. 'This is the Great Khan's Minister!'

They needed no second bidding but carried the insensible Marco down to the quayside and placed him on a waiting boat. Once they were across the other side, their shame-faced military escort, who had been relaxing on the verandah of one of the teahouses, hastily summoned a sedan. Marco was placed gently inside, his body propped up by cushions on either side. It was already the Hour of the Monkey before they reached the House of Serenity. Purple-Skin and Mai-da rushed out and helped the unconscious man to his bedchamber. Mai-da would have taken over now but Su-Ling shook her head, examining the blow on Marco's head carefully.

'It's a cut and a bruise, that's all. He'll have a sore head when he awakes.'

She ordered Purple-Skin to bring her water infused with herbs and told the others to leave. Mai-da would have objected but Purple-Skin intervened. Su-Ling sat on the side of the silk-caparisoned bed. Every so often she would bathe the cut then feel the blood pulse in Marco's neck or wrist.

'Are you a physician?' Raphael asked from the other side of the bed, amazed by this opulently furnished chamber.

'I only know enough to distinguish between what is serious and what is not. Our friend needs rest and sleep – that will be the best cure. See, Raphael, the swelling is coming up; the bruise is making itself felt. If there was no bruise, no swelling, I'd be more concerned.'

'We were in great danger, weren't we?' Raphael demanded.

'More serious than we ever thought,' came the reply. 'Azrael has grown stronger. He can draw on the malice of the souls he possesses, on the evil they have nurtured.'

'Why didn't he just kill us?' Raphael asked.

'Because it would have been too difficult to carry out the killings and then escape. Those possessed were blinded for a moment, but to move someone's will towards the urge to kill, to commit murder, requires time.' She sighed. 'But, yes, I would recommend that if we ever walk the streets of Cambaluc again, we go well protected.'

She put down the bowl of water, came round the side of the bed and stood next to Raphael.

'Is there nothing we can do?' the Franciscan asked.

'Oh yes, at the appointed time. Until then we can pray, fast, and call on the Lords of Light.'

'And?'

Su-Ling leant down and kissed him chastely on the lips.

'We can love, Raphael, like we have.' Her eyes filled with tears. 'Like we have loved before and, no doubt, we will love again. In the end it will be love, and the sacrifices it demands, which will defeat Azrael and all his bloody handiwork.'

PART THREE

The Hour of the Monkey

Chapter 12

Lin-Po and Wei-Ning had travelled many miles. Where possible, they kept to the narrow country roads. Wei-Ning seemed well furnished with monies. Immediately they'd left the Province of Saitchu she bought new clothes and did her best to disguise Lin-Po and herself. The master sorcerer felt both intrigued and embarrassed. He had been born in Cambaluc and found the prospect of wandering the narrow lanes and roads of the Western Provinces an eerie experience. Matters were not helped by the rain which fell steadily, turning the trackways to mud. Lin-Po found it difficult to avoid slipping over into the wet morass of the paddyfields. He tried not to moan but the discomfort proved too much.

Sometimes they begged. Other times, at Wei-Ning's insistence, Lin-Po had to work in the fields. He plucked the half-grown rice from the rain-soaked soil and helped the farmer move it to a new planting ground. Lin-Po's hands, soft and delicate, were not used to heaping manure, pulling up rice, removing wild grasses or helping to push a plough pulled by the farmers' womenfolk.

His clothing stank of night soil, mud and the fusty smells of the alleyways and humble cottages where he had to sleep. The countryside itself he found sombre and unexciting. Rice-fields stretched as far as the eye could see, broken by copses of trees and the occasional village or hamlet. Lin-Po's stomach curdled at the food he was forced to eat: holding the small hand bowl up to his mouth, scooping up the smoking rice with none-too-clean chopsticks and having to regard as delicacies items like pickled cucumber, beancurd, red salted turnip, ground nuts and the occasional piece of fruit.

Wei-Ning insisted they keep themselves to themselves; though when they reached the great roads, they mingled with pedlars and hucksters as well as hordes of peasant farmers with their peculiar gait, caused by the constant use of the hoe. Royal messengers, riding good horses, dressed in the Imperial Insignia and wearing official hats, thundered by. Scholars moved from shrine to shrine. There were porters, poets, landless men, former soldiers wandering around at a loose end, looking for mischief. Now and again the roads became choked with rock slides and the pair were forced to pick their way through the slush and mire and climb over sharp pointed stones. Wei-Ning was strangely silent. Since their escape from the underground caverns, she had refused to discuss what they were doing or where they were going.

'The Province of Saanxi awaits us,' she would say. 'After that we return to Cambaluc.'

She impressed upon Lin-Po how dangerous their situation was, and kept him well away from Mongol soldiers who, with banners and pennants displayed, would come riding down the road shouting at them to stand aside.

'Why can't we travel by river?' Lin-Po whined. 'We could rest our feet and sleep under the awnings. We have enough money to buy passage.'

Wei-Ning tolerated this moaning for three days before snorting in indignation. She dragged him from the road, slopping through paddyfields across the narrow trackways which separated these until they reached a riverbank. There, Wei-Ning took shelter under a willow tree and shared out their meagre provisions. Lin-Po studied her carefully. She was no longer the great beauty, the delicate lady of the court. She looked more like a filthy urchin, with her sandals fashioned from bamboo, rotting trousers, ragged shirt and leather jerkin.

'Why are we here?' Lin-Po moaned.

'Watch the river!' she snapped.

He did so, his eyes growing heavy. Suddenly, a barge nosed its way round the bend: cumbersome, pushed by poles, the vessel was full of farmers supplementing their income with a little fishing. Lin-Po watched its progress with interest. He even thought of jumping to his feet and hailing it, though Wei-Ning warned him not to. A bank of mist was rolling in. Abruptly the sound of gongs and cymbals could be heard, and an imperial junk, sails all spread, banners and pennants snapping in the breeze, appeared. Lin-Po glimpsed the Imperial Insignia, white tiger faces and red snarling dragons painted on shields along the side. The junk moved with surprising speed and bore down on the fishing barge, which was forced to heave to. Lin-Po watched the soldiers clamber down rope-ladders into the barge to carry out the most thorough search.

'That's the way they expect us to travel,' Wei-Ning hissed. For the first time since they had left the cavern she grasped his hand, rubbing his fingers between hers. 'We have protection,' she murmured, 'but we must be careful. Soon the news of your disappearance will reach Cambaluc. Imperial messengers will be despatched; border guards and mounted patrols will have your description and mine. If we are taken, we can expect little mercy. You have broken the terms of your exile, remember. We will be hustled to the ground, our necks stretched and our heads cut off.'

'I have magic,' Lin Po replied defensively.

Wei-Ning made a rude sound with her lips and dropped his hand.

'Magic!' she scoffed. 'Lin-Po, you may be a great conjurer but *real* magic?'

'I was Demon Father in the Water Lily Society.'

'Charlatans and counterfeits!' she jeered.

'We made the blood sacrifice.'

Wei-Ning's face grew solemn. 'Yes, yes, you did.' Her lips smiled but her eyes remained watchful. 'However, what you call up and what you control, Lin-Po, are two different things.'

She spoke so matter-of-factly that Lin-Po felt uneasy. Staring across the brown-tinged river, the mist now creeping along the bank, he heard the lonely call of the birds and felt the rainwater trickle down his hot, sweaty back. Lin-Po shivered. He was so used to controlling the game, like one of those wandering gamblers who stop in a village and fascinate the peasants. This was all so different.

'Why must we enter Saanxi?' he demanded.

'The Jade Crown,' she replied. 'Among other things.'

'What Jade Crown?'

'I have told you enough times: a Jade Crown and its guardians await us.'

'I have never heard of it.'

'Very few people have.'

'And what will we do? Simply march up to some temple and take it?'

Wei-Ning bit her lower lip. She patted the ground.

'It lies beneath the earth. You will see things, Lin-Po, you have never seen before. It promises to be a dangerous enterprise.'

Staring intently at Wei-Ning, the master sorcerer tried to use his gift to catch her thoughts like a child would butterflies in a net. The more he tried, however, the less confident he became, for he picked up nothing but a deep sense of unease. Wei-Ning was staring at the junk pulling away from the barge.

'My mind is my own, Lin-Po. The door is firmly closed except for the Master.'

'The Master?' Lin-Po pulled his cloak around him. 'What do you mean, the Master?'

'Do you think you are him?' Wei-Ning mocked. 'You and your Water Lily Society?'

'I have thought about what happened in Cambaluc,' he told her.

Lin-Po leant back against the tree trunk and closed his eyes. It had all been so mysterious. He and Shunko had been leading sorcerers in Cambaluc. They had made a small fortune and bought a bigger house, a veritable mansion in the new city with gardens and orchards, carp ponds and fountains. They were garbed in silk and were deferred to by all members of the Water Lily Society. They had basked like wealthy cats in the sun until Wei-Ning appeared. Lin-Po opened his eyes and stared at his companion.

'Who are you?' he asked abruptly.

'Lin-Po, I am Wei-Ning, a member of the Water Lily Society. I came from Hangchow.'

'Yes – yes, you did,' he replied bitterly. 'And you brought disaster with you, you and your lover at court.'

'What lover?' Wei-Ning edged closer, her black eyes steely hard. 'What lover, Lin-Po?'

He glanced away. 'There were rumours,' he mumbled. 'About you being Ahmed's mistress.'

'That's right,' she replied soothingly. 'I did have powerful friends. I also paid you gold and silver to perform the blood sacrifice. Don't you remember, Lin-Po?'

'I remember,' came the surly reply.

How could he forget? He, and the others, abducting travellers, wandering scholars, lonely storytellers, peasant girls on their return from the markets. Gagged and bound, eyes blazing with terror, these victims were carried out, sometimes to the fields beyond the city, more frequently to the shady groves of Lin-Po's house. How could he forget the roaring fires, the magical powders and potions, the dreamlike trances and, occasionally, under the influence of opiates, terrible visions. Lin-Po himself had experienced hideous nightmares: of rats, teeming over the fields, so many it looked like a sea of shiny fur rushing towards him. Every ritual ended with his sharp-bladed knife slitting throats and spilling blood into a bowl as an offering to the demons of the night.

Oh, what times they were! The gold and silver had poured in. Lin-Po lived like a great lord. He and Shunko could even buy precious imports from the islands off the coast, gems and stones from beyond the Great Silk Road. Lin-Po had one gift, the ability to read minds. He had exploited that, but murder had proved a more lucrative source of income. He had not questioned Wei-Ning. She bore the emblem on her shoulder, mysterious in her ways though never once did she break a promise. Lin-Po had tried to question her but all he received were evasive answers. Then disaster had struck.

'Why?' Lin-Po glared at Wei-Ning.

'Why what, Master Sorcerer?' she teased back.

'I didn't know it was Ahmed.'

She made no attempt to reply.

'It was Ahmed, wasn't it? He sent you.' Lin-Po crossed his

hands and tried to rub some warmth into his arms. 'It all happened so quickly,' he murmured.

One morning, just before dawn, the imperial soldiers broke into the house, pillaging and looting. He and Shunko had been seized, bound and confined in some smelly prison box. Others of their society had joined them. At first Lin-Po had been confused. Had Wei-Ning been a spy? But more news had arrived from members of the Water Lily Society who had escaped. A ruthless hunt was on for Wei-Ning whilst the Great Khan's First Minister Ahmed had faced summary assassination. Lin-Po had expected to die. He and Shunko had gone on trial. He had used his gift to anticipate what the magistrate would say and, surprisingly enough, he and Shunko had been sentenced to perpetual exile on the borders of the Great Desert until . . . He glanced at Wei-Ning. She'd often appeared so beautiful, so comely, it was hard to believe this ragged, dirty figure was a confidante of a great one of the land and yet . . . ?

'There must have been a traitor,' he mused. 'Someone high-ranking.'

Wei-Ning lifted her head. 'They thought it was you.'

Lin-Po was so startled he leapt to his feet. 'That's impossible!' he wailed.

Wei-Ning jumped up and imitated him, dancing up and down, feet squelching in the mud, arms flapping like the wings of an injured bird. Lin-Po's face flushed with embarrassment.

'You are like a child,' she sneered. 'You moan and you whine! Why couldn't it have been you? Ahmed was killed. I had to flee for my life. Others died terrible deaths: the garrotte, the sword.'

'But you know I am not the traitor!' Lin-Po shouted.

He picked up his bundle as if to walk away; Wei-Ning caught him by the arm.

'I know you are not.' She smiled.

Lin-Po tried not to feel like a chastened child; he slumped down beneath the willow tree.

'Then, if you trust me, why don't you tell me more?'

'Because, if we are captured,' Wei-Ning replied, 'you can't tell what you don't know.'

'But we will go back to Cambaluc?'

'Oh yes, Lin-Po, and it will be dangerous.'

'But if we are successful?'

'If we are successful, palaces and mansions, parks and gardens, treasure chests, beautiful women – they'll all be yours. All ripe for the plucking.'

'But Ahmed's dead.'

'The Water Lily Society isn't,' Wei-Ning retorted. 'And where there's life, there's hope.'

'What about the traitor?' Lin-Po said doggedly. 'How do I know you are not the traitor? How do I know that you are not taking me back to a horrible death in Cambaluc?'

'You don't.'

Lin-Po snorted in annoyance.

'But is it likely, Master Sorcerer? My head will roll just like yours.'

'The traitor?' Lin-Po repeated obstinately.

'I don't think there was one.' Wei-Ning squatted and stared across the river. 'You and I kept faith. Perhaps Ahmed made a mistake? There are more spies in the palace than there are mice in a granary.' She sighed. 'And that's all it would have taken: one mistake. Ahmed, of course, kept lists but he destroyed them. For that, we thank good fortune. If the magistrates had learnt about our victims and the sacrifices we made . . .' she sliced a finger across her throat, 'we would both be wandering demons, headless vapours in the Netherworld.'

'But why are they looking for us now?' Lin-Po asked. 'I mean, if the Water Lily Society has been crushed, its members killed, in hiding or exile, if Ahmed's corpse has been fed to the dogs – why should they spend so much time and energy looking for you and me?'

'Because there is someone in Cambaluc they can't control.'

Lin-Po shook his head, baffled. 'Who?'

Wei-Ning just stared at him. Lin-Po shivered. He recalled those bloody sacrifices in dark groves and lonely places: the hot, spilling blood, the calls into the night. He had been paid to summon up the Plague Lord, that great demon from the courts of Hell. But he had been unsuccessful. Oh, sometimes he had experienced phenomena, shifting shapes, a cold so harsh, it chilled the blood.

'Was I successful?' Lin-Po's heart leapt with pride.

'Of course you were.'

'But I never saw anything, nothing happened.'

Wei-Ning chuckled deep in her throat.

Lin-Po became aware of the swirling brown river, the drops of rain falling from the leaves, the deathly stillness of the countryside, the skies above grey and lowering. For the first time since his escape from the underground caverns – indeed, for the first time in his life, despite his capture and imprisonment in Cambaluc – Lin-Po felt genuinely frightened. For years he had played the great wizard in a number of forms: the diviner with the sixty-four sticks, or the three coins in a tortoiseshell box, the usual methods for divining the future. He had pretended to be an exorcist making up mysterious prayers, offering scrolls with enigmatic writing. He was a master of the genuflexion and strange, unfamiliar signs. He'd worked wonders to surprise and astonish even the clever ones in both countryside and city. However, if the truth be known and Lin-Po, in moments of lucidity, did confess it, he actually believed in nothing. Now this young woman was telling him the opposite, that he had achieved something: he'd called out into the night and the darkness had answered.

'How do you know?' he stammered.

'Oh, I know, Lin-Po. That's why I came for you. You are truly fortunate. The Plague Lord has risen. He is waiting for us in Cambaluc.'

'If he's so great,' Lin-Po croaked, worried as the illusions of a lifetime were shattered like a porcelain vase dropped on cobblestones, 'if that's really happened, how come we are skulking under a rain-soaked tree on the edge of a dirty river? My belly's empty, my arse is sore, my feet are callused.'

'All great deeds demand sacrifice,' Wei-Ning said blandly. 'You have to break the soil to plant. Bend the back before you can reap.'

'Yes, yes – but shouldn't it be easier? Can't we at least be guarded?'

Wei-Ning just smiled, and Lin-Po experienced a cloying terror. Was she mocking him? He became aware of something or someone standing behind him further up the bank. He wanted to turn but daren't. Then he heard a growl. Lin-Po spun round and gaped: a pack of dogs, high-tailed, with jet-black eyes and coats of a dirty yellow mange, were thronging there, lips curled, teeth bared.

Lin-Po sprang to his feet as the dogs advanced threateningly. Then a whistle shrilled and the dogs fled as a large water ox came over the hill, its huge circular horns sweeping up to meet each other, its light coat glistening. A boy sat astride its back blowing a simple flute. The boy had his head down; the sorcerer glimpsed matted blond hair, a body naked except for a loincloth, and stubby fingers clutching the flute, which gave off an eerie, blood-chilling sound.

Something was wrong. Lin-Po felt as if he had drunk too much wine. Was this a dream? He looked back over his shoulder. Wei-Ning still squatted, staring at the scene behind Lin-Po. The self-proclaimed Master Conjurer whirled round and stifled a scream. The boy had lifted his head to reveal skin of a ghostly grey pallor: his lips were red, as if he had sucked on blood, whilst his eyes were large black holes. Lin-Po began to shake. Surely this was a phantasm? It had been raining, in fact a drizzle was still falling, yet the boy's body was as dry as a fallen leaf.

'What's this? What's this?'

He stared back at Wei-Ning, who was muttering under her breath. The boy? Lin-Po looked again but the water buffalo had turned and was going back over the hill. Lin-Po followed, determined to get to the bottom of this. He had created enough illusions in his time. He'd seen the tricks of the travelling magicians from across the borders of Cathay. Panting, he reached the brow of the hill: no boy, no ox, no sound of an eerie flute but something much more frightening. On the banks, the narrow paths which dissected the rice-fields, figures stood, still and grey as statues. They were wraiths, not real people. Their eyes glowed like coals. All gazed towards him hungrily as if they wished to cross and join him.

Lin-Po shook his head dazedly. Had Wei-Ning given him some sort of a drug? He could tolerate it no longer. Crouching down on his haunches, he closed his eyes, wishing that his dead wife were here. As if in answer, he felt his hair being caressed; gentle fingers moved down but their touch on his hot face was icy cold. Lin-Po opened his eyes and stared up. Shunko was standing before him, a greenish hue to her face, her black eyes blazing with anger. Her mouth open, teeth bared, she was touching her chest at the terrible rent which pierced it.

Lin-Po began to scream. He could hear it himself. He didn't

care if the soldiers heard it. He didn't really care if they came and chopped off his head, put an end to all these nightmares. Then he fainted. He was only aware of the water splashing on his face and the cold mud oozing through his weather-worn clothes.

When Lin-Po awoke it was dark. He felt warm and secure. They were still on the riverbank but had moved to higher ground. Wei-Ning had lit a fire which crackled merrily. Lin-Po sleepily wondered where she had collected the wood and whether she was frightened? He moaned, more to attract her attention than because he felt pain. Indeed, he was warm and comfortable. Smiling, she came across with a bowl of steaming rice and fed him.

'What happened?' he whispered.

'You've travelled far, Lin-Po. Perhaps I pushed you too hard. Too much walking, too little food – it numbs the mind and stirs all forms of fantasy in the soul. Hush now!'

Lin-Po hungrily finished the bowl of rice. Wei-Ning then served a small cup of aromatic rice wine, quite unlike the coarse fare of the wayside taverns or cookshops. Lin-Po had not drunk such wine for ages, not since those heady days in Cambaluc. Afterwards, he felt sleepy and allowed his head to fall back. He was aware of the stars whirling above him, then he fell into a dreamless sleep.

The next morning he woke refreshed. The rain had stopped, the clouds had broken and a strong sun was already climbing high in the sky. He sat up. Wei-Ning was busy packing their belongings into the usual bundles, securing the clasps. When Lin-Po looked down at his clothes, they were dry. His feet and legs no longer ached. He stared around; he was sure he had slept on a bed of flossed silk but it was only their blankets and cloaks with a padding of grass and leaves.

'What happened?' he demanded.

'You had a fever.' Wei-Ning stood over him. 'I told you last night. You travelled too far and ate too little. Your body was fevered.'

'But the bedding, it felt like silk?'

'When you are tired, my friend, the hardest wood becomes the softest pillow.'

'But my clothes are dry, and they are also clean.'

'I took them off, washed and dried them.'

'And the food, the drink?'

Wei-Ning pointed across to a small farmstead.

'You shouldn't have undressed me,' he reproached her.

Wei-Ning laughed and turned away. 'I don't understand you, Lin-Po,' she called over her shoulder. 'If you are uncomfortable, you moan and when you feel better you moan. Anyway, it's time to be gone!'

Lin-Po got to his feet. He took his bundle and slung it over his back, slipping his feet into his sandals. Wei-Ning knelt down and tightened the thongs.

'Take courage,' she murmured. 'Let your belly glow and your heart leap. We are not alone, Lin-Po. If we use our courage and wit, all will be well.'

Before he could prolong the discussion any further, she picked up her bundle and walking stick and, with her straw hat tied firmly on her head, Wei-Ning was soon splashing across the fields back towards the road.

In the days that followed, Lin-Po felt stronger, more determined. He didn't know what was the cause – whether it was something Wei-Ning had given him, what he had seen or that long dreamless sleep – but his fear and trembling were now a distant dream. Lin-Po felt angry. Someone in Cambaluc had betrayed him. He had been forced to lose face, suffer degradation, feel the full rigours of exile and, of course, there was the death of Shunko. Wei-Ning offered the means for revenge and he would take it.

They left the country roads and, once they had reached the highway, Lin-Po took a more active role. At a small town he bought some new robes and assumed the part of a seller of snuffboxes, which he stole from a trader who lay drunk, snoring like a hog in a tavern yard. They mingled easily with the dregs of the highway: sneak-thieves, swindlers, the sellers of bogus wares who offered imitation silk really made of paper, or lumps of lead and copper which, generously painted, could be traded as small ingots of gold and silver. At Wei-Ning's insistence, he cut plants: at teahouses or cook-shops, he diced the plants up and poured them into small sealed jars to sell as powerful potions or drugs. Wei-Ning acted her part, too: sometimes she was his daughter, at other times his assistant and, on one occasion, his wife.

The closer they came to Saanxi Province, however, the more aware Lin-Po became of a strong military presence: guards posted at crossroads, the same at the entrance to towns and villages. Wei-Ning became anxious.

'We can pass for a while as labourers,' she said, 'moving from one village to another, but the more we travel . . .'

'What do you mean?' Lin-Po asked.

'You know the Mongol's system of spies and police – they will be on the lookout for both of us. Now we have changed our appearances, we travel with people who can vouch for us. However, I have noticed when we are stopped, the soldiers ask their usual questions.'

'What about the scribes?' Lin-Po asked her. 'Those men who sit behind the soldiers?'

Wei-Ning patted him on the shoulder. 'Your wits are returning, Lin-Po. The scribes are taking careful note of who passes. We give different names, different occupations but, the further we travel north-west, the more dangerous it becomes. Our descriptions are passed on by couriers. The reports are sifted and, sooner or later, we will be detained and more closely questioned.' She paused. 'Once we have finished in Saanxi, it will be easier.'

'Why?'

Wei-Ning smiled. 'Oh, don't worry, Lin-Po, you'll see.'

Two days later, they entered a large provincial town. Guards stopped them, but Lin-Po was able to answer their questions adroitly enough and they were allowed through. They entered the dusty marketplace where the stalls were busy. The towns-people milled about whilst stopping to watch the travelling mountebanks, fire-eaters and shadow-dancers ply their arts in return for a coin or a bowl of rice. Lin-Po and Wei-Ning went into a cookshop, broke their fast and bought extra food for their journey. They were about to leave when a strange procession forced them back into the courtyard. Petty criminals were being paraded: pickpockets, market thieves – their punishment was public humiliation, being forced to wear signs. These were decrees from the city council or even new edicts from Cambaluc. The boards were painted white and, held by ropes, hung down the front and back of the unfortunate malefactor. People gathered not only to scoff and ridicule but to read the news. Lin-Po was about to step forward when Wei-Ning nipped his wrist.

'The second criminal,' she whispered. 'Study him closely!'

Lin-Po did so. The malefactors were seven in number, guarded on each side by bored-looking sentries, trailing spears and shields. He jostled amongst the crowd, reached the second prisoner and quickly read the board which hung down behind him. The writing, in clear black paint, proclaimed his name, Lin-Po, and that of Wei-Ning: it gave their ages and fairly accurate descriptions. It advertised how these two criminals wanted for treason were travelling to or were already in the Province of Saanxi. The board boldly announced how both these criminals were to be arrested on sight, and even Lin-Po was astonished at the rich reward offered for their capture. All his doubts disappeared. He'd truly seen visions on the banks of that river: Wei-Ning was *not* wandering in her wits. The sweat broke out on his skin. Wei-Ning pinched his wrist, a sign to keep calm.

He turned away, going back to the cookshop.

'At least we've changed our appearance,' he whispered. 'But I need something to drink.'

They went back inside and sat at a table. Lin-Po's heart lurched at the greasy-faced young man who sauntered over and sat down opposite them. He leaned his elbows on the table, hands clasped, and smiled at Lin-Po and Wei-Ning.

'Travelled far?' he asked.

Lin-Po's throat went dry. Even without his gift, he was astute enough to recognise a Government spy when he saw one.

Chapter 13

The spy was dressed in a long, grey shirt and green trousers, an ornamental belt around his slim waist. Lin-Po noticed his fingers were stubby and chalk-stained; he was a dangerous man, with his mean mouth and ever-shifting eyes. Lin-Po had met his kind before. The Mongol overlords had crushed all resistance: the native rulers, the Sung Dynasty, had been wiped out. The Mongols, however, had quickly taken over the habits and customs of Cathay but they kept a watchful eye on their newly conquered subjects, not just with soldiers tramping the roads or cavalry patrols criss-crossing the countryside. A legion of spies also flourished. Lin-Po smiled. After all, years earlier, hadn't he acted as a paid informer?

'Well?' The stranger leant over the table, beating a tattoo on its slop-covered surface. 'I only want to be friendly. I am hungry and have stopped here for a meal. My name is Zao Tse. I am a tailor by trade.' He held up his hands and playfully tapped Lin-Po on the shoulder. 'You know what I am, don't you?'

'I can read your mind,' Lin-Po retorted.

'Where are you going?'

'We are travellers,' Wei-Ning answered. She gestured at Lin-Po. 'This man is my uncle: we are visiting kin.'

'Are you truly?' Zao Tse studied Wei-Ning. 'And where are your kin? I know this town well.'

'On the outskirts,' Wei-Ning replied defensively. 'Near the Silver Peacock Pagoda.'

Lin-Po hid his surprise.

'And you are travelling far? You have passes?'

'I thought you were a tailor?' Wei-Ning said. 'You have no authority to stop or question us.'

The young man wrinkled his nose and got to his feet. 'Please excuse me. I am going to relieve myself.' He went out into the back yard where the latrine buckets stood.

'Let's go now,' Lin-Po whispered. 'I have read his mind: he's an informer!'

'Don't be stupid!' Wei-Ning hissed. 'That's what he wants us to do.'

'He suspects,' Lin-Po murmured. 'We should go.'

'You know what he is, Lin-Po, a government informer. They never hunt alone: he'll have a friend outside.'

'Why doesn't he just send for the police or soldiers?'

'He daren't do that. He has to be certain. If we are wrongly arrested, we could demand dreadful retribution, he knows that.'

She stared round the ill-lit cookshop. 'I wonder which of these is his companion?' Then Wei-Ning threw her head back and laughed. 'It's not too fine outside,' she declared loudly. 'And I am tired and thirsty.'

Zao Tse came back in, striding towards them, arms swinging.

'Do you want to buy some new clothes at a bargain price?' he asked, sitting down. 'My old mother always taught me to be kind to strangers. I'll show you to your kinspeople, too.'

'You said you were hungry,' Wei-Ning replied casually. 'And so are we. I am not turning up at my cousin's house starving. He'd think we've just come for food.'

Zao Tse looked a little disconcerted. Wei-Ning ignored him and called across to the cook, ordering rice-flour dumplings stuffed with sweet apples boiled and wrapped in plantain leaf. After breaking her fast earlier, she had little appetite, but she and Lin-Po would have to eat heartily – that, or arouse suspicion.

'And you, Zao Tse?'

The informant pointed to a large vat of water: it contained small crabs which could be eaten alive after being dipped in a sauce of vinegar and salt.

'Two of those, please,' he cheekily requested. 'And some steamed buns of wheatflour filled with diced pork and lumps of apple.'

'You *are* hungry,' Wei-Ning grinned.

As she engaged him in a patter of conversation, Lin-Po sourly watched the cook fire the mobile charcoal oven with a hollow bamboo tube. He looked around, listening with half an ear to his companions chatter about the weather, the crops. The rest of the customers were a nondescript group: a travelling singer, two farmers in from the fields, market vendors and an old Buddhist monk slumped on a stool, half-asleep. It was a noisy, cheery place, none too clean, but the food smelt savoury and tasted good, as they knew from eating here earlier, and the cook apparently enjoyed his trade. One of his daughters served them, placing the steaming bowls on the table and bringing chopsticks which, she assured them, had been cleansed in boiling water.

Lin-Po marvelled at the change in Wei-Ning's character. She had loosened her hair and unbuttoned the top of her shirt. When she ordered rice wine, her coolness and her iron resolve were infectious. Lin-Po joined in the conversation, demanding that

Zao Tse contribute something towards the meal. The informant became nervous. He ate and drank fast. Wei-Ning began to tease him, ordering skin of pig stewed in oil. The man ate like a dog, wolfing his food.

'Where do you live?' Wei-Ning asked. 'I mean, we've answered your questions, but who are you?'

'I told you, I'm a tailor.'

Wei-Ning ordered more rice wine, kicking Lin-Po under the table as a sign to be careful what he drank. Lin-Po obeyed. While he ate, Zao Tse's eyes flickered several times over to the far corner. Lin-Po waited a while then turned. Wei-Ning was correct: a wandering scholar had now come in and was pretending to pore over a tattered manuscript. He was undoubtedly Zao Tse's companion.

'I just wondered.' Wei-Ning again nudged Lin-Po. 'My companion and I are travel-stained.' She shovelled more rice into her mouth then put the bowl down. 'I could go to a bath-house but, if you are a tailor, we'd like to buy new clothes.' She leant over. 'Something nice to wear? Perhaps a wash? That would be fine, wouldn't it, Uncle?' She stared innocently at Lin-Po.

'I don't know,' Zao Tse murmured.

'Surely your wife won't object?' Wei-Ning teased.

'I don't have a wife,' the young man replied. 'I live alone, I inherited my father's shop.'

'You are a bachelor?' Wei-Ning replied breathlessly, opening her eyes wide. 'I wager you are plagued by the matchmakers, a handsome young fellow like you, with a good trade and your own shop!'

Lin-Po kept his face impassive. He prided himself on being a conjurer, an illusionist, but Wei-Ning was better. She had transformed herself from the hard, gritty traveller to the coy, simpering young woman who had drunk a little too much rice wine. She had turned the tables completely, showing no fear, pushing Zao Tse into a corner. After all, he had introduced himself, insisting on helping. If he retreated now, Wei-Ning could get angry: he might lose face and, of course, he was still suspicious.

'Come on.' Wei-Ning got to her feet. 'Uncle, you settle with the cook.' She smiled at Zao Tse. 'We'll pay for the food in return for the use of your bath-house, eh? A little hospitality wouldn't go amiss.'

Zao Tse had no choice but to agree.

The three of them left the cookshop and walked along the narrow streets. Wei-Ning was now openly flirting with Zao Tse, slipping her arm through his, talking and laughing loudly, drawing the attention of curious onlookers. Zao Tse, much the worse for drink, was now clearly regretting what he had done.

Lin-Po, trailing behind them, grinned but kept his head down. Due to the Mongols, customs were slowly changing: women were to be seen but not heard. The practice of binding the feet of young girls was becoming a fashion. If Zao Tse was seen by friends and neighbours with a flat-footed woman laughing loudly, touching him in public, they would consider he was consorting with whores and harlots. Zao Tse would occasionally turn, looking over his shoulder as if trying to draw Lin-Po into the conversation, but in reality he was searching for his companion. The travelling scholar had also left the cookshop: he was now following but some distance behind.

They crossed the market square just as the gong sounded the end of afternoon business. Zao Tse hurriedly led them along an alleyway and stopped at a garden gate. He opened this and waved them through. The courtyard was small with raised footpaths to keep it clear of the rainwater draining from shabby grass patches and overgrown flowerbeds. The house inside was fairly clean but bleak and rather bare. Lin-Po deduced that Zao Tse was not a very good tailor and had decided to supplement his income by collecting information. By now, Wei-Ning was trilling like a songbird. She helped Zao Tse light a fire in one of the braziers, then demanded that he serve some wine, asking him to bring from his workshop any new clothes as well as bricks to warm the water tub. Zao Tse, though nervous, had no choice but to obey. Time and again Wei-Ning reminded him how they were now his guests and, after all, they had paid for the food. She was openly flirting and teasing. Only once did she glance at Lin-Po and wink quickly.

Eventually the bath-tub water was ready and Wei-Ning prepared herself. She shook her long black hair loose and, using a silver comb, deloused it, popping the lice into her mouth to crack them, laughing and chattering all the while. At last she was finished. Lin-Po had never seen her look so beautiful. Wei-Ning's face seemed to have changed, become more refined, framed by the glossy black hair which cascaded down to her shoulders. She kept moving her neck as if to relax, straining forward to talk to Zao Tse who, like Lin-Po, sat on a cushion watching her.

'I need to bathe. You have soap? Something fashioned out of peas and herbs?'

Zao Tse swallowed hard and nodded.

'And the water is ready?'

'Oh yes,' came the throaty reply.

Wei-Ning got to her feet. 'Well, come on, show me.'

They left the room and went down the corridor. Lin-Po heard the splash of water, Wei-Ning's singing, more laughter, then a small scream. Getting to his feet, Lin-Po walked down the ill-lit passageway. He stood at the entrance to the chamber and stared through the latticed curtain. Wei-Ning and Zao Tse were lying on a bed of rush matting. Wei-Ning's glistening body was twisting beneath Zao Tse, her legs slightly up, her hands on his back. She was moaning, screaming. Abruptly she turned and smiled at Lin-Po. Zao Tse gave a low groan of pleasure then rolled off. Wei-Ning turned. Lin-Po saw the knife flash and, in one swift cut, Wei-Ning sliced Zao Tse's throat from ear to ear. She sprang to her feet as if to escape the splashing blood, hastily dressed then kicked the still jerking corpse. She gathered her hair up, pushing in the combs and pins which held it in place.

'A little fox.' She smiled and, coming over to Lin-Po, tweaked his nose playfully. 'He was very dangerous. There was no other way. If we had tried to escape, he would have raised the alarm. We also need a corpse. You can do the blood sacrifice tonight. Tomorrow morning we cross into Saanxi Province.'

Lin-Po's mouth and throat went dry, not so much at the sudden brutal death but at Wei-Ning's coldness.

'You would have made a marvellous actress. You play so many roles.'

'He was dead as soon as he met us,' Wei-Ning grinned. Again she tweaked Lin-Po's nose. 'But that's the problem with men. They often talk too much and act too little.' She sighed. 'We can stay here the night, eat and drink to our hearts' content, sleep in soft beds.'

'You are forgetting his companion.'

'No, I'm not,' Wei-Ning told him. 'Wait there!'

Lin-Po heard her run down the passageway in a patter of sandals, the door opening and Wei-Ning's voice in the garden. A short while later she returned, holding the scholar by the hand.

'Are you sure?' The man was trying to lie. 'I came here to see Zao Tse. We are old friends.'

'As are we,' Wei-Ning said warmly. 'Now, he's getting a bath. Sit down on the stool.'

Confused, the scholar scratched at his ill-shaven cheek.

'Sit down! Sit down!' Wei-Ning pushed him onto a stool and thrust a cup of rice wine into his hands.

Only a second or two later, Lin-Po heard a gurgle, the cup fall to the ground. He glanced back: the scholar was still sitting on the stool, a look of horror on his face as the blood pumped out of the wound in his throat. Wei-Ning stood behind him, wiping her dagger on the scholar's gown. The man opened his mouth then slumped to the floor as if in prayer, his blood forming a pool around him.

'Now we have nothing to fear,' Wei-Ning replied matter-of-factly. 'Lin-Po, we need two cups of blood, two lamps.' She swept the pots from the table. 'These will do.'

'Aren't you frightened of their ghosts?' Lin-Po asked.

The scholar's body was still convulsing in its death throes. Wei-Ning tipped the corpse onto its side with her foot.

'He was more dangerous alive.' She went back and closed the door. 'Daylight is fading, it's dusk. The best time for the ceremony is now.'

Lin-Po obeyed. He went into the bath-house, collected blood in a bowl and did the same at the scholar's corpse. He placed these on the table whilst Wei-Ning brought two lamps. She then knelt beside him, clutching a small stick of incense she'd found somewhere in the house. For a while they just waited as the darkness grew deeper and the sounds from outside faded. Lin-Po glanced sideways. Wei-Ning seemed asleep; her eyes closed, her face serene, only those lovely lips moving.

Where do you come from? Lin-Po wondered. Just who are you? His mind raced back to that cookshop. Wei-Ning laughing and flirting, loudmouthed and raucous in the street, teasing and titillating, then killing as coldly as any marauder. Lin-Po recalled her squirming beneath the now-dead Zao Tse, moaning and squealing in pleasure, acting the courtesan. Lin-Po felt excited, more so than he ever did with Shunko. He glanced at the table. The lamplight had grown stronger: its reflection was caught in the blood-brimming bowls. Somewhere a dog howled, not the usual *yip, yip* – more like a wolf in some wood-filled valley. He jumped as Wei-Ning began to speak in a tongue he could not recognise.

'Who are you talking to?'

The words were out before he could stop them.

'The General of the Nine Gates.'

Lin-Po shivered. Wei-Ning was calling on the Guardian of the Courtyards of Hell. Outside, the silence was broken by the squeak of flitting bats. Wei-Ning's breathing was becoming deeper, slower. She now knelt up, eyes fixed on a point between the two candles. Lin-Po shivered. He tried to control his panic. Two grey shapes had appeared.

All his life Lin-Po had lived in the shadow world, a mixture of light and darkness, trading on and exploiting the fears of others. Even as a young boy he had been a teller of tales; keeping well away from his widowed mother, he'd slip off to watch the conjurers in the marketplace and do anything to learn their tricks. Now he knew true terror. This was no illusion. The shapes were getting firmer; he could make out a head, shoulders, body.

Lin-Po began to shake, his whole body coursing with sweat as if he had run a long distance. The room was darker, the silence oppressive and hot like the noonday breeze from the desert. Somewhere a fly hummed loud, discordant. Lin-Po wanted to look away but he couldn't. The shapes took on a clearer form, revealing angry, contorted faces. He recognised Zao Tse and the scholar but they stood, hands bound like prisoners being taken out for execution. A mixture of grey and green, their eyes were tinged red as well as their lips and the gashes in their throats. They glared at him but did not move, more like statues or acolytes. Lin-Po closed his eyes and opened them again. A black plume of smoke was twisting between the two ghosts. The column rose then sank. It reminded Lin-Po of a typhoon. Sometimes it shifted, opening up to reveal tongues of burning fire.

The heat was now intense. Wei-Ning sat unperturbed, unconcerned about the ghosts, her eyes on that sinister black column. She began to speak in the strange tongue again. Her tone was relaxed, as if she was speaking to a friend rather than praying to a demon. Lin-Po tried to make sense of what she was saying but couldn't. He sat, terrified. The black smoke shrouded a demon; the two ghosts were its guardians. Even after death the Lords of Hell had their retinue. Lin-Po stared: faces, skull-like, appeared in the column of smoke. Wasn't that Shunko, his wife? And others, members of the Water Lily Society, people he had known and dealt with in the heady days of Cambaluc? The faces were glaring at him, only to fade and be replaced by others.

Lin-Po could stand it no longer. He closed his eyes and bowed his head. He did not know whether he had swooned or not but Wei-Ning was shaking him by the shoulder. She was offering him food, strips of dried meat, a bowl of cold rice, some juice. It tasted like apricot, or was it pear or apple? He stared around. The small kitchen was now empty: only the scholar's corpse lay stiffening on the floor. He felt slightly sick but still hungry so he gobbled the food. Wei-Ning was her usual self.

'What was that?' Lin-Po croaked between mouthfuls. 'And who *are* you?'

'Come outside, Lin-Po. The evening has turned warm and the stars are in the Heavens. We'll sit and talk.'

He obeyed her, getting up, easing the cramps from his legs

and back. He stepped over the corpse and followed her out to a bench near a flower trellis. Wei-Ning let him finish his food. She sat there, hands clasped on her knees, more like a young girl getting ready to speak to her parents than the cold-blooded killer, the demon-raiser.

'An exciting day,' she murmured.

Although it was dark, Lin-Po knew she was smiling.

'What is all this?' he asked wearily. 'Wei-Ning, I confess: I am a conjurer, a shape-shifter. I can play tricks which astonish, fascinate but, even in Cambaluc when I made the blood sacrifice, that never happened. What did you do?'

'I called up the dead,' she replied lightly. 'Zao Tse and his friend. They were humble enough and acknowledged their mistakes, for which they paid with their lives.'

'And the other?'

'Oh, a messenger,' she said evasively. 'A shape, a phantasm.'

'And?'

'Tomorrow we cross into Saanxi. In the hills near the city of Xian is the hidden Tomb of Zheng, the Tiger of Qin, the First Emperor of Cathay, founder of the Celestial Kingdom.'

'People say he is only a legend!'

'No legend,' Wei-Ning informed him. 'He was, he is, and he will be.'

'What do you mean?'

'One thing at a time,' Wei-Ning replied. 'You asked about me.'

'No, no, the tomb,' Lin-Po insisted.

'We are going to the tomb,' she said. 'We shall travel to Xian.'

'But the legends?' Lin-Po stuttered. 'I've read the histories. They tell of underground caverns filled with armies of jade soldiers, costly treasures.'

'And? Go on!' Wei-Ning looked impatient.

'There are hideous traps. Lakes of acid.' Lin-Po shuddered. 'Hidden pits: weapons armed and primed. So, how will we get in? And, more importantly,' he added: 'How do we get out?'

Wei-Ning smiled and leant closer. She smelt fragrantly of some costly perfume.

'I shall tell you my story.' She paused and stared up at the sky.

Lin-Po followed her gaze. She was looking at the bats flitting round the eaves of the house.

'They are really flying rats,' Wei-Ning murmured dreamily. 'They have bodies of ashy colour, their fleshy wings join all four limbs into one. They swallow their breath and keep their heads down because of their heavy brains.'

She made a hissing sound deep in her throat and held out her arm. Fascinated, Lin-Po watched a bat float down and perch on her outstretched hand. He had never seen one so close to, and was repelled by its sleek head and those macabre wings. Not so Wei-Ning. She spoke again, lifted her hand and the bat disappeared like a falcon leaving its perch.

'Where did you learn all this?' Lin-Po asked in awe.

'My name is not Wei-Ning,' she replied, 'but Xie Yang. I am the sister of Bing Di.'

Lin-Po couldn't hide his astonishment. Bing Di was the last Emperor of the Sung Dynasty.

'You are lying!' he stammered.

'Am I?'

'You are a member of the Water Lily Society. You have the emblem on your shoulder.'

'Listen now, Lin-Po: my sister and I are true-blooded Princesses of Cathay. Our father and our brother after him, were the last emperors of the Sung Dynasty. We are the true rulers of the Middle Kingdom, the Celestial Ones who, because of the Mongols, lost Heaven's mandate!'

'I thought the Emperor's family had been wiped out?'

'No, Lin-Po. My father died fighting the Mongol invader. My brother, with his Admiral, fought his last battle at Lantao. They both threw themselves into the sea rather than surrender. Hangchow fell, and the Mongol's writ now runs through the Celestial Kingdom.'

'You talked of a sister?'

'She follows her own path.'

'And you?'

'According to my estimate, I am twenty-eight years of age. For the past sixteen years I have been Wei-Ning. The Water Lily Society, before the death of my father and brothers, included the most powerful in the kingdom. My sister and I were initiated into its rites, then I was sent away. I was supposed to remain hidden, but the column I was travelling with was betrayed and ambushed by Mongol horsemen. Can you imagine what it was like, Lin-Po, to be a daughter of the Celestial One? To know nothing but silk, marble palaces, fragrant gardens – and then to fall into the hands of Mongol tribesmen who beat, raped and humiliated me? I escaped with one idea, one dream: to exact terrible retribution. When I travelled back to Hangchow, I learnt of other members of the Water Lily Society, including high-ranking courtiers, who were in hiding. Some of them were great sorcerers – no, no, not like yourself. They knew the ancient rites and secret words. They taught me about the General of the Nine Gates; they mapped out the roads to the Courtyards of Hell: the importance of the blood sacrifice and how to speak to the Plague Lord. We plotted and we planned. I was sent to Cambaluc and won the heart of Ahmed.'

'Then,' Lin-Po intervened, 'you sought me out. You were sent by Ahmed, weren't you? We never dreamt the conspiracy reached so high and included such powerful men.'

'Yes, yes.' Wei-Ning smiled. 'It included the most powerful.'

'So, what happened?' Lin-Po asked.

'I don't know,' Wei-Ning replied so quickly, Lin-Po was sure she was lying. She would only tell him what she thought he should know, rather than the whole truth. 'In my education,' Wei-Ning continued, 'I was also taught about the Wheel of Life, how many times we step onto it, the same soul but manifesting itself in different times and different places. Yet, in essence, all is the same.'

'I don't believe that.' Lin-Po shifted on the bench.

'Don't you, Lin-Po? Haven't you ever dreamt of places and times you could never have visited? Life *is* a wheel,' she repeated, drawing closer and pressing her fingers against his forehead. 'Think now, Lin-Po.' Her voice took on a dreamlike quality. 'Look into your soul.'

Lin-Po felt sleepy. He closed his eyes. Images, snatches of dreams appeared, gabled halls, ivory columns. He was dressed in silk and stood in a chamber made all of jade. An emperor, a Celestial One, was sitting on a throne also made of jade. His gold-slippered feet rested on a silver footstool; clouds of incense rose to hide his face. Soldiers dressed in red and black guarded him either side of the throne. Two people stood nearby. Lin-Po was sure that one of them was Wei-Ning. He opened his eyes.

'Do you remember now, Lin-Po?'

'If you are so powerful,' he enquired grumpily, 'why do you need me?'

'Oh, but I do. Tell me, when we were in that cookshop, why didn't you use your gift, Lin-Po? Why didn't you try and read the mind of Zao Tse?' She looked sternly at him.

'I did and I didn't,' he stammered. 'I knew what he was. I took your word. I met no opposition . . .'

'But if you had?'

'I'd have used it,' Lin-Po replied defensively. 'I have to concentrate. In the cookshop I knew there was no real need. Zao Tse was so obviously treacherous!'

'But the scholar?'

Lin-Po shook his head, confused.

'I followed Zao Tse's gaze.'

'Did you now?' Wei-Ning smiled. 'Did you really? Or were you using your gift and not realising it? You possess a talent,' she whispered, unbuttoning her jacket, 'which I do not have: that is one of the reasons, Lin-Po, why you have been chosen. And, when we reach Saanxi, you must use that gift for the sake of the One we serve.'

Chapter 14

Wei-Ning and Lin-Po were up before dawn. They plundered the house of Zao Tse for fresh clothes, footwear and food. Afterwards they locked the property and were on the outskirts of the town before sunrise. For a while they hid in a bamboo grove then joined a procession of traders, tinkers and itinerant pedlars making their way out to the countryside. Wei-Ning had searched through Zao Tse's possessions and they were able to furnish themselves with new identities. Lin-Po was now a tailor, Wei-Ning his niece. They were allowed to pass unmolested, though cavalry patrols were more numerous, pounding along the rough paths or broad highways. The presence of troops, officials and bureaucrats became more noticeable but Wei-Ning and Lin-Po were able to lie, change their appearance and safely crossed the border into Saanxi.

'Do we break into the tomb by ourselves?' Lin-Po asked. 'How do we find the entrance?'

'Everything has its place,' Wei-Ning quipped. 'Everything in its order, dear Uncle.'

Eventually they entered the town of Xian, and Wei-Ning hired a chamber in a wayside tavern. The innkeeper, a surly, balding man, served them dishes of shrimps boiled in oil and cups of rice mixed with eggs and noodles.

'This is the House of the Bronze Lady?' Wei-Ning enquired.

'You saw the sign,' the fellow replied shortly. 'What do you think it is? – the Palace of Infinite Joy? Eat your grub while it's hot. You'll find two beds in the out-house.' He licked his lips and studied Wei-Ning from head to toe. 'Of course, if you want to leave your uncle, you can always bed down with me. You'd make a merry handful.' He grinned sly-eyed at Lin-Po. 'And if you want, your uncle can watch!'

Lin-Po coloured with anger. He had not forgotten Wei-Ning making love to him in Zao Tse's house: hungrily, passionately as if she was determined to bind him to her in flesh as well as soul.

'This is the House of the Bronze Lady?' Wei-Ning repeated.

The innkeeper was about to reply with an obscenity when Wei-Ning lifted her hand and made a sign in the air.

'And the lilies are blooming,' she said clearly.

The fellow's mouth opened and closed.

'The lilies are blooming,' Wei-Ning said again. 'And the waters still run deep . . .'

'But hide many things . . .' the innkeeper replied slowly, his leering grin replaced by a look of fear. Indeed, he would have gone down on his knees but Wei-Ning made a sharp gesture with her hand. 'This place isn't good enough for you,' the man pleaded. 'Come, honoured guests, come with me into my private quarters.'

He walked over to the doorway where the other customers couldn't see him and gestured frantically.

'I am dreadfully sorry,' he apologised once they were alone in the smelly chamber which served as his own personal quarters.

He pulled up stools for Wei-Ning and Lin-Po then knelt on the rush matting before them.

'By what name are you called?' he asked respectfully.

'I am the Water Lily,' Wei-Ning told him.

The innkeeper put his face in his hands and moaned quietly. 'I didn't know who you were,' he whined, shoulders shaking. 'I knew you were strangers, but . . .'

'No, no, you did right,' Wei-Ning reassured him.

'There are soldiers in the town,' the innkeeper continued in a rush. 'They are circulating descriptions, but . . .' he smiled in a show of blackened teeth '. . . I wouldn't have dreamt you are the Water Lily.'

Wei-Ning undid her jerkin, pulling back the rush shirt beneath. Lin-Po glimpsed the number tattooed on her shoulder, a water lily beside it.

'I wasn't always an innkeeper,' the man said heavily. 'Once I studied in the Halls of Examinations. I refused to bow the knee to the Mongol. My family were killed and I fled.'

As he talked, Lin-Po noticed how the man changed. The greasy smile, the slovenly way he held himself disappeared; even his speech altered, becoming more cultured, refined.

'I am supposed to be dead,' he told them, 'but I took a little treasure with me,' he gestured around the shabby room, 'and bought this. Quite a change from the Ministry of War.'

On and on he chattered. Lin-Po realised the innkeeper had once served the Sung Dynasty. In the subsequent execution of its adherents, this fellow had been fortunate enough to flee. Wei-Ning let him gossip on, listening carefully to the marketplace chatter about troop movements, where they could stay and what they should do.

'The Khan's messengers come through here, do they?' she interrupted.

'Yes. They stop here,' he confirmed immediately, 'just for something to eat or drink. A few chatter.' He shrugged his shoulders. 'But, apart from descriptions being circulated and your names being proclaimed, I don't know what's going on.'

'I need help,' Wei-Ning declared.

'There are other members of the Society in the city.'

'No, no.' Wei-Ning shook her head. 'I need professional help.'

'Such as?' The fellow became all attention.

'The Tomb of Zheng!'

The innkeeper's face turned an ashy pallor.

'I've heard the stories,' he whispered. 'They say the tomb is not far but that's just legend.'

'Well, it isn't,' Wei-Ning assured him. 'I can offer those who help unlimited wealth: treasure and plunder men only dream of.'

'Can I come?' The innkeeper's fear was replaced by greed. 'I can help.'

'Of course you can.' Wei-Ning smiled. 'But you are an innkeeper. You have your place on the outskirts of the city. Strangers come here at night, yes? Outlaws, fugitives – men who live by the dark rather than the light of day: desperate men?'

'We have the *Feng Shu*,' the innkeeper agreed.

'And what are they?'

'A group of outlaws who live in the hilly country. They consist of former soldiers, escaped criminals and the like, and are led by Lon Ta, who calls himself Marshal of the Hills. He's a former officer in the Sung Army.'

'How many men does he have?'

'The band is about thirty strong, well armed. In the summer and autumn they raid, in the winter they retreat to the mountains.'

'I want to meet this Marshal of the Hills,' Wei-Ning informed him. 'Tomorrow night, here.'

'But the entrance to the tomb?' the innkeeper enquired.

Wei-Ning made a cutting movement with her hand and the fellow backed away.

'Tell the Marshal of the Hills nothing about what I've said except that I can make him rich beyond his dreams, and can promise him that he will see things few men ever see in a thousand lifetimes. Now, there's a Buddhist temple on the other side of Xian, isn't there: the Altar of the Earth?'

'Yes, yes, that's right. Beyond the Gate of Pearls on the main highway out of the city. It stands in a grove of trees, a semi-derelict place served by an old Buddhist monk and two acolytes. Very few people go there.' The innkeeper shrugged. 'It's not fashionable.'

'No, no, of course it won't be.' Wei-Ning smiled. 'Ah well, Uncle and I will now finish our meal in here. We want your best food, mind, and the clearest rice wine – none of that muck you serve your other guests. I want two good beds: a chamber at the back of the house will serve. Uncle and I will retire for the night now. We'll be gone before dawn and return at dusk. You'd best hurry!' she added warningly. 'We haven't got much time to waste: this time tomorrow the Marshal of the Hills had best be here!'

The man scampered off. Wei-Ning followed him out, made sure the passageway was empty then closed the door behind him. Then she came and knelt on the matting before Lin-Po. Once again she had changed, and was now more like a daughter prepared to listen to her father's advice.

'Tomorrow morning,' she whispered, 'we will travel to the Altar of the Earth. We are going to have to kill its guardians.'

Lin-Po hid his fear. 'Why? What will happen?'

'The old Buddhist priest is the keeper of the secret, the entrance to the tomb,' Wei-Ning breathed. 'It's handed down by mouth from one generation to another. Somewhere in the carvings of the temple the secret lies etched into the stonework: however, it would take years to find and decipher it. You, Lin-Po, will have to read the old priest's mind.'

'What happens if I can't?' He felt a fleeting panic.

'Oh, you will. Most people cannot put up any defence.'

'But he will be suspicious!' Lin-Po exclaimed.

'Nonsense! We will pose as travellers making an offering at the shrine and asking for information. He may understand what you are doing. Before we leave tomorrow morning, I'll collect weapons. So, given a little luck, some help from you and the protection of the Master, we will be successful.'

Lin-Po had other questions. Wei-Ning answered these abruptly: her mind was set and there would be no turning back.

'How do I know if that's all you need me for?' Lin-Po asked as they finished the meal. 'What will happen to me afterwards, if I'm successful?'

'You are one of us,' Wei-Ning reassured him. 'The Master needs you in Cambaluc. Now, come on: let's get a good night's sleep. Tomorrow is a busy day.'

Lin-Po didn't know whether Wei-Ning had slipped a slight opiate in his drink but he had a dreamless sleep and woke to his companion shaking him, her face bathed in the light of a small lamp. As Lin-Po struggled up, yawning, Wei-Ning pointed to a far corner.

'The innkeeper has left us two bows and a quiver of arrows,' she said. 'There's also a slightly rusty sword and a dagger and some food for the journey.'

They left shortly afterwards, slipping through the alleyways and byways of the town. Wei-Ning stopped at a shop boasting the sign of a rice bowl. She knocked on the shuttered window, and when it creaked open, she whispered a password. A short while later the gate to the courtyard was unlocked and a boy led out a pack pony. Wei-Ning stowed the weapons in the baskets provided, and covered them with a leather sheet, tying it down securely.

'There!' She smiled at him through the darkness. 'Uncle and niece on their way to visit relatives.'

They paused for something to eat at one of the cookshops on the corner of the marketplace and waited for the sound of the horn, the clashing cymbals and the thunderous beat from the drum tower to mark the beginning of the day and the opening of the city gates. They passed through these safely into the open countryside. Wei-Ning took directions from a peasant and other travellers, after which they left the main highway and set off up a narrow trackway. The morning mist still hung heavy, blocking any view, though Lin-Po soon realised they had left the open countryside and were climbing a steep hill, dotted with trees and boulders. It was an eerie, silent place, with no sound apart from the echoing patter of their heavy sandals and the clatter of the sure-footed sumpter pony.

Lin-Po always mocked people's imagination. Indeed, he'd played so many times on the gullibility of customers that he'd learnt to ignore fanciful notions. Nevertheless, this place oppressed him: it exuded an atmosphere of fear, of being watched, as if the hillside on either side of the trackway was full of armed men waiting to pounce. Or was it a haunt of demons – a gathering-place of the undead? He breathed in deeply and glanced across at Wei-Ning. Then he made one real attempt to read her mind, to see if he could break through the barrier. Pulling back the hood of her cloak, she glanced across at him, her face flecked with mud and sweat.

'Don't worry, Lin-Po.' Her voice carried strongly. 'There is nothing to fear!'

When they reached the top, the mist curtain shifted, and before them rose the temple of the Altar of the Earth. A square-fronted edifice, the dome at the top had originally been painted vermilion and green, but this had long since faded, cracked and peeled. The pillars outside were covered with crawling ivy which concealed the guardian lions, dogs, tigers and griffins on either side of the shabby entrance. The door was closed but a shutter above it abruptly opened. Lin-Po glimpsed a face then the shutter fell. Wei-Ning hobbled the pony; they walked across the cracked paving-stones and pulled at the dirt-engrained rope. Deep inside echoed the hollow sound of the bell. They heard the patter of feet. A young man, dressed in a grimy satin robe, finally opened the door.

'Visitors!' he exclaimed, his round, monkey-like face lit by a smile. 'You've brought us food? Gifts for the god?' He pointed to the ladder just inside the doorway. 'I saw you coming. I couldn't believe it. I told the master, he's ready.'

Lin-Po stared round. The temple smelt like a stable. It was none too clean, and the bamboo matting was frayed and cut. The place was devoid of any ornament, apart from a huge statue of Buddha at the far end. This was poorly illuminated by flickering torches set on the altar beneath. The Buddhist priest was already waiting seated on a cushion, the other acolyte on a small stool beside him.

'Well, you'd best come forward!'

The acolyte ushered them to what looked like a mattress placed on the foot of the steps before the altar space. The old Buddhist priest sat, cross-legged, a serene look on his face. The acolyte sitting on his right looked like a twin to the one who had ushered them in. Lin-Po and Wei-Ning knelt on the mattress and stared up into the wizened face of the Buddhist priest. A charlatan, Lin-Po thought contemptuously. This place was filthy but they got fed and took charity from the local peasants.

The small house behind the temple was no doubt comfortably furnished.

'Why are you here?' The Buddhist priest's words came in a floating whisper.

'We are travellers, Reverend Father,' Wei-Ning replied, 'come to make sacrifice. We have food and drink with us. We are also . . . curious.'

The old priest's milky-white eyes studied them carefully. Lin-Po concentrated, but he felt a little giddy and had to put his hand out. He knows we are lying, he thought. He could sense the Buddhist priest's flow of thought. He's in pain, Lin-Po concluded: there is something wrong with his stomach. He's hungry and resents us coming here so early. He's also very wary, but the two acolytes are no better than thugs. They are not above a little robbery and have weapons concealed behind the altar.

'Are you well?' Wei-Ning sweetly asked.

'I am well, beloved niece,' Lin-Po replied. 'And we can do what we want.'

'What's this? What's this?' The old priest cupped his hand to his ear.

'I am a scholar,' Lin-Po explained, 'as well as a tailor. I have heard that somewhere in this region lies the Tomb of Zheng.'

The reverend father cackled with laughter.

'Legends!' he muttered. 'Nothing but legends. You are wasting your time.' He lifted a vein-streaked hand. 'Make your sacrifice now!'

'Please tell us – where is the entrance to the tomb?' Wei-Ning insisted.

At this, the old priest lost his reverential pose.

'There *is* no entrance,' he snapped. 'It is all legend, and even if it were true, the tomb would be far away from here!'

Lin-Po nodded serenely. 'We have made a mistake, niece.' He

smiled at Wei-Ning. 'The reverend father is correct. We should make a generous offering for disturbing his family.'

Lin-Po stared at the old priest. He's laughing at us, he thought. He believes we are stupid. Lin-Po concentrated on what the priest was thinking, and clear and strong came the answer to their question.

'We should leave, niece,' Lin-Po told Wei-Ning. 'Let us go out and bring back our gifts.'

Wei-Ning unhobbled the horse and glanced up at Lin-Po, who gazed to where the acolytes were waiting expectantly near the temple door. 'What is the matter?' she asked quietly.

'He's laughing at us,' Lin-Po murmured, keeping a polite smile on his face. 'He's a bit suspicious but he thinks we're idiots.'

'The entrance – where is it?' Wei-Ning asked through gritted teeth.

Lin-Po felt a glow of satisfaction: this was one gift Wei-Ning did not possess.

'Don't worry – it's not far to the Tomb,' he teased her.

Wei-Ning got to her feet and gathered the reins.

'What do you mean, it's not far?' She beamed coyly at the acolytes, who were becoming impatient.

'The secret is passed from priest to priest. The old man thought we were fools, but I now know that the entrance is right there in the temple itself – beneath the altar. The only problem is, the altar has to be smashed before the entrance is uncovered.'

Wei-Ning looked greatly relieved. 'You are sure?'

'The old priest is often asked the question and comforts himself with the answer.'

'Well done, my friend. We have gifts,' Wei-Ning called out to the acolytes, coming forward, 'but we cannot bring our donkey into the temple. Please will you ask Reverend Father to come to the door.'

When one of the men scurried off into the darkness, Wei-Ning walked ahead, one hand in her jerkin, gesturing at the other man to come over and help. Instead of stopping, however, she carried on moving towards him. The acolyte stopped, a look of puzzlement on his face. Wei-Ning had her hand on his shoulder and the dagger was deep in his belly before he even knew what was happening. Lin-Po, meanwhile, ripped off the leather covering taken from the pony, now skittish at the scent of blood, plucked a bow from the pannier and notched an arrow. The second acolyte came to the door. He stood stupefied by the scene before him but, before he could recover his wits, Lin-Po's arrow thudded into his chest. Wei-Ning was already running through the entrance. The old priest was hobbling towards her, head down, hand grasping a stout cane. By the time Lin-Po entered the temple the old man was dead, body crumpling to the floor, blood gushing out of the fatal wound in his neck.

'Easier than I thought.' She smiled over her shoulder. 'Quick now, make sure there's no one else here!'

'What's the matter?'

Lin-Po spun round.

A young woman was standing in the doorway, a plate of food in her hand. She glimpsed the priest's corpse and turned to flee. Lin-Po chased after her, arrow to the bow. He stopped, aimed and loosed it: the young woman's hands flew up into the air and the bowl of food clattered to the paving-stones as she collapsed into a bush growing at the side of the temple. Lin-Po ran up and checked the blood beat in her neck: she was dead.

'A temple servant!' he called back. 'I'll make sure there are no more!'

The small well-furnished house which stood in its own garden behind the temple was empty, but the kitchen was full of savoury cooking smells. Lin-Po doused the fire, filled two bowls with what was cooking and rejoined Wei-Ning: she was sitting outside the temple staring up at the sky.

'It was well done,' she declared, scooping the food into her mouth with her fingers. 'We will hide the corpses, meet this bandit chief and start tomorrow morning.'

They finished their food and dragged the four corpses away from the temple, burying them in a narrow ditch and covering them with loose leaves and bracken. The pony which had bolted now returned. They took water from the well and washed the bloodstains from outside the temple and closed the door.

'So, do we go back?' Lin-Po demanded.

'No, *I* go back.' She smiled. 'You stay here.'

Lin-Po made to object but she pressed a finger against his lips.

'Do what I say,' she urged. 'This temple is deserted but, who knows, there may be visitors. If any come, you must either remain silent or, if they become too curious, kill them. I shall be back at first light. Promise me now!'

Lin-Po promised. Wei-Ning kissed him quickly on the lips, wrapped the cloak around her, gathered the pony's reins and walked into the gathering mist.

Lin-Po went back into the temple and stared at the massive altar on its heavy rock plinth. He pushed one of the altar corners but both altar and plinth were firmly fixed into the rock floor: Wei-Ning would certainly need the help of her bandit group.

Lin-Po found the place eerie and uncomfortable. He made the sign against wandering ghosts and returned to the house, spending the day eating, sleeping and going through the dead priest's possessions. He discovered nothing about any treasure or secret entrances.

'A secret passed from priest to priest,' Lin-Po murmured to

himself. 'And, of course, the altar is too heavy for one man to move, and was guarded by the acolytes.'

Lin-Po sat in a corner. Once, as a student, he had read about the Emperor Zheng. How was he described in one of the chronicles?

He has the nose of a hornet and large, all-seeing eyes. His chest is like that of a bird of prey and his voice like that of a jackal. He is merciless, with the heart of a tiger or a wolf.

Lin-Po shivered. What dreadful secrets awaited them in that underground tomb?

When darkness fell, Lin-Po lit lanterns and the small stove to give warmth and comfort. He found a jar of rice wine and drank it too fast, falling asleep on the floor. When he awoke he felt cold: mist was seeping in through the half-open shutter. Lin-Po rubbed his arms and stiffened with fear. Was that a sound? He ran to the doorway. It was still black as night outside, but the sky showed the occasional streak of light. Mist boiled and curled in the trees around the temple. He glimpsed torchlight and, hearing the clink of harness, he ran along the side of the temple, opened the door and slipped inside. Whoever was approaching was taking a different direction from the one he and Wei-Ning had used. He climbed up the steps, looked through the shutter at the two groups in the forecourt and sighed with relief. Wei-Ning had returned; men with horses were grouped around her.

'Lin-Po!' she called. 'Where are you? Lin-Po!'

He hurried down, opened the door and went outside. There must have been thirty men in the forecourt: a few on foot, most on horses. Lin-Po recognised the innkeeper. Wei-Ning introduced the Marshal of the Hills: a fierce, ill-kempt thug dressed in scraps of armour, with a straggling beard and moustache, and long matted hair falling to his shoulders. The small black eyes in the harsh Tartar face glared ferociously as the

Marshal looked Lin-Po over from head to toe. He cleared his throat and spat.

'I hope you are not wasting my time.' The Marshal rubbed a tendril of Wei-Ning's hair between his fingers.

'It will involve some hard work,' Wei-Ning countered, 'but at the end, there should be enough treasure for us all to live like emperors for the rest of our lives.'

Lin-Po looked carefully at the band of outlaws. The innkeeper he dismissed as near-harmless. Lin-Po had lived with dangerous men, creatures of the twilight who would kill, rape and rob without a second thought. These men were the worst kind: scavengers, bandits without a spark of pity or compassion. They came from all parts of the empire. One was dressed like a Tibetan, another like a desert wanderer. Their harness and armour were a motley collection of what they had taken. One was even dressed in the robes of a woman, his long, evil face garishly painted. Wei-Ning, however, was not abashed. She told the Marshal of the Hills to leave two men to guard the horses, then took the rest of them to the temple and showed them the altar.

'Destroy this,' she instructed, 'for beneath it lies the entrance.'

The bandit chief rattled out an order. Some of his men disappeared through the door and came back with heavy mallets and hammers. Torches were lit and the temple was soon filled with clouds of dust, so thick and intense that for a time they had to break off their hammering and go outside to gulp in the fresh morning air. The Marshal, of course, directed everything: Lin-Po and Wei-Ning he ignored.

'Is this wise?' Lin-Po whispered as they left to stand beneath the trees. 'They'll cut our throats as soon as share the treasure. You do not have to read minds to know that.'

Wei-Ning's eyes glittered with excitement.

'We are protected, Lin-Po. We need them to break in. You see, they are decoys. They will test the danger: remember that we are about to enter a place of demons. I intend to take the Jade Crown of the First Emperor of Cathay; his time and that of his servants has come again.'

'And afterwards?' Lin-Po asked.

'If we have the Crown,' Wei-Ning murmured, 'we will have protection.'

'By magic?' Lin-Po scoffed.

'No, not magic.' Wei-Ning looked up at the brightening sky. 'We will take the Crown and its little guardians to Cambaluc. Only this time, there will be no more danger, no more threat. We will travel swiftly and unimpeded.'

Lin-Po was about to question her further when excited cries sent them hurrying back into the temple. Inside, the statue of Buddha gazed down at a sea of destruction. The Altar of the Earth and the stone plinth on which it rested had now been destroyed, and were now no more than a heap of rubble in a swirl of white dust which made them cough. The Marshal of the Hills was pointing triumphantly at the wooden trapdoor that had been uncovered, its iron ring clear for all to see. Around it his men, sweating and exhausted, shared out water-skins, pouring the precious liquid over their faces to cleanse the dust.

'If we hadn't found it,' the Marshal bellowed, waving his hand, 'I'd have cut your throats!'

'There will be blood soon enough,' Wei-Ning whispered.

'What was that?' The Marshal came forward, sword in hand, his heavy leather gloves in the other.

'Let's open the trapdoor,' Wei-Ning told him.

A rope was put through the iron ring. At first it wouldn't move but with a massive creak it eventually came back on its well-formed hinges, revealing a flight of stone steps leading down into the darkness. The Marshal bellowed an order. Two of his men immediately went down. Suddenly from below came the most horrifying scream. The bandit with the torch clambered swiftly back. His companion, his face contorted with terror, crawled up the steps but collapsed at the top: a strange froth spilt out of his lips.

The Marshal ordered three of his archers forward: fire arrows were loosed into the pit. Wei-Ning, drawing her dagger, went to the top of the steps and stared down. She glimpsed a door, a fire arrow deeply embedded in it, its flame flickering. In the dancing shadows she could see the writhing snakes.

'I warned you about the ambushes,' she said. 'There's a snake-pit below.'

'Snakes!' the Marshal exclaimed. 'How can snakes live for hundreds of years?'

'Small recesses,' Wei-Ning shrugged. 'The ground beneath the temple and the hills around have a warren of caverns, galleries, caves, chambers.' She turned to one of the men. 'Go into the house. Find oil, anything that will burn.'

A short while later the entire pit was put to the torch, flames leaping up, clouds of smoke billowing through the temple. At Wei-Ning's insistence they waited until the fire had burnt itself out. Once it was safe, Wei-Ning herself went down to inspect. Some snakes had been burnt, were no more than heaps of ash, but the rest had retreated back through narrow crevices and cracks away from the heat. A makeshift ram was brought and the first door was battered down. Wei-Ning urged caution but the Marshal ordered torches to be lit and they went straight into the cavern. The entrance chamber was musty, dank and dark. With a sense of foreboding, Lin-Po realised that this was probably the nearest he would come to seeing Hell before death. The nightmare had begun. Wei-Ning, however, seemed impervious to the atmosphere, and Lin-Po was curious about the small wooden box she'd brought with her.

The Marshal was astute enough to realise that such elaborate precautions must hide a great treasure but his lust to seize it cost the lives of several of his men. They made their way along the gallery, but not cautiously enough. At one spot the entire floor gave way beneath them, and a group of outlaws fell screaming through the hole onto the sharpened spears embedded below.

Similar traps had been set in different chambers. Gaps in the floor had been carefully hidden over; lay waiting beneath them, lined with rock and filled with a sharp acid substance. Some traps, of course, had rotted with age but, by the time they had reached the end of the gallery, Lin-Po reckoned that they must have lost a third of their number.

The air was surprisingly clear despite the deep darkness which stretched ahead of them. Wei-Ning declared that there must be shafts, small cracks high up which allowed in air. Some doors led to nothing but, once opened, caused a fall of earth. The Marshal, however, now staying at the rear with Wei-Ning and Lin-Po, was impervious to the losses, driving his men forward with the prospect of unlimited wealth. More makeshift torches were lit. One of the bandits, in an attempt to avoid a pit, threw himself against the wall and screamed as the spear-head embedded there dug deep into his side. The Marshal bent over him, whispered a few words of comfort, then summarily cut his throat.

Wei-Ning was praying, talking swiftly in that tongue Lin-Po had heard her use before, calling on the powers of darkness to protect them. The Marshal, however, now used caution, keeping his men away from the sides. They advanced slowly, testing everything before them now, the walls, ceiling and floor. There were more rock falls, special packs of earth, stones carefully prepared, ready to crash down at the slightest touch or pressure.

The deeper they went, the more cunning the pits became. The Marshal's men were beginning to rebel, some openly declaring it wasn't worth the risk. The Marshal killed the leading protester, taking his head clean off his shoulders with one glittering swipe of his sword. The mutiny was quelled and they continued their journey.

Eventually the galleries ended in a broad timbered door. The Marshal of the Hills made Wei-Ning and Lin-Po open it. The door was not locked or stuck but swung back smoothly, revealing a long chamber. The bandit chief pushed two men forward, furious at the losses he'd sustained. Lin-Po could read his thoughts: once the treasure hoard was revealed, he and Wei-Ning would be disposed of.

They made their way tentatively along the main gallery; more caverns and chambers stood off it. When torches were brought, Lin-Po exclaimed in surprise. At first he thought a group of men were hiding there, waiting to pounce but, as the torches flared into life, they revealed clustered figures carved out of terracotta, statues of soldiers in perfect battle formation. Every statue was lifelike in detail: studs on an archer's shoes, metal breastplates, hair tied up in a queue on the top of the head. The second chamber was no different. This time the soldiers were lightly clad for swift movement. Some wore half-armour; officers stood with epaulettes on their shoulders; there were even horses with red lips and dilated nostrils.

'It's an army!' the Marshal of the Hills whispered. 'An entire army!'

'The Emperor Zhing's Companions,' Wei-Ning informed him. 'Waiting for their master to come back to life.'

All fear of traps had now disappeared. Each chamber revealed more mysteries and treasures – books written on silks, porcelain vases, costly decorations in gilt, bronze, copper, gold and silver. Precious turquoise stones glittered in the torchlight. Other chambers held huge sculptures of elephants, griffins, tigers. There were chests and coffers brimming with silver and gold ingots, Heavenly horses cast in gilt bronze, tigers carved out of white ivory, precious lanterns and lacquered furniture: the treasures of a mighty Emperor awaiting his return. Some few chambers held more grisly artefacts – the skeletons of those buried with Zheng. Lin-Po and the rest moved amongst these sights in silent awe. The Marshal of the Hills, however, clapped his hands and shouted with pleasure. Now and again he would run into a chamber and come out brandishing some precious object. Wei-Ning plucked at Lin-Po's sleeve and stared up at the ceiling; he could see nothing up there but the beams. Then Wei-Ning held out her hand and a few grains of dirt fell into it.

'Come with me,' she whispered.

The bandit gang was now breaking up as each person seized what he wanted. Wei-Ning and Lin-Po, however, hurried ahead. The gallery ended at a small door which Wei-Ning opened. Lin-Po nearly dropped his torch when he saw what was inside: the room within was literally lined with gold plate – floor, walls and ceiling. Precious jewels winked from the corners where the gold plate met. The floor, despite the passage of time, still glowed like a golden mirror. In the centre of the chamber, on a marble plinth, lay the body of a man sheeted completely in jade, which gave off a strange greenish light. On a small case at the end of the tomb rested a Jade Crown decorated with gold-red, snarling dragons and, in the centre, framed by a circle of gold, glowed a dark purple amethyst.

'The First Emperor of Cathay!' Wei-Ning whispered.

She moved gingerly across. Lin-Po noticed that now she was wearing gauntlets like those used by a cavalry officer. As she took the crown, he expected some trap to be sprung, but nothing happened except a patter of dust and dirt from the roof. Looking up, he noticed how one of the gold plates was slightly buckled, letting the packed earth trickle through. Wei-Ning, however, was busy in the far corner: she removed a gold plate, opened her wallet and placed some cheese-curd down on the floor.

'What!' Lin-Po exclaimed.

'Hush!'

Wei-Ning put the wooden box on the floor, releasing a small flap: Lin-Po recalled the rat-catchers of Cambaluc. He went to question her but she raised a hand then began to gibber in that foreign tongue, an odd clicking sound. Lin-Po heard a squeaking then two, three, four rats appeared: he watched fascinated as Wei-Ning grasped a rat and slid it into one of the compartments in the box; she seized a second, inspected it but let it go and replaced it with a third.

'Why are you doing that?' Lin-Po demanded.

'These are the Guardians of Zheng.' She smiled.

Lin-Po felt more dirt trickle onto his head.

'What's happening?' he whispered. 'Why are there no traps?'

'It's all one big trap,' Wei-Ning whispered back. 'The gallery, the chambers, this place. The opening of the doors has released some mechanism. In a short while the ceiling will cave in and we'll all be buried alive. Come on, we must get out!'

As they left the chamber, Wei-Ning shouted to the bandits and pointed to the place from where she had come.

'Gold!' she screamed. 'More than you've ever seen!'

Hearing this, the Marshal shoved them roughly aside and ran down towards the royal burial chamber, followed by his men. Wei-Ning, pushing Lin-Po before her, went back the way they had come, sliding the door shut behind her. They hurried now, threading their way through the galleries, Wei-Ning accurately remembering the different traps and hidden dangers. They paused at the sound of a low distant rumble, like a thunderstorm brewing on a summer's day.

'They have found their gold,' Wei-Ning said, 'and I have kept my promise. They'll have wealth for as long as they live!'

When they reached the temple, Wei-Ning pushed the Crown and box into Lin-Po's hands, then seized her bow and quiver of arrows and edged towards the temple door, where daylight now streamed through. Lin-Po was going to stay behind when suddenly the temple shook as the earth trembled beneath him.

'Get out!' Wei-Ning hissed.

As they hastened down the steps, the tremor was beginning to make itself felt, frightening the horses. The two bandits left on guard were doing their best to quieten the restless animals. One glimpsed Wei-Ning and came hurrying towards her. She crouched, ignoring the turmoil around her, and drew back the bow. The feathered shaft caught the man full in the face; the other, now terrified out of his wits, tried to mount a horse and escape, but Wei-Ning despatched him with an arrow in the back.

She then seized Lin-Po by the arm, pushing him along the path down the hill. In the fringe of trees they paused. The tremors were still continuing, whole sections of the hill sliding as the earth cracked. The temple shook as if made of paper and paste before toppling sideways, pushed by an invisible hand, disappearing in a resounding crack and a boiling white cloud of dust. Clutching the sack and box, Wei-Ning urged Lin-Po on down the hillside towards the dirt track which would lead them to the main highway. At last Lin-Po could go no further but crouched by a tree, holding his side. He looked up at Wei-Ning, her face stained with sweat and dirt.

'Magic?' he whispered.

'If only it was,' she gasped. 'The hill and the land around has been tunnelled out centuries ago, the earth held up by timbers and columns. The collapse of the burial chamber was like a wave rippling: it brought the rest down as well.'

She gently wiped the smudges from his face.

'We have the Crown and its Guardians,' she said triumphantly. 'The innkeeper, the Marshal of the Hills and all his men have paid for it with their lives. I can feel no pity for them. Now we are for Cambaluc!'

She cupped one of his hands in hers. 'The danger is past,' she told him. 'No more threats.'

'We've faced enough,' Lin-Po shuddered. 'Why doesn't the Demon Lord help us more? We could have been killed in there.'

'We must have faith. We must do our part, Lin-Po. At this moment, the Plague Lord needs *our* help. We are not shadow-actors. We have to prove ourselves and we have done so.'

Lin-Po picked up the small wooden box containing the rats and stared through the eye-slits.

'I've never seen the like of these,' he said wonderingly. 'Rats are usually brown. Is this a new species?'

'No, no.' Wei-Ning took the box away from him. 'They can be found in provinces to the north.' She pointed back up the hill. 'The temple and the caverns beneath are a warren of tunnels: the rats managed to survive. Last night, when you were asleep, I spoke to the innkeeper. Some of these rats have been found near the town. But,' she added in a half-whisper, 'there is still no trace of the disease.'

'What?' Lin-Po exclaimed.

Wei-Ning stroked his cheek. 'The time for questions is over. Vengeance is within our grasp. The Plague Lord's coming is at hand!'

PART FOUR

The Hour of the Horse

Chapter 15

'Around the silken bed
Bright moonlight shines,
Dully though,
More like frost on the ground.
Lifting my eyes,
I study the bright moon.
Then, closing my eyes,
I dream that I am home.'

Su-Ling finished her poem, opened her eyes and smiled at Brother Raphael.

'It is the custom,' she explained, 'to recite poetry in a garden as lovely as this.'

She gestured at the miniature waterfall, gurgling over the specially carved rocks, spilling into a small pool where carp caught the sunlight and shimmered like moving bars of gold. Raphael leant back against the tree and stared up at the silver cages containing the songbirds whose liquid, fluting cadences provoked bittersweet memories of green fields, high in the Alban Hills around Rome.

'It's well named the Garden of Pure Delight,' he said.

Su-Ling studied his face, now shaven and oiled. However much the friar protested, the Venetian's servants were insistent on providing his every luxury, be it a warm scented bath, or a bright, sharp razor and perfumed oils. At first Raphael had objected, but soon realised he would cause so much hurt that grateful acceptance was more virtuous than righteous self-denial.

Two weeks had passed since the attack on the Venetian. Marco had kept them all safely behind the high walls of the House of Serenity whilst despatching furious messages to the court. Sanghra had launched a thorough search of the entire city but there was no sign of the Tartar executioner, whilst the mysterious deaths amongst the Guild of Pourers had ceased altogether. Sanghra had also visited them on a number of occasions to assure Marco that all was being done.

'We can find nothing,' the minister had concluded two nights earlier at a special banquet arranged by Marco. 'The murders have ended; the Tartar executioner has disappeared – the city has returned to normal. I have, however, issued an edict: every official must report any suspicious circumstance to me.'

'Normal?' Su-Ling queried.

'True, true.' The minister was savouring the special shellfish which Marco had imported packed in ice from the coast. 'The deaths amongst the pourers caused grave disruption. Several parts of the city are polluted but now perhaps, the crisis is past.'

Marco had refused to accept this and so had Su-Ling.

'Sadly, I believe this to be the quiet time before the storm,' she commented. 'Is there any news of Wei-Ning and Lin-Po?'

Sanghra shook his head. 'Vague reports and rumours, but nothing substantial.'

'They will be well-protected,' Su-Ling had declared. 'As we say at home, and I am sure you will have a similar proverb: "the demons look after their own".'

Raphael could see Su-Ling was anxious though she hid it well. She was so secretive he could not decide what their relationship was supposed to be: brother and sister, or lovers? The young friar was confused. He wanted to hold and kiss her but felt guilty at this violation of his vows, even though it was only in his mind's eye. His overriding desire was simply to be with her: then he felt calm, complete, harmonious. Raphael was more aware of her than he was of the thousands of miles' absence from Rome and the familiar rhythm of his life as a friar.

'Are you homesick?' asked Su-Ling, sitting on the edge of the fountain. She flailed her fingers in the water and flicked drops at him.

'Yes and no,' he replied, dodging the drops. 'I feel like a hypocrite.' He glimpsed the puzzlement in her eyes. 'I am a priest, a friar,' he continued in a rush. 'Yet here I am, sitting with a beautiful woman in a garden of delight.'

'And what is wrong with that?' she asked smilingly. 'The sun and the water are God-made. He provided this beautiful day for us to enjoy.'

'You know full well what I mean,' Raphael answered more confidently. 'I took a vow, a solemn oath to be celibate, chaste in thought, word and deed.'

'And aren't you?' Su-Ling teased. 'Have you been chasing the serving-girls? Or have you asked our host to import some courtesans from the city?'

'I love you, Su-Ling, and you love me.'

Raphael was deliberately blunt. Over the last few days he had examined his conscience about this lovely-faced Buddhist nun. He felt guilty enough without hiding their relationship beneath childish flirtation or the courtly romance so beloved by the rich young men of Rome. Su-Ling was not surprised by his declaration. She smiled and replied in an enigmatic burst of poetry.

> '*My flower shall not cease to live.*
> *My song shall never end.*
> *I, the singer, intone the words.*
> *They become scattered,*
> *They are strewn about.*
> *The words come back,*
> *And I, the singer,*
> *Sing them again.*'

'So, you love me, too?' Raphael asked huskily.

Su-Ling took some of the water and patted her brow.

'Yes, I love you.' She leant across and stroked him gently on the cheek. 'That is our destiny. We were born to love each other.'

'But love,' Raphael answered, quoting from a poem of his own country, 'must be consummated.'

'And what is consummation?' she teased him. 'Tell me, Friar, is it two bodies becoming one? But that happens when a whore goes with her clients. No, of course, it doesn't.' She answered for him. 'Is not consummation more than two minds, two souls becoming one?' The teasing tone in her voice disappeared. 'Our love will be consummated, Raphael: that is why we are here. I have nightmares that it will be consummated in our struggle against this great evil.'

Raphael sat up, plucking at the grass. Su-Ling had referred to this before, as if some dark menace lurked beyond the walls of the House of Serenity. He found it difficult to accept, half-persuaded by Sanghra that the crisis had passed.

'Where did you learn so much about love?' He tried to lighten the tone. 'And everything else you know? You say you were a foundling and lived your life in the Temple of the White Dove.'

'You don't have to travel the world to know the heart of man.' Su-Ling kept her head down. 'True, sometimes I feel a deep sadness, at times even anger. How can those who gave life to me have forsaken me so quickly? But anger and hate, you must let them go.' She trailed her hand through the pool. 'Just like water, let it run off, let the sun dry it, what does it matter? My temple has many books and manuscripts. I prayed and I studied: the holy ones, the old priests, also allowed me to sit with them when people came to confess or ask for their advice. Husbands in conflict with their wives. Men and women possessed by demons or pursued by them. If the human heart had a problem, sooner or later, it was brought to the Temple of the White Dove.'

'And?' Raphael asked.

'I learnt a lot. I realised how different people are, yet how much the same. Each of us has a great desire to love and be loved. People search for the good, they want to live in peace with themselves, their families, their neighbours. Yet life is like this house, beautiful, calm, serene but there's evil within and without ever ready to break in.' She sipped from a bowl. 'Is that not true of you, too, Raphael? Are you so different from me, or those you have met? Kublai Khan rules this empire and makes his presence felt. Do not your princes do the same? And isn't the Khan's First Servant Sanghra a reflection of those great men who wield power in your own country?'

'But what we face now,' Raphael said sombrely, '*that* is different.'

'Oh yes, it is different,' Su-Ling agreed. 'And only God knows why it is happening in this place at this time.'

'Do you really believe we lived before?' Raphael interrogated her. 'My Church condemns that!'

'Your Church may condemn the rising of the sun but it will still rise. We are locked together, Raphael, and will be for all eternity. Each soul is given a task. You and I, we share that task. We may go into the darkness because of it. If we keep faith, one day we could break free of the Wheel and know true freedom, true life. True love.'

'I find it so difficult,' Raphael confessed, 'all these strange, unfamiliar images and sensations. I used to wonder if I became a friar simply to escape a house full of women.' He smiled. 'My mother and sisters. Or was it because I was frightened by life, repelled by its cruelty? Do I truly love God and my fellow man?'

'And now?' Su-Ling asked.

'Now I am changing,' Raphael told her. 'Being here in this garden, sitting next to you, is like entering a room which I've been striving to enter for years. It's dark, it's ill-lit but this room contains the truth, the reason for my existence.' He glanced across the gardens at the high tower overlooking the orchards. 'And our host?' he asked. He pointed to the crenellated top of the tower. 'He's in there now with his strange-looking clerk Purple-Skin. You know he's watching us?'

'I have since we sat here,' Su-Ling replied. 'He's a strange one, Raphael, even for a Venetian, but he's a good man. His heart is in the right place. He loves the things of this world and relishes the adulation and power the Great Khan has given him. Yet he's sharp-witted, he has a lively soul and a keen mind. He senses the danger which threatens: he is the best ally we could have in facing what is to come.'

*   *   *

If Marco Polo had heard Su-Ling's praise he would have blushed. He was, indeed, leaning against the wall around the top of the tower, staring across the garden at the Franciscan priest and Buddhist nun, at the same time dictating letters to Purple-Skin who sat at a table beneath his parasol patiently copying down what his master said. Nevertheless, Marco's mind was not on the task in hand. True, the Great Khan required reports, even if there was nothing to tell, but Marco would have much preferred to be with his guests. He felt intrusive in their company yet it was fascinating just to sit and watch them. Marco gingerly fingered the now fading bruise on his forehead. In truth he felt comfortable and safe when he was close to them.

'You are still worried, Master, aren't you?' Purple-Skin asked.

'Yes, I am still worried,' Marco said. 'I still feel uneasy.'

'But no danger threatens, surely?'

Marco shook his head and walked across to the other side of the tower, where he stared down at the travelling fair which, at this time of year, always arrived in the fields outside the House of Serenity. He half-listened to the sounds drifting up. The reality was that he did not believe what Sanghra had lightly declared about the danger being past. True, the deaths amongst the pourers may have ceased – yet there was no sign of the Tartar executioner. More importantly, the Great Khan's secretariat had written to say that Lin-Po and Wei-Ning had apparently vanished from the face of the earth, although vague reports had come in from the city of Xian and officials in the Province of Saaxi, of a man and woman visiting an isolated Buddhist temple which had later been destroyed by a minor earthquake.

Deep in thought, Marco ran his finger round his lips. The Great Khan had his messengers, patrols, officials and legions of spies only too eager to earn the substantial reward posted, yet the missing pair had still not been tracked down. Su-Ling claimed that Lin-Po and Wei-Ning would be protected by the same great demon which had attacked them. Marco did not accept this: he might live in Cathay but he was a Venetian born and bred. If the good Lord needed human hands and will to do His bidding, the same was true of Satan and all *his* hosts. Suddenly, he beat his fists against the wall of the tower in a burst of frustration. How could Lin-Po and Wei-Ning just disappear off the face of the earth?

'Shall I finish this report?' Purple-Skin asked tentatively.

'Oh, what does it matter!' Marco answered as if talking to himself.

'Of course it matters,' Purple-Skin said. 'Master, when this crisis passes, cases will still be waiting in the courts. It has passed, hasn't it?'

Marco stared across the fields: the sowing was now completed, the farmers anxiously waiting to see what summer would bring. The waterlogged fields stretched as far as the eye could see, broken only by the occasional copse of trees or rise in the ground where the peasants had their village. He couldn't tell Purple-Skin what he truly felt: like a traveller on a dusty summer road, the sky above him was blue and the sun was hot – but a storm was undoubtedly brewing.

During the day, all was well: Marco immersed himself in various tasks, but at night, when the moon bathed the courtyard in a silver light, he would leave Mai-da sleeping softly beside him and pace the corridors of the House of Serenity. Sometimes he would go out into the courtyards, on occasions climb up here and sit under the stars listening intently to the sounds around him. It was always the same. A sense of unease clung to him, of being spied on, of unpleasantness hiding deep in the shadows. In the moonlight he would watch the white winding trackway leading to the city. On a few occasions he'd glimpsed shadows racing along it. One night he had fallen asleep and dreamt that a nightmare army was making its way towards them.

Sometimes, Marco refused to leave his bed but lay staring up into the darkness for hours on end. He would try to talk to Mai-da, but she'd pretend to be asleep; yet she, too, was becoming nervous. Marco wanted to interrogate her about the Water Lily Society but the promises they had exchanged when their relationship had begun, prevented this. Was she involved in this affair? Marco wondered. How about Purple-Skin? They were both acting strangely. Was it some secret they shared – or were they just victims of *his* own anxiety? He no longer made love to Mai-da. Indeed, he had asked Brother Raphael to shrive him and, in the last two weeks, had attended Mass more often than not.

Purple-Skin coughed. Brought back to the present, Marco stared down at the travelling fair.

'You may go if you wish,' he murmured.

'Master, will I see the manuscripts?'

Marco looked over his shoulder.

'You know the ones,' Purple-Skin reminded him. 'They arrived yesterday.'

The Venetian shook his head. 'Su-Ling is insistent they are only for her eyes and Brother Raphael's.'

'What are they, Master?'

'They come from the Imperial Archives and the libraries of the Buddhist priests, and contain accounts of terrible plagues which have ravaged the Middle Kingdom and elsewhere.' Marco shrugged one shoulder. 'Su-Ling believes they may hold an answer to this danger.'

The scribe sniffed and glanced at Marco from under heavy-lidded eyes; his long face was creased by an angry sulk.

'She has set herself above the Master,' Purple-Skin muttered.

Marco glanced away. The growing tension between Su-Ling and Raphael on the one side and Purple-Skin and Mai-da on the other could not be resolved. His concubine was becoming more distant and hostile by the day and, where possible, she kept well away from Su-Ling and Raphael. Marco tried to soothe matters over. Su-Ling remained as serene as ever; Mai-da, however, grew more vociferous.

'You lust after her, don't you?' she accused him. 'You and that foreign devil, looking at her, all ox-eyed!'

To distract himself, Marco stared down at the different stalls which had been set up on the great pebbled path in front of the main gate. There was a whole row of them, selling items such as artificial flowers, false hair in long tresses, and boxes of red ceremonial candles; pedlars held trays full of sharp knives for shaving, and bamboo back-scratchers shaped like tiny hands. Booths covered by tattered awnings offered steaming bowls of food. Lanterns had been lit, pennants displayed, an array of tawdry colour to draw in the peasants and travellers. Usually Marco enjoyed visiting the fair, but on this occasion, he had ordered the gates and doors to be locked. No strangers were to be allowed in. He glanced back across the garden. Mai-da, in a leaf-green silken robe, was either going or coming back from some flowery arbour hidden behind the trees. He sighed and stared back at the makeshift market.

Suddenly, a flash of white caught his eye, and Marco repressed a shiver of fear. He looked again: the man in white moved behind a stall. Marco was sure it was the Tartar executioner, staring towards the main gate. Just then, Tanglefoot the beggar came hobbling away from the market along one of the side walls of the House of Serenity. Curious, Marco watched. Tanglefoot was a common visitor to the house: with his misshapen face and uneven gait, Marco always felt sorry for him. Now there was something different about him – as if Tanglefoot was acting, rather than being genuinely lame. A cold sweat broke out on Marco's back.

'Purple-Skin!' he shouted. 'Bring me my bow and arrow, a sword!'

The scribe was at the doorway on the steps leading down. 'Master?'

'Just do it!' Marco bellowed.

He edged along the parapet of the tower. From here he could see Tanglefoot, who was no longer hobbling; hidden in the shadows, he was moving as swiftly as a hunting cat towards a side entrance, a small garden door near where Su-Ling and Raphael were sitting. Marco couldn't believe his eyes. The nearer Tanglefoot got to the gate, the more purposeful his walk became, almost a run. Marco could wait no longer. He rushed through the doorway and down the steps. There was no sign of Purple-Skin or the arms he'd demanded. Seizing a halberd that was fixed on the wall as decoration rather than for defence, he ran along the galleries and passageways and through the courtyards, knocking servants aside, shouting and screaming for his retainers to arm themselves and follow him.

When Marco burst through a doorway into the garden, Su-Ling and Raphael, heads together, were sitting on the edge of the ornamental waterfall, conversing quietly.

'Take care!' he shouted, and raced towards them.

Su-Ling, sensing something was wrong, got to her feet. The shadow was already threading its way through the orchard towards her.

'Over there!' Marco pointed.

Raphael was still bemused, had not moved. Su-Ling turned round, just as Tanglefoot burst from the trees, grasping a broad-bladed scimitar.

No longer the beggar but now a master swordsman, Tanglefoot's cowl was pushed back, his skeletal face transformed by a grin. Adopting a fighting stance, knees slightly bent, he edged his way towards the Buddhist nun and Brother Raphael. The Franciscan grasped an ash pole, pulling it from one of the trellises, waving it threateningly, trying to come between Tanglefoot and Su-Ling. The beggar was just as fast. He moved sideways. Raphael lashed out with the pole. Tanglefoot's sword shimmered, slicing it in two. Marco was closer. He shifted the halberd in his hand, getting ready to throw it. He could hear a screaming and realised it was him. Tanglefoot moved closer, taking a swiping cut at Su-Ling. She darted back. The beggar regained his stance, measuring the distance, watching Su-Ling carefully.

'Tanglefoot!' Marco was within throwing distance.

The beggarman turned, his usually gentle face contorted into a mask of ghastly hatred: upper lip curled back, narrow eyes gleaming with battle fury.

Marco stopped to regain his breath, shifting the spear carefully. 'Old friend, what is all this?'

'The foreign devil,' Tanglefoot whispered. He moved his sword threateningly. 'But Tanglefoot will take care of him. Chop, chop, like a woodcutter slicing sticks.' The voice was low and grating. 'Then I'll start on these two lovelies here.' The beggar's bushy eyebrows rose in mock surprise. 'Did you think I had forgotten you, Venetian? I've been busy.' He lowered the sword. 'Have you been busy, too?'

Suddenly he was moving forward, his weapon snaking out. Marco held his ground and used the spear to block the parry. Tanglefoot stepped back. Drawing up the scimitar in both hands, he acted the master swordsman, watching Marco intently. The Venetian recalled all the tricks and moves the Great Khan's sword officers had taught him. Tanglefoot was measuring the distance. He would try two cuts. The first would be mock, to throw him off-balance: the second would be the killing blow aimed direct at Marco's neck. Tanglefoot would expect him to step back. The beggarman blinked: the first cut was coming. Marco didn't wait but charged forward, jabbing the halberd at Tanglefoot's face. Scimitar and spear met in a screeching clash. Marco then turned the pole, using the butt end, still driving at Tanglefoot's face. Confused, his adversary stepped back and brought the scimitar up again. Marco, twirling and twisting the halberd, brought the sharp end down and, without any hesitation, drove it deep into Tanglefoot's chest. The beggarman writhed like a speared fish. The scimitar dropped from his flailing hands. He clutched at the blood-spurting wound. Marco ruthlessly drove him back under the outstretched branches of a tree. He pushed him against the trunk, gripping the spear hard, watching Tanglefoot in his death throes, coughing and spluttering on the blood pouring through his chapped lips and disfigured nose.

Marco waited until the old man's body stopped jerking then, using his foot, he freed the halberd and stepped back, watching the corpse crumple to the ground. Su-Ling and Raphael stood, hands joined. The Franciscan's olive-skinned face had turned pallid. Su-Ling remained serene. Only the rapid blinking of her eyes betrayed any agitation. She walked forward and placed her hand on Marco's shoulder.

'I thank you,' she whispered.

Marco looked into those lovely eyes. 'He would have killed you,' he panted, still breathless.

'I know,' she said. 'The Executioner is very close.'

Marco, breathing deeply, turned towards the garden gate. Su-Ling clutched him by the sleeve of his gown.

'The Demon will have returned.' She pointed to the corpse. 'Poor Tanglefoot was only a weapon.'

Marco strode off into the trees. He wanted to compose himself, wipe the sweat from his face, control the shaking in his limbs. He found the garden gate off the latch. He closed it, pushed the bolt home and went back. Purple-Skin, Mai-da and others had arrived by now, the scribe forlornly holding a bow and quiver of arrows. Raphael was graphically describing what had happened. The servants clapped their hands in appreciation of their master's bravery. Marco stepped onto the edge of the fountain and spread his hands as a sign for silence.

'The garden gate should have been locked,' he declared strongly. 'Someone opened it.'

'Master,' Purple-Skin interrupted, 'servants have been leaving for the market. 'It was probably an oversight.'

Marco drew in a deep breath.

'Very well, but I want every gate and doorway locked, bolted and closely guarded. No one is to enter without my express permission!' He climbed down. 'The lives of our guests are precious. My orders are to be followed on pain of death! Sister,' he glanced at Su-Ling, 'Brother Raphael, I must ask you to stay within doors.'

Then Marco walked away down the path, eager for a bowl of wine. He turned at the patter of slippered sandals behind him. Mai-da, her lovely face painted white, her black glossy hair piled up and held in place by jewelled combs, came hurrying up. She paused, slipped her hands up the voluminous sleeves of her gown and bowed.

'What is the matter?' Marco asked.

'There is nothing, Master.' The title was added more as an insult than a term of respect. 'I am leaving.' She smiled at Marco's surprise. 'Are you astonished?' she enquired. 'Did we not agree from the beginning that I was free to go when I wish, where I wish?'

'But why now?' Marco stepped forward.

She held up her hand. 'The flower blooms and fades. So it is with us two, Venetian. You only have eyes for the Buddhist nun. I do not wish to stay here where crazed beggars can enter to cut and slice. I have my own treasure, my own possessions. With your permission, I will arrange for servants to take me into Cambaluc.'

'Where will you go?'

'See?' Mai-da stepped closer and grasped Marco's hand. 'The flower has faded. You do not even ask me to stay. I shall be gone before dusk.'

And, stepping round him, Mai-da made her own way into the house.

Marco sat down on one of the garden walls and put his face in his hands. He could not stop Mai-da leaving. In fact, she was right – he did not want her to stay. His life had changed since the arrival of Su-Ling. Mai-da was only a shadow from the past.

'Are you well, *signor*?'

Marco took his hands from his face and looked up. Brother Raphael and Su-Ling were standing before him.

'I told you to go into the house.'

'Then you must come with us.' Su-Ling smiled and stretched out her hand.

Marco grasped it, marvelling at its cool softness. He led them into the Room of Perfect Stillness, his personal writing office deep in the house. Already Marco was noticing a change in atmosphere. He espied one servant, a bundle over his shoulders, threading his way down towards the main door. Mai-da was not the only one leaving.

'Let them go.' Su-Ling followed his gaze. 'You cannot force them to remain.'

Marco agreed. He had never faced danger himself, having always been protected by the Khan, but his servants knew something hideous was about to happen, against which there was no real defence. Su-Ling grasped him by the shoulder, forcing him to turn. She cupped his face in her hands.

'What you did out there,' she murmured, 'was very brave. You truly have the courage of a tiger. Now you must have the cunning of the fox. We must plot and we must plan.' She let her hands fall away. 'I suspect Lin-Po and his companion Wei-Ning have reached Cambaluc. Tanglefoot was used to clear any opposition, to give them time. Let me use this chamber to study the manuscripts. You and Raphael can help me. Through prayer, study and courage we can confront and defeat these Demons!'

Chapter 16

In the days that followed, the House of Serenity became an abode of ghosts, as one servant after another packed their belongings and quietly slipped away. Su-Ling and Raphael immersed themselves in the manuscripts brought from the principal archives and Buddhist temples in Cambaluc. Marco tried to help but, like Raphael, he'd found some of the script unintelligible, difficult to translate. What they could do in a day, Su-Ling could read, study and absorb within an hour. Raphael acted as her clerk. Marco offered the services of Purple-Skin who, since Mai-da's departure, had become even more sullen and withdrawn. Su-Ling shook her head, her sea-grey eyes full of sadness.

'I don't think so,' she declined. 'I need to discuss that with you some time.'

Marco found her response enigmatic but Su-Ling returned to her studies, and Marco went back to whatever duties still required his attention.

When the Great Khan heard of the attack on the House of Serenity, squads of soldiers were sent down to camp around the building. Cavalry patrolled the roads and bowmen set up camp in the nearby villages. Kublai also sent personal messages of reassurance whilst his First Minister Sanghra became a constant visitor to the house. Nevertheless, not even these precautions could protect them fully. During the day all was well but, at night, strange lights appeared on the walls. Footsteps echoed in the corridors, eerie cries shrieked from the gardens. Marco woke one night, sweat-soaked, and saw a shape like a grey column of smoke moving through his bedchamber towards the windows. He experienced an intense feeling of panic. When he shouted for help, Purple-Skin came running, only to find nothing, no sign of any disturbance, except that the bedchamber had grown cold and its perfume-sweetened air was gone as if someone had opened every window.

Marco wished his uncle would return. He had even begun to regret Mai-da's leaving so abruptly. One night in the courtyard he looked up to see that horrid ghost from his past. The woman Sforza came rushing towards him, her face bluish-white, eyes red-rimmed, lips purple. He had been tending a lantern and the sight so shocked him he covered his face like a child. Yet, when he took his hands away, there was nothing, leaving him wondering whether it was a phantasm of the night or the result of a tired mind and taut nerves.

The soldiers, camped beyond the walls, experienced similar phenomena. They talked of shifting shapes, of cold mists which would sweep in during the dark hours. Sentries were disturbed by creatures prowling on the edge of the camp and blood-chilling calls which they swore came from no known animal or bird. The officers found discipline so difficult to enforce, Marco was forced to seek Su-Ling's advice.

'It is nothing but nasty tricks and evil games,' she assured him. 'Lin-Po and Wei-Ning are now back in Cambaluc, and what we are experiencing are petty annoyances. Brother Raphael will say prayers and carry out an exorcism. Yet,' she sighed, 'you still look worried.' She grasped Marco's hand. 'I will send a letter to my monastery. We have our own guards: soldiers who serve the Buddha and protect our precincts, spearmen and archers. I will ask Mother Abbess to send them.'

She was true to her word and, four days later, a squad of Buddhist soldiers, about sixty in number, led by a mounted officer, entered the Gate to the World.

Marco had heard of such men, but this was the first time he had ever met them. Most of them were former soldiers who had forsaken a military career to take up the Buddhist life. They were dressed simply in saffron robes, and wore leather, metal-studded helmets with little armour except wrist- and shoulder-guards, although they were armed expertly enough with sword, dagger, spear and bow. The difference between them and the imperial soldiers was more in attitude. They moved and drilled precisely, quietly, and there was little chatter or talk: none of the usual coarse language or false bonhomie. A self-possessed unit, they would take orders from no imperial officer or Marco, only from Su-Ling, who arranged their deployment around the gardens near every door and gateway.

Marco found them rather chilling. These men, their heads and faces completely shaved, were devoid of any of the insignia or ornament much loved by Cathay and Mongol soldier alike. They ate and drank what was offered, practised a rigid self-discipline and reminded Marco of the crusading knights of the West, the Hospitallers and Templars, albeit bereft of the ostentation and arrogance so characteristic of such Orders. To all intents and purposes the House of Serenity became their temple. They followed their prayer rituals, morning, noon and night. The House of Serenity was soon filled with the sweet smell of incense sticks which they constantly burnt before their portable shrines.

Within a very short time, the eerie phenomena and phantasms of the night no longer troubled the house. Marco calculated that only Purple-Skin and five or six of his retainers now stayed. Sanghra offered others but Su-Ling intervened.

'News of this will be all over the city,' she said. 'They'll only panic and flee. Moreover,' she tapped the manuscripts, 'we do not know who might come in here under the pretence of being a servant or a cook. It's very important that no one, not even the soldiers, be allowed to stay within the precincts of the house.'

'Does that include me?' Sanghra asked.

Su-Ling gave the most graceful bow. 'I am your Excellency's most humble servant. I can only advise.'

Sanghra took no offence. Marco could see he was fascinated by the development and impatient to discover what measures Su-Ling would recommend to counter the dangers. He was often reluctant to leave and dispensed with all the court ceremony so beloved of the Great Khan's ministers.

Eventually Sanghra was rewarded. Su-Ling announced that the following morning, at the Hour of the Pig, she wished to meet both him and Marco in the Room of Perfect Stillness.

'No one else is to be present,' she warned.

Sanghra was so delighted, he delayed his return to Cambaluc and said he would stay overnight in the House of Serenity.

It was still dark, Marco had to light the lanterns, when he and the Great Khan's First Minister sat on cushions before the low black lacquered table. Su-Ling and Raphael sat opposite, the manuscripts they'd studied piled high on a table behind them.

'You have no report?' Sanghra began.

'What I have to say,' Su-Ling told them all, 'cannot be committed to paper. Nor can I prove anything I suggest.'

'Which is?' Sanghra said impatiently.

'In Cambaluc . . .' Su-Ling paused. 'No, let me begin again. The Great Khan should know that a grave danger now faces him in Cambaluc. One which could topple his empire, bring chaos, blood, war, fire and the sword.'

'From whom?' Sanghra intervened. 'The Great Khan's writ runs over the face of the earth. No man dare oppose him.'

'The danger is threefold,' Su-Ling replied. 'The first is the Water Lily Society, of which Lin-Po and Wei-Ning are leading members. They have a strong loyalty to the Sung Dynasty which the Great Khan has overthrown. Secondly, the Water Lily Society not only dabbles in sorcery but masters it. Its members have used their powers and the blood sacrifice to summon up a great Demon of Hell, the Plague Lord – whom Brother Raphael calls the fallen angel Azrael. This Demon can live amongst men. To quote Christian scripture: *"He goes about like a roaring lion seeking who he may devour"*. Azrael wishes to spread a great plague which will wipe man from the face of the earth. He is prepared to use others in this attempt: Lin-Po and Wei-Ning have entered into a compact with him and all the Lords of Hell. Finally, there are the deaths amongst the pourers, the scavengers in the city. Chaos has been caused, sewers and cesspools remain uncleaned. Every day the sun grows stronger. Summer will soon be here, bringing hot winds and cloying heat. Contagion will spread like dirt through clear water.'

'And this contagion will disrupt life?' Sanghra asked. 'Cause resentment?'

'Your Excellency is correct,' Su-Ling replied. 'In any country, particularly in the Middle Kingdom, devastation and plague are seen as Heaven's rebuke to whoever sits on the Dragon Throne.'

'But the Great Khan is all-mighty,' Marco intervened. 'Such unrest can be easily crushed.'

'Ah yes.' Su-Ling glanced at Brother Raphael. 'Each of the dangers I have listed can be dismissed as nothing but straw in the wind. However, together, clasped and bound, they'll give birth to appalling evil.'

'And what is that?' Marco asked.

'A plague, the like of which has never been seen before. Since my youth,' Su-Ling continued, 'I have dreamt of cities, which I have never visited, suffering hellish devastation. From the chronicles, I discovered these were not figments of my imagination. In the West stands a great city called Byzantium. Brother Raphael calls it Constantinople.' She stumbled over the strange-sounding word.

'Yes.' Marco nodded. 'It is a great trading city.'

'Our writings mention how, seven hundred years ago, a terrible plague ravaged that city,' Su-Ling went on. 'No one was spared. The sickness struck like lightning in the sky. Men who were healthy in the morning had fallen dead by noon, of a raging fever and a terrible thirst, of buboes and boils appearing in the groin and armpits. So intense was the pain, some people even took their own lives. The dead carpeted the streets. There were so many, they took the roofs off houses, threw the corpses inside, drenched them with oil and set them alight. The same chronicler also mentions how, many years before that, in the centuries preceding the birth of Christ, a similar plague ravaged the great city of Athens.' She smiled. 'Brother Raphael helped me with this. He described a city which both of us have seen in our different dreams and visions of the night.'

Marco felt a chill of fear. He recalled the dirty, narrow lanes of the old city, the brimming sewers and cesspools. But how could that be so dangerous? Pestilence often occurred in the hot months but nothing like Su-Ling described.

'So, this plague is from Hell?' Sanghra demanded.

'I have told you,' the Buddhist nun replied. 'The Lords of Hell could only use what is available.'

'Then I'll order every street, every alleyway to be cleaned!' Sanghra retorted. 'Refuse will be taken out and burnt. Troops called in from the provinces to help. Prisoners released.'

'No, it's different from that, isn't it?' Marco demanded. 'Lin-Po and Wei-Ning have brought something into Cambaluc. Something which will turn the pestilential fires into a raging inferno.'

'Yes.' Brother Raphael now spoke up. 'An inferno which will sweep the face of the earth. This month Cambaluc, next year Genoa, Marseilles, Paris, London and north to the great German cities.'

'Then what is it?' Sanghra asked.

'A similar plague,' said Su-Ling, 'occurred in the Middle Kingdom some fourteen hundred years ago during the reign of Zheng, the tiger of the Qin Dynasty who took the title of *Shi Hu Ang Di*, the First August Emperor of the Middle Kingdom. A man who ruthlessly removed all opposition, Zheng ordered the Great Wall to be built in the north. He was deeply superstitious. For his own protection, each night he slept in a different place. Desirous of immortality, he regularly consulted soothsayers and sorcerers, sought life-giving elixirs and even sacrificed virgins to the devils. According to one historian, Sima Quian, he built a great tomb in Saanxi Province filled with every imaginable luxury and countless attendants. The tomb was also protected by traps.' She paused.

'Saanxi is where Lin-Po went,' Marco said.

'I think he discovered the tomb,' Su-Ling replied. 'According to one legend, the First Emperor made a pact with Hell. When his Jade Crown returned to Cambaluc, he would reign again and make a holocaust of victims to the demons who supported him.'

'Superstition!' Marco scoffed.

'You do not know what you say.' Su-Ling shook her head. 'And if Lin-Po brings the Jade Crown back?'

'If it is brought back here, we will seize it,' Sanghra said emphatically. 'The Great Khan will be delighted to wear the Jade Crown of Cathay's First Emperor.'

'I don't know.' Su-Ling shook her head. She glanced quickly at Marco. 'There are gaps in my conclusion.'

'They are bringing something else, aren't they?' Marco asked.

Now Raphael spoke up. 'The physicians of the West,' he said, 'know very little about pestilence and plagues. Here in the Middle Kingdom the medical practitioners have studied infection and contagion most closely. Did you know that most of the great plagues which have ravished humankind, all originated in the same part of Asia?'

Marco shook his head.

'The scholars of Cathay,' the young friar continued, 'believe infection is caused by dirt and polluted water. But what feeds on that?'

Marco shrugged. 'Flies? Rats? Mice?'

'The author of a treatise called *The Bee Sting* advances the theory that just as a bee can sting its victim and thrust venom into the blood, so can a flea, be it one from a rubbish heap or those which gather in clouds above some marsh or swamp,' Su-Ling informed them. 'The author then concludes that some of the terrible plagues which have ravished this kingdom, and others, are not really caused by polluted air or dirt but by fleas.'

'In which case,' Sanghra declared drily, 'we should all be dead. There's not a tavern or guesthouse in Cambaluc which doesn't have its fleas. Even the imperial palaces are plagued by them.'

'But what happens if only a certain type of flea carries a deadly contagion?' Su-Ling asked.

'If that is the case,' Marco intervened, 'once the hot weather passes, the bamboo snaps under the cold and the water freezes over, such fleas disappear. It is well-known, be it butterfly or bee, that they are creatures of the summer.'

'That's what puzzled the author of *The Bee Sting*.' Su-Ling paused. 'He concluded that some fleas are unlike those which hover over the marshes to sting and bite then die when the weather turns cold. He argued that they lived comfortably on a warm supply of blood in the fur of some animal – dog, cat . . .'

'Or *rat*?' Raphael added. 'In my Order we have physicians who have argued that filth, rats and contagion are three demons which walk hand in hand.'

'And have Lin-Po and Wei-Ning brought these into Cambaluc?' Marco asked.

'It's possible,' Su-Ling nodded. 'The author of *The Bee Sting* claims that a certain type of rat, black in colour, was responsible for the raging contagion in Byzantium and Athens. Zheng discovered this and, in his desire to form a compact with Hell, brought some of these rats into the Middle Kingdom.'

'He sacrificed his own people!' Marco exclaimed.

'Yes, he was evil enough to plan that.'

'But,' Sanghra leant forward, 'if this has happened before – true, hordes may have died, yet mankind continues to prosper.'

'Each time, the Lords of Light have fought and blocked such rampant evil,' Su-Ling pointed out. 'They have their servants too but, each time, the devastation is greater.'

Marco knew she was referring to herself and others.

The nun went on: 'Zheng was finally defeated. He died in agony but he vowed to return. According to one chronicle, he was not only buried with the Jade Crown but also with what he called "its Guardians", a colony of rats. They may have survived.' Su-Ling spread her hands. 'The author of *The Bee*

Sting alleges that only one creature, apart from man, seems to have a genius for survival: the rat. If Wei-Ning broke into Zheng's tomb, the Jade Crown is not the only thing she will bring back to Cambaluc.'

'To cause a war of contagion?' Sanghra queried.

'And why not?' Su-Ling pointed to the manuscripts behind her. 'When the Mongols invaded Cathay and the Great Khan's grandfather laid siege to its cities, they often catapulted cadavers of dead animals into these cities to spread contagion.'

'True,' Marco agreed. 'In campaigns, opposing forces always pollute wells and rivers.'

'Whatever Lin-Po and Wei-Ning intend,' Su-Ling said, 'they are in agreement with Azrael, a pact truly forged in Hell. We have a city where people live cheek by jowl, whose traders send wares and goods to all the ports of Cathay. Silks and other precious objects are exported to the West, even to the provinces of the frozen snows in the North. It's like a play. The stage has been set: everything is ready. Cambaluc is on the verge of summer with its sewers and cesspools not properly drained, its scavengers and pourers demoralised and confused. The city's funeral pyre is stacked high with wood and kindling. Lin-Po and Wei-Ning are a flame – and what a conflagration they will cause!'

'I find this difficult to accept,' Sanghra said slowly.

'You have little choice,' Su-Ling retorted. 'I suspect it's already begun.' She smiled and bowed her forehead, almost touching the black lacquered table. 'Your Excellency, if you will excuse this humble servant, she needs to talk on a private matter.' She gestured at Marco.

Sanghra clambered to his feet, his sly, narrow face betraying his anxiety and unease; all protocol and etiquette were forgotten in this crisis.

'I shall return to the Khan,' he said. 'Cambaluc must be

searched.' He bowed towards them and walked out into the corridor shouting for his escort.

'I'm glad he's gone.' Su-Ling listened to his fading footsteps. 'Signor Marco, we must have words with you.' She glanced at the half-open door.

Raphael got up and closed it.

'When you first journeyed to the imperial palace,' Su-Ling began, 'you reported how the table-server Kwei-Lin stalked your cortège?'

'Yes, that's true.'

'Who knew you were going to the imperial palace?'

'Well, my household did.'

'But how did Kwei-Lin know?' Su-Ling persisted. 'Chance and fortune are fickle things. Isn't it a coincidence how, on the very day this matter began, at the very hour you were taken to meet the Great Khan, Kwei-Lin strides into your life looking you up and down as one swordsman would another?'

'But surely someone didn't leave my house to search him out?' Marco paused. 'But we are not talking about Kwei-Lin, are we?' he continued: 'Rather the demon?'

Su-Ling gathered the cups and put them on a table before her.

'Azrael can move from body to body. We have seen that. But there's always one which he regards as his home that he leaves for other dwellings to carry out his will. Now, victims like Kwei-Lin or the executioner are more like sticks waiting to be picked up. They have no choice or will in the matter. Their evil lives and mean souls are like these cups, just receptacles waiting to be filled.' She pointed to the small porcelain jug containing rice wine. 'But the real dwelling-place is elsewhere.'

The blood drained from Marco's face as the truth began to dawn on him.

257

'And the phantasm in the courtyard?' Su-Ling asked. 'How many people know about the nightmare you experienced in Venice so many years ago? Or the afternoon Brother Raphael and I were attacked – how did Tanglefoot know we were alone and unprotected? Why did the Tartar executioner come on that day, at that very same hour? Who opened that garden gate? When we went down to the prison, Kwei-Lin accused you of lusting after me. Now, Azrael may be a demon but he is not a Lord of Light. He has no entry to your mind or mine. So how could he make such an accusation unless he had learnt it from elsewhere?'

Marco rubbed his arm. His throat was parched; he found it difficult to swallow.

'Mai-da!' he gasped.

'I could cite other proofs.' Su-Ling glanced sadly at him. 'Why did Mai-da choose that particular day to leave? Was it because her task was finished? Because she must return to meet others of her ilk, Lin-Po and Wei-Ning? And, more importantly . . .' At this point, she got up and walked quickly to the door, opened it to satisfy herself no one was eavesdropping and returned to sit beside Marco. She grasped his hand.

'I did not wish to say this whilst Sanghra was present. However, we have Wei-Ning leaving Cambaluc and travelling to Saanxi. She is not troubled or arrested. We know that she met Lin-Po. They have travelled to Saanxi, seized the Jade Crown and returned immediately to Cambaluc. Now, they may be protected by the forces of darkness – but how can these help on an open road? They got past endless imperial patrols and border guards, not to mention all those professional informers and spies only too eager to earn the reward offered for their capture. Think!' she urged. 'How did Wei-Ning get out of Cambaluc? The journey to Saanxi would be relatively easy but, remember, the Khan's servants were on the lookout for a man and woman travelling back to Cambaluc: the nearer they drew, the more dangerous it should have become but, apparently, not for them.'

'It's only a matter of time,' Raphael agreed, 'before Sanghra or one of the Imperial Council also wonder how these two criminals, for whom everybody is searching, can pass like a mist from one place to another without the slightest challenge.'

'They were helped,' Marco conceded dully. 'If someone issued a pass, sealed by one of the Great Khan's council, no one would dare challenge them. You know that. In the Middle Kingdom the Great Khan's writ, and that of his ministers, must be accepted at face value.'

'And who could issue such a writ?' Su-Ling asked quietly. 'Sanghra? Why should he do that? Or was it a member of the Imperial Chancery? They may write out the writ but they must get it sealed. However, there is one minister, the Khan's favourite . . .'

'Myself,' Marco interrupted, his face flushed with anger. '*I* carry the imperial seal. *I* possess the vermilion ink, sheaves of imperial paper. However, I never authorised that!'

'No. Purple-Skin did,' Su-Ling murmured.

Marco would have sprung to his feet but Su-Ling pressed her hand on his shoulder.

'You have been betrayed, my friend. In your heart you know what I say is true. Did you not once mention how Mai-da and Purple-Skin entered your service at the same time? They are both members of the Water Lily Society. Perhaps you suspected that?'

'I did of Mai-da but why? Why come to me?'

'Because the Great Khan trusts you,' Su-Ling replied gently. 'You have all the trappings of power and enjoy Kublai's confidence. He values your sharp wit.' She ignored Marco's scoff of self-mockery. 'And, like all his councillors, you hold the vermilion seal, the mark of the Dragon Throne. You listen to what Kublai says, the chatter of the court. Purple-Skin and Mai-da were suitably placed to learn everything you did. Purple-Skin is a professional scribe. He writes out warrants and writs all the time, doesn't he?'

'And in my arrogance,' Marco said bitterly, 'I seal whatever he puts before me. The warrant could have been drawn up weeks ago.'

'Even months,' Raphael intervened, 'when the names Lin-Po and Wei-Ning meant nothing to you.'

'Then why has Purple-Skin stayed on?' Marco sighed and lifted a hand. 'Of course, Mai-da needed a spy here, didn't she? Someone to watch me, to report comings and goings.'

'Perhaps there was another reason?' Su-Ling added kindly. 'I can tell from Purple-Skin's eyes that his soul is troubled. He may have begun this treachery with a clear mind but he has come to like, even admire you, Signor Marco.'

Marco felt torn between fear and anger. He closed his eyes and quietly thanked God that Sanghra was not present to hear the consequences of his own foolishness. He had prided himself that he was not a member of any court faction, aloof from the intrigues, yet he had been unwittingly drawn in.

'Why?' he said only.

'According to our reckoning,' Raphael told him, 'ten years ago, the last Sung Emperor, Bing Di, tried once more to drive the Mongols out of the Middle Kingdom.'

'I know, I know.' Marco stared at the far wall.

'There was a terrible sea battle,' Raphael said, 'which lasted three weeks. They say over eight hundred Sung warships were captured and over one hundred thousand men perished. The young Emperor Bing Di tried to escape. Others claim his leading minister took him into his arms and both committed suicide by jumping into the sea. Whatever, the corpse of the last Sung Emperor was found on a nearby beach and the Great Khan gave him honourable burial. Now, Bing Di had two sisters, daughters of the imperial concubine Yang. Yang was a formidable woman, a high-ranking member of the Water Lily Society. She died – but her two daughters disappeared.'

'And both eventually arrived in Cambaluc,' Marco declared despairingly. 'One became the concubine of the First Minister Ahmed and the other, calling herself Mai-da, became mine.'

'So it would seem,' Raphael said gravely.

'We can only speculate,' Su-Ling took up the story, 'on what really happened to Ahmed. Perhaps he made a mistake – or became terrified of what Wei-Ning planned? The conspiracy led by him collapsed. Wei-Ning didn't care. She had, through the Water Lily Society – particularly the good offices of the sorcerer, Lin-Po – entered into a pact with the Plague Lord Azrael. When Lin-Po was exiled, Wei-Ning fled. She was probably hidden and helped by her sister Mai-da and your scribe, Purple-Skin. She had a mission to carry out – to free Lin-Po, seize the Jade Crown and, through her pact with Azrael, knew what she had to bring back to Cambaluc to begin a contagion that would spread throughout the world. The Demon Azrael responded because he had found two souls consumed with hate and murder. They provided safe sanctuary as well as the opportunity to wreak terrible damage.' The Buddhist nun shook her head. 'I suspect Wei-Ning, rather than Mai-da, was the more possessed. After she left Cambaluc, Azrael took up residence in other souls to perpetrate those terrible murders, a virtual massacre amongst the Guild of Pourers. Now Wei-Ning, Lin-Po and Mai-da are together again.'

'Where?' Marco felt the fury boil within him. 'You seem to have all the answers. Tell me – *where are they?*'

'Of all the murders committed by Kwei-Lin,' the Buddhist nun said quietly, 'each one had a certain logic except those in the Temple of the Red Horse. *Think*, Signor Marco. Lin-Po and Wei-Ning would need a sanctuary, a deserted place, wouldn't they?'

Marco drew a deep breath. 'Of course! If there's one place shunned by the citizens of Cambaluc, it's a temple where murder has taken place. Local people would regard it as a House of Demons.'

'That is true,' Su-Ling replied. 'I've already sent urgent despatch to Mother Abbess, who wrote back immediately to say that the Temple of the Red Horse is regarded as accursed; never again will it be used as a Buddhist shrine. Perhaps in a year or two it will fall derelict, be razed to the ground. The land will be exorcised and left for others.'

'It should be surrounded!' Marco exclaimed. 'I'll summon imperial troops to—!'

Su-Ling grasped his hand. 'No, no, you must not do that. There could be spies at court, other members of the Water Lily Society. What needs to be done, must be done tonight.'

'Which is?' Marco asked.

'First, you must make sure Purple-Skin does not know.'

'I will deal with *him*,' Marco rasped.

'Then we will leave the House of Serenity,' Su-Ling went on, 'taking with us the Buddhist soldiers only and no others. When we arrive at the Temple of the Red Horse, whatever happens, please, do exactly as I ask!'

Marco instinctively felt like refusing.

'It's for the best,' Su-Ling said, reading his mind.

Marco caught the note of warning in her voice.

'If you send a courier to the imperial palace it may be too late. Wei-Ning and Mai-da will negotiate. The Great Khan would love to get his hands on the Jade Crown, use it as further proof that he enjoys Heaven's mandate. Signor Marco, *please*.'

Marco stared at this remarkable young nun and, once again, quietly cursed his own arrogance. He had behaved like a child.

'Don't blame yourself,' she smiled. 'The ways of this country are mysterious. Now let us go! There are preparations to be made!'

Marco strode off down the corridor, pausing only to seize a scimitar from the wall, throwing the sheath on the floor. Purple-Skin was in his chamber, the door half-open. He was seated hunched over a table, head in hand. He shaded his eyes as he stared up at the Venetian.

'Master, what is wrong?'

Marco moved the sword, grasping the hilt in one hand, the tip of the blade in the other.

'I know everything, Purple-Skin.' Marco found it difficult to speak. 'About Mai-da, about her leaving.'

Purple-Skin turned, took a small jar from the side table and filled his cup. He drank it quickly and refilled it.

'I thought you would find out eventually.' His long face creased into a smile. 'I am sorry. In a way, I truly am. You came to this court like a child running into a house full of demons and ghosts, rivalries and hatreds. The powerful Magistrate, friend of the Great Khan! Did you really think you could read our minds and hearts?'

'Aye, and like a child I trusted you,' Marco retorted.

'Did I not warn you?' Purple-Skin appealed to him. 'Did I not say, when I first entered your service, to trust no one? Everyone here wears a mask. Oh, you might be the learned judge, sifting the evidence, proclaiming your verdicts. Our minds, hearts and souls are, in fact, closed to people like you. To be one of us you must think like one of us, and you could never do that.'

'I thought you were my friend.' The Venetian found it hard to keep his voice steady; tears stung his eyes.

'You have no friends,' came the harsh reply. 'You are a foreign devil. No, no.' Purple-Skin shook his head. 'I am wrong. The very first night I met Su-Ling, I thought, She is his friend and she is very dangerous.' He hunched his shoulders. 'I could have left but I did not. Mai-da asked me to stay but, in the end . . .'

Purple-Skin pulled on his lower lip. 'Look at me now – I'm still lying. I like you, Venetian. I truly do. You never took a bribe, were never corrupt. For that I had respect. You also have a kind heart.'

'And now?' Marco asked, more curious than angry.

'I wondered how long it would take the Buddhist to discover the truth. In a day or two I would have left but I had to prepare.' He filled the cup again. 'I'm beyond all threats, Master.' He lifted the cup in a mocking toast. 'I have already drunk more of the poison than I need. Better this way, slipping into an eternal sleep than the execution yard. Promise me – for the little good I did, an honourable burial? A prayer, a libation to my ghost, so that the Goddess of Mercy will understand what I did?' He toasted Marco again and leant drowsily against the cushions. 'We shall meet again, *signor*, during the time of the Rats' Great Flitting . . .'

Purple-Skin let the cup fall even as his eyes closed and his body shuddered.

Chapter 17

Towards the end of the Hour of the Snake, as the sun set in bright bursts of red against a pink-blue sky, Marco led his companions and the troop of Buddhist soldiers out through the Gateway of the World. Matters had moved swiftly. Marco could do little but arrange Purple-Skin's body in the pose of death. Su-Ling and Brother Raphael offered quick prayers for his soul and then the orders were issued.

'No gong, no drums, no banners!' Su-Ling warned. 'We will take the country routes skirting the city.'

She had quiet words with the officer who despatched two scouts ahead of them. By the time they reached the edge of the park near the Temple of the Red Horse, the scouts were waiting under the shade of a willow tree which overlooked one of the small canals. Marco could tell from their faces that they were uneasy. He himself felt the oppressive atmosphere. Despite the lovely sunset, the cool evening air, the silence was ominous.

'The temple is definitely inhabited,' one of the scouts reported, 'though we don't know by whom. We smelt fire-smoke, cooking odours. We also discovered a corpse: a man dressed in the dirty white garb of an executioner.'

'That would be the Tartar,' Su-Ling declared grimly. 'They will have no use for him now. Where is he?'

The scout pointed across the parkland.

'There's an arrow deep in his back, and his throat has been cut for good measure.'

'You didn't approach the temple too closely?' Su-Ling asked.

The scouts shook their heads.

'Beloved Sister, it's truly a place of ghosts and demons.'

'But you searched as I asked?'

'Yes, beloved Sister. The temple windows are high in the wall, just widened slits. The front door is barred and bolted, but it's been opened. It's only been made to look as if no one has entered.'

'And?' Su-Ling prompted.

'It is as you've said, beloved Sister. All around the temple are small drains or sewer-holes.'

'What would those be for?' Marco enquired curiously.

Su-Ling shook her head. 'The temple is very old. Perhaps, once, there was running water inside, a spring or fountain? Or the holes were used to drain the oils and juices from sacrifices?'

The other scout nodded. 'You are right, beloved Sister. The land both beneath and around the temple is criss-crossed with small streams and canals. Some are natural, others man-made. Many are choked with rubbish or undergrowth.'

Su-Ling thanked and dismissed them. She then sat beneath the tree, reminding Marco of a young girl preparing for a picnic. She sat serenely, while Raphael crouched beside her; he and the officer were invited to do likewise.

'I ask you now,' she began, 'by all you hold sacred, to swear that you will do exactly as I ask.'

The officer agreed quickly enough. Marco was still reluctant. He nursed a deep feeling of unease, of matters moving too swiftly. The cart Su-Ling had ordered them to bring was piled high with casks of oil. Indeed, the cellars and storerooms of his home had been ransacked for them as well as small tubs of pitch and tar. Su-Ling had been most mysterious. On their journey here, she and Brother Raphael had insisted on walking behind the cart, asking others to stay away whilst they conversed quietly together.

'Give me your word, *signor*. If you do not . . .' She let the words hang in the air.

Marco finally agreed. Su-Ling held his hand and that of the officer, as if by very touch she could persuade them of what she was about to say.

'This evening,' she declared, 'life is about to change. A terror is to be released on the world which will leave its mark for hundreds and hundreds of years.'

The officer fidgeted but Su-Ling held his wrist tightly.

'Listen, my brothers. Others, my superiors at the Temple of the White Dove, yea, even the Great Khan himself, will ask questions. You will be our witnesses. You will tell them what we had to do. A great demon resides in the Temple of the Red Horse. He possesses one, perhaps all three of the souls who hide there: the two imperial sisters who call themselves Mai-da and Wei-Ning, and the master sorcerer and outlaw Lin-Po. Wei-Ning and Lin-Po have brought rats to Cambaluc. A species not known in this city but one, according to ancient wisdom, that was the principal cause of a devastating plague. We do not know whether it is their bite or their urine or some other infection which lives on their bodies and is responsible, but these rats are the harbingers of a terrible doom. The ground has been well-prepared. Summer is close. The Guild of Pourers has been thrown into disarray. Even you, Brother,' she glanced at the Buddhist officer, 'have reported how great is the stink in the city. It will grow even worse in the months ahead.'

'And the rats have been released?' Marco asked.

'Yes,' Su-Ling replied. 'And any farmer will tell you how many litters rodents have in one year. This plague will undoubtedly come, be it in a year or ten years' time. The infection will start here in Cathay: it will spread across the world, be a respecter of no boundaries, persons, creed or colour. It will be fanned and encouraged by Azrael and his disciples who, by then, will have turned the Middle Kingdom into a sea of blood. One province will be at war against the other. The Water Lily Society will raise the Sung flag, the banner of revolt. Cities will be devastated. All civilised life will come to an end. The Four Horsemen of the Apocalypse will gallop the face of the earth.'

'And we cannot stop this?' Marco asked.

Su-Ling released both their hands and joined hers as if in prayer.

'We cannot truly stop the evil men do but we can lessen its impact. As I have told you before, Azrael needs the human soul as a place of habitation. At this moment in time he is at his weakest.'

'Of course,' Marco broke in. 'They have been hiding in that temple for days.'

'Very good, Brother.' Su-Ling smiled. 'Now he is at his most vulnerable. That is why nobody, except Brother Raphael or myself, must enter that temple.'

'No!' Marco objected fiercely. 'That cannot be!'

'It will and it shall be!' Su-Ling replied softly. 'They will not expect us. They were to stay there for a while to ensure the success of what they have done. They feel safe, even if they are surrounded by imperial troops. They hold the Jade Crown. They know Sanghra or any minister will be open to negotiation. But, remember this, in the last resort Wei-Ning, Mai-da and Lin-Po are fools. They are wicked and their arrogance has blinded them. Azrael is a liar, the Lord of Lies. From the essence of his being he does not care for them, or any of us. All his will, his soul dwells in eternal night and breeds a festering hatred for both God and man. He does not care whether all three die. He will seek out and possess another soul, a dwelling to continue his villainy. It is Azrael who must be stopped. Once bereft of any human soul, he should be sent back to the edge of Eternity, confined to Hell: that is all we can do.'

Marco stared in astonishment. His body prickled with the cold sweat of dismay. He suspected what Su-Ling and Brother Raphael had decided upon and, from their faces, how they were resigned to it. The Buddhist officer, however, was almost in shock, hands trembling. He stretched out his arms as if to embrace Su-Ling but she drew away, shaking her head.

'Listen!' she ordered. 'You have sworn to do what I ask. Soon it will be dark. Brother Raphael and I will go into the temple then. They will accept us. They will not understand the sacrifice we intend. Once we are in, this is what you must do . . .'

It was dark when Marco walked across the hump-backed bridge, a flaring torch in one hand, a sword in the other. He followed Su-Ling's instructions carefully but kept his mind clear lest Lin-Po used his skill to trick them. The door was sealed by wooden bars nailed across but he could see how someone could get under that and open the door. He pounded on it with the hilt of his sword.

'Mai-da!' he bellowed. 'The woman known as Mai-da, her sister Wei-Ning and Lin-Po! Your whereabouts are known. I order you to open up in the name of the Great Khan!'

Again he repeated this before retreating hastily across the bridge. At first he thought he had been mistaken: that the temple was empty. Abruptly the door creaked open. He made out a shadowy outline.

'Who dares disturb us?' It was a man's voice, calm and mocking.

Lin-Po, Marco thought.

'In the name of the Great Khan, I order you to surrender!' Marco shouted.

'You can tell that Mongol,' the voice was sneering though Marco sensed a touch of fear, 'how the wearers of the Jade Crown do not bow before some horseman from the Steppes.'

'The Jade Crown!' Marco exclaimed. 'You possess the Crown of the First Emperor?'

'We possess much more than that.' This time it was a woman's voice, sharp, precise. 'There is no need for bloodshed.'

'In which case,' Marco bellowed back, 'the Great Khan offers envoys: the Buddhist nun Su-Ling and the priest Raphael. They enjoy his favour.' Now he closed his eyes and prayed.

'They may come forward,' the woman replied, 'but they must come unarmed. No one else is to cross that bridge.'

Or what, Marco thought? What can they do? Smash the Jade Crown to pieces? He recalled Su-Ling's words: how Wei-Ning and her accomplices fully trusted the Demon Lord and how this trust was ill-founded. Marco lowered the torch and walked back into the darkness.

Su-Ling and Raphael had prepared themselves. Brother Raphael looked nervous. Su-Ling, resolute. She came forward and grasped both his hands in hers.

'Once across the bridge, you must show no remorse or regret, not a second's hesitation. If they notice anything untoward, what they think is foolishness will be revealed as trickery.

Once we are in the temple and the door is closed, do as I've told you.'

Standing on tiptoe, she kissed Marco on the lips then on each cheek. Brother Raphael embraced him, hugging the older man tightly.

'Remember me,' he whispered. 'Make sure Masses are said for my soul and that of Su-Ling. Go back to Italy and, one day in some sunwashed piazza, take a glass of wine and toast us. Say a prayer for Su-Ling and Brother Raphael.'

Marco, his eyes filled with tears, found it difficult to reply. Raphael stood back and sketched a cross in the air.

'*Pax et bonum*, Brother,' he breathed. 'Peace and goodness to you all. We shall meet and feast again in the Halls of Light.'

Su-Ling now pushed the torch back into Marco's hand. The evening breeze fanned its flame and sent sparks fluttering up into the darkness.

'Will not Lin-Po read your minds?' he asked hoarsely.

Su-Ling laughed. 'He can try but he will fail: thanks to you, he will not have the time. Now, we must go!' she urged. 'Quickly!'

They left the trees and crossed the hump-backed bridge. This time Marco smelt the refuse and rubbish which had piled up there. He recalled Su-Ling's words and stared fearfully at the outline of this grotesque temple, now a shrine to plague and death. In the middle of the bridge he stopped as instructed.

'I bring you the nun Su-Ling,' he shouted. 'Brother Raphael is with her.'

'Let them come forward,' a voice called. 'You must retire.'

'Go back!' Su-Ling hissed.

She watched Marco return to the other side, the torchlight becoming a pinprick in the gathering darkness. Then she clutched Raphael's hand.

'Are you ready, Brother?' she asked him. 'And when you walk forward with me, remember this. I loved you before you were born.'

Her face was faint in the darkness, her voice a mere whisper but Raphael could feel her intensity. He feared nothing now. He felt warm, calm and protected. He accepted what Su-Ling had told him earlier. This was the sacrifice, the altar was their bodies and their souls a prayer to God.

'Let us go now!' he urged.

'Don't be afraid,' she counselled. 'I am with you and so are the Lords of Light. Do not be baited, do not show temper.'

As they walked forward, the door to the temple swung open, the makeshift beams nailed across being roughly kicked away.

'Enter!' a mocking voice called out.

Su-Ling and Raphael stepped across the wooden beams and into the temple. Its murky interior was lit by candles and little votive lights set in the niches along the walls.

'As they like it,' Su-Ling murmured. 'Darkness and dancing shadows.'

'Don't stand there like children, whispering to each other,' scolded the voice. 'Come forward and show yourselves!'

Su-Ling heard the door slam shut. Someone slipped by them in the darkness. Her eyes now accustomed to the gloom, she made out the huge statue of Buddha and, on the dais beneath it, two, no, three figures. She recognised Mai-da on her right; the other two must be Wei-Ning and Lin-Po. Wei-Ning sat in the priest's chair like an empress, the beautiful light-green Jade Crown resting in her lap. The votive lights arranged along the top step showed up their faces but little else.

'Approach!'

Su-Ling and Raphael walked forward. Two cushions were thrown before the steps followed by a curt order to kneel.

Su-Ling, still holding Raphael's hand, pressed his fingers as a sign to obey. They both knelt down. Raphael glanced at Mai-da. She was dressed in some dark gown: her round, high-cheeked face slightly pale under its coiffured hair. The woman sitting in the middle was even more beautiful. She had painted her face like a highborn lady: jewelled combs held the glossy coils of black hair in place. She looked like Mai-da but her face was firmer, eyes larger, chin and mouth more determined. She was dressed in a costly gown of green silk shot through with gold thread; precious pearls hung from her ear lobes and a jade bracelet adorned each wrist. The Crown which she held in her lap caught the light in glittering flashes so it seemed as if a fire burnt within the precious stone. Lin-Po appeared nondescript: a tired-looking, middle-aged man. Raphael did not like his secretive face and sly black eyes which studied him carefully.

'You must tell Lin-Po,' Su-Ling announced, 'that he cannot read our minds.'

Lin-Po chuckled behind his hand. Wei-Ning did not move. Mai-da's glance was full of malevolence.

'So now we are all here,' Su-Ling began, 'all six of us . . .'

'Six?' Mai-da queried.

'Which one of you houses the Lord Azrael?' Raphael asked. 'All three? Or just one of you?'

'Keep a civil tongue in your head!' Wei-Ning's voice was low and deep; her lips hardly seemed to move. 'You are a foreign devil. You have no right to be in the Middle Kingdom. When you kneel before Princesses of the Sung Dynasty, you must show the same respect, even more, than to some Mongol horseman.'

'So,' Su-Ling replied almost sweetly, 'it is you, Wei-Ning, who houses the Lord of Hell. Did you leave him here when you fled Cambaluc? What are you going to do now? You have released the rats, have you not?'

'I told you Purple-Skin could not be trusted,' Wei-Ning rasped. She half-glanced at her sister.

'We knew that without his help.' Raphael spoke up. 'Purple-Skin's soul has gone to God and, in time, so will we all.'

'Sooner rather than later for some of us,' Wei-Ning retorted, lifting her head. 'Our only failure was not to kill both of you.'

'But you have made this mistake before,' Su-Ling replied. 'On the Wheel of Life, one confrontation after another. Have you not dreamt, Wei-Ning? Is there not some kinship between us? Are we not locked in a terrible struggle which defies time? Are we not guardians of life and death?'

'Not this time,' Wei-Ning said triumphantly. 'As you say, Purple-Skin now rots and the rats are busy in the sewers. They'll carry their poison through the city and, from there, to the ends of the earth. No life, no human soul, will remain: as it was in the beginning, as it should have been, as it shall always be. Total war until human life is extinguished.'

'Who speaks now?' Su-Ling taunted. 'The Sung Princess or the Demon Lord? What is your plan? To cause disruption in the city and the empire? To flee to some other province where the Water Lily Society will protect you? To raise the banner of revolt? Do you really think you are going to be allowed to walk out of this temple unscathed?'

For the first time since he had met her, Raphael saw a look of concern in Mai-da's eyes, whilst Lin-Po shifted uneasily on the seat. He felt Su-Ling's fingers brush his hand. The Franciscan glanced across the temple floor and glimpsed it, just a gleam, a mere shimmer from the oil Marco and the Buddhist soldiers were pumping through the rivulet holes of the temple.

'Do you really think you'll walk out of here alive?' Su-Ling repeated. She was eager to draw them into debate, keep their attention. She could feel the tension as both Lin-Po and the demon which possessed Wei-Ning tried to enter her mind, discover her thoughts. Raphael would be experiencing the same mental invasion but they were both prepared, strong enough to resist.

'You are envoys of the Great Khan,' Wei-Ning sneered. 'You are what he calls "Holy Ones". It is well-known that the Mongol lord treats his envoys with respect, whilst the Venetian lusts after you and would not see one of his priests injured.' She laughed. 'Tanglefoot proved that. No, the Khan will confirm whatever you agree. He'll want you safely returned.' She picked up the Crown and held it. 'And, above all, he'll want this.'

'You are a liar, Azrael, and the Father of Lies!' Su-Ling retorted. 'What does the legend say? How that wicked First Emperor of the Middle Kingdom will once again return when the Jade Crown goes to Cambaluc? Has the Demon Lord told you that? Well, it has returned, but does that mean you or anyone else should wear it? You have all been deceived! Do you think the Lords of Hell worry about who moves where or when? Do they care if this temple is stormed? Does it matter to them whether you live or die?' She pointed back towards the door. 'If imperial troops force that door, I am sure Wei-Ning here will touch someone: an officer, a soldier, a servant – so as to continue Azrael's work.' Su-Ling paused, then leaning forward, she spoke in that language Raphael had heard her use before. The nun had described it as an ancient tongue from beyond the borders of the Middle Kingdom, used by Buddhist priests only in the most solemn exorcism. The change in Wei-Ning's face was remarkable. The arrogance disappeared in a licking of the lips and swift blinking of an eye.

'What is this?' Lin-Po screeched. 'Why can't I read their minds? You said we would be safe – that the Great Khan would not see his envoys hurt. That we would trade the Crown and be allowed to leave!'

'*No one* will leave this temple alive,' Su-Ling said forcefully. 'We are to die here and so are you.'

'This is nonsense!' Mai-da gasped, clutching her sister's wrist.

'What does it matter?' Su-Ling continued. 'You are led by a liar and the Father of Lies. Did he promise you safety? Do you think he really cares? I've also asked him who is there for Wei-Ning to touch. How can the demon now move to another soul?'

Wei-Ning thrust the Crown into her sister's hands and rose. She came down and grasped Su-Ling's face, her eyes seething with fury.

'You lie!' she whispered hoarsely. 'You cannot do that!'

'But we will,' Su-Ling told her.

'Too late – the infection has been released!'

'True,' Su-Ling smiled sadly. 'War and plague *will* come, but not like you dreamt of! You yourself will be despatched by fire across Eternity, and locked in Hell until you are released again. How much time will pass before you can return?' Her smile became radiant. 'Look at you,' she said, 'so cunning, so arrogant, so confident that you don't even ensure all is safe!' She glanced at Lin-Po and Mai-da. 'Did you think you could really live like hogs, not caring about others or what might happen in the future?'

Goaded, Wei-Ning brought her fist back and smashed it into Su-Ling's face. Raphael went to intervene even as Lin-Po jumped to his feet.

'The floor!' he screamed. 'Look at the floor!'

Raphael looked around. The oil was now seeping across, catching the light. Wei-Ning stood puzzled even as the first fire arrow smacked against the brickwork outside, only to flutter down in a flurry of sparks. The second and the third aimed true: piercing the small windows even as Marco and the Buddhist monks thrust burning cloths and twigs into the rivulets. Wei-Ning jumped from the dais. She was running towards the door when the whole floor was simply engulfed in flames. It licked around her sandals and, in the blink of an eye, transformed her into a screaming human torch. Lin-Po and Mai-da tried to run behind the statue to the hidden recess, but they, too, were caught by a sheet of flame. Su-Ling, her face bloodied from Wei-Ning's blow, turned to face Raphael, grasping him by the arms, drawing him close, tenderly, like a lover.

'Be brave,' she whispered. She felt him clutch her like a child, and she kissed the side of his face. 'Only a short while,' she promised. 'Only a little pain. I love you, Raphael. I always have and I always will. For this we were born, for this we will die, and for this we will find life again!'

Raphael's eyes closed. As he clasped her, he was aware of the terrible screams around him, of the flames roaring. He smelt Su-Ling's perfume, fragrant and soft. He wanted to reply and was about to when the fire reached them. One swift gust caught them, a scarlet flame which leapt up, roaring against the darkness.

Outside the temple, Marco, tears running down his face, watched the main front door buckle under the heat and caught the glow of fire in the high windows.

'Is there nothing we can do?' the Buddhist officer asked hoarsely.

'There is nothing,' Marco replied sadly.

'And has the evil gone?' the officer wanted to know.

'All have returned to the places they chose,' Marco murmured. 'Perhaps the plague will not come now. Perhaps it will be delayed or, even if it does come, it will not have the intensity that was planned, nor will it cause the devastation so greatly desired by the Lords of Hell.'

The Buddhist officer withdrew and Marco stood watching as

the flames consumed the entire building, cracking the masonry. He did not move until the domed roof splintered and fell and the Temple of the Red Horse was reduced to a heap of blackened rubble.

Afterword

When he was dying, Marco Polo was questioned by his family and friends on the veracity of what he had written. Marco's reply was just as enigmatic and enticing as his entire account: *they didn't know the half of it!*

Historians are not too sure just what Marco did in China, though there is no doubt that he was favoured and patronised by the Great Kublai. His omissions are tantalising in the extreme and probably occur because Marco did not want to get into trouble when he returned to the Catholic West. Indeed, several historians have argued that some of these omissions are so glaring (e.g. Marco never mentions tea!) that his whole story is a fiction. I disagree. I have studied the different editions of his works, and in my view Marco Polo stands as one of the greatest travellers-cum-storytellers in Western culture.

The plague known as the Black Death did eventually strike Western Europe, appearing and reappearing in a series of devastating epidemics. The origin of the black rat is equally mysterious, though there is a medical consensus that the species (*Rattus rattus*) is different from its cousin the brown rat (*Rattus Norvegicus*). Debate also rages about whether *Xenopsylla Cheopsis*, the flea which carries the infection, is totally dependent on the rat. The Russian archaeologist Chwolson points out that the rat could have originated in Semiriechinsk in Central Asia. However, if its origins are doubtful, the effects of the plague were not.

P.C. Doherty